BLOWOUT IN LITTLE MAN FLATS

And Other Spine-Tingling Stories
of Murder in the West

BLOWOUT IN LITTLE MAN FLATS

And Other Spine-Tingling Stories of Murder in the West

Edited by

Billie Sue Mosiman and Martin H. Greenberg

RUTLEDGE HILL PRESS®
Nashville, Tennessee

Published in Nashville, Tennessee, by Rutledge Hill Press®, Inc., 211 Seventh Avenue North, Nashville, Tennessee 37219. Distributed in Canada by H. B. Fenn & Company, Ltd., 34 Nixon Road, Bolton, Ontario, L7E 1W2. Distributed in Australia by The Five Mile Press Pty. Ltd., 22 Summit Road, Noble Park, Victoria 3174. Distributed in New Zealand by Tandem Press, 2 Rugby Road, Birkenhead, Auckland 10. Distributed in the United Kingdom by Verulam Publishing, Ltd., 152a Park Street Lane, Park Street, St. Albans, Hertfordshire AL2 2AU.

Cover and book design by Harriette Bateman.
Typography by E. T. Lowe, Nashville, Tennessee.

Library of Congress Cataloging-in-Publication Data

Blowout in Little Man Flats, and other spine-tingling stories of
   murder in the West / edited by Billie Sue Mosiman and Martin H.
   Greenberg.
     p.   cm.
    ISBN 1–55853–573–X
    1. Detective and mystery stories, American—West (U.S.).
  2. Murder—West (U.S.)—Fiction.   I. Mosiman, Billie Sue.
  II. Greenberg, Martin Harry.
  PS648.D4B58   1998
  813'.087408—dc21   98–4798
                                        CIP

Printed in the United States of America

1 2 3 4 5 6 7 8 9 — 03 02 01 00 99 98

CONTENTS

INTRODUCTION

The western United States during the period of its settlement was known widely for its lawlessness. Today the law prevails, just as it does in every section of the country, but there is still an Old West mentality among some of the West's maverick citizens and a feeling that, sometimes, death can be decreed without interference from the court system.

In these mostly contemporary stories there is a definite flavor of the Old West; where gunslingers made the laws and ruled the land; where the sheriff, when there was one, was not always feared by the criminal; and where even minor disagreements might result in murder.

It may not be accurate to describe this part of America as the "Wild West" any longer, but calling it "possibly safer to mind your own business" wouldn't be out of order.

Read Richard Matheson's "The Conqueror" to recreate what Texas was like in 1871. Instead of viewing cars speeding past on a freeway, relive the stagecoach era and meet a young man who hopes to snare an illusory place in Old West history.

In "Bull and Bear," by R. L. Stevens, we find an Idaho wilderness trail and two men who accidentally happen upon one another—and a bear. We also discover that even in the wilds, nothing is quite what it seems to be.

In "Craps," by Joyce Carol Oates, you're invited to the tables in Vegas where fate is always the dealer. There is no place wilder and no place more typically western than Las Vegas, Nevada. Oates takes us into the casinos, into the lives of people on the edge, and tells a story flavored with that particular brand of poignancy and horror she unfailingly conjures up for the reader.

No matter how strange we think the West was or might still be, this part of the country shares with all the rest the undercurrents of greed and passion that can lead to murder, escape and pursuit, and the inexorable grip of justice.

From Texas and Arizona to Alaska and Washington state, you'll find in these stories a variety of experience as wide as the land itself.

Bar the doors from the cold mountain winds of Colorado, draw the blinds against the leaching sun of California, and let the imagination and story-telling gifts of some of America's best authors guide you through a tour of terror in the West.

Billie Sue Mosiman

1997

Kathleen Dougherty's novels have been described as "explorations of the dark underbelly of the mind." After reading this story, it's easy to see why. She has worked as a sales manager for an artificial intelligence company and as a research associate in pharmacology. This story doesn't draw on any of those experiences, simply because it doesn't need to. Instead, it's a look at rationalization, fear, and the human psyche, surrounded by an arctic wasteland.

When Your Breath Freezes

Kathleen Dougherty

There are seven of us.

I am Sister Ellen: the youngest, the ugliest, the least devout, the most fragile. I need the vast silences of northern Alaska and the imposed silence of this cloister. The souls of these women are quiet, their musings as distant as the Chukchi Sea. The nuns have taken me in for the winter, an act of charity, a charity they might well regret. But they don't know about my special ability, my accursed gift. If they did, they'd shun me as others have. Their unspoken thoughts, though, are safe from me. Nothing could compel me again to peruse the mind of another. What you see there are the ugly shapes of nightmares.

Under my white robes, the color for a novice, are a pair of expedition-weight long johns, the fabric a heat-retaining, sweat-wicking synthetic; then a pair of wind-blocking pile pants. We have no television, no radio, yet we have the latest in underwear.

Off come the sturdy black shoes and on go the insulated knee-high boots. I unpin the white novice's veil from my hair and hang the veil on a wall peg. I slide a black ski mask over my head, position the mouth and eye holes. I like wearing the mask; its blank anonymity hides my facial scars. There is only one mirror here, in the infirmary. I have little use for mirrors.

I wrap my neck with the wool scarf knitted by Sister Gabrielle. I think tenderly of her gnarled hands, twisted by arthritis, the black yarn, and the slow clack of the needles. She had embroidered "Ellen" on a cloth tag. My fingers work a stretch cap on top of the ski mask, then I shrug on the anorak with its thick pile of yellow fleece lining, its rich fringe of fox fur around the hood. The drawstring snugs the hood low on my forehead and up over my mouth. The fur tickles and has that dusty aroma of animal skin.

Last are the glove liners and the padded mittens with Velcro wrist bands. Even before I open the heavy wooden door, I imagine I hear the cows lowing, though that's not possible. The wind's voice whips away sound and, deceptively, mimics the wail of a cat, a distant locomotive, an unhappy ghost.

I flick on the outdoor lights and step beyond the door, pulling it closed behind me. The frigid air steals my breath. Outside all is the white of an unusually bitter February. Though midmorning, there are hours before dawn bleaches the sky. My teeth chatter. It is colder than death out here.

The north wind pauses in its cold rush. I spit. The saliva crackles, freezing in midair, and shatters like glass on the walkway. Cold, very cold, even by the standards of northern Alaska. More than seventy below. Gusts sweep snow pellets, hard as gravel, across the covered walkway to the barn. That wooden structure, like the convent, appears to sprout from the mountainside.

During the Yukon gold rush, miners hewed these caverns, clawing from granite the shelters that shielded them from brutal winters. The south-facing walls are wood; north-facing walls and much of the ceiling are the smoothed underbelly of the mountain. Snaking into the earth from those north walls are tunnels; a few lead to steaming pools of hot springs, potable—though slightly sulfurous—water. After the Second World War, the exhausted claim was purchased by the Immaculata order, and this remote land, once brimming with the harsh voices and greed of prospectors, became the refuge of silent nuns.

The gale blasts against my long skirts and I cover the walkway in a graceless stagger. The barn door sticks, its hinges cranky with cold. I wrench open the door and step inside to rich aromas: cow hide, dung, hay, bird droppings, wood smoke. The miners had used the large room as a barracks. Humid air fogs a tunnel entrance, one which leads to the hot springs, where the nuns take paying guests during the brief summers.

The barn houses two cows, a mangy good-for-nothing goat, and a chicken-wire enclosure with a dozen hens and an irritable cock. The hens set up a comical squawking and fluttering, shocked to their very cores every few hours when I come to tend the wood stove. The cows regard me with their calm brown eyes, aware that it's morning and hoping for fresh fodder. These are, as far as I've seen, the only cows in Alaska, a gift from a rancher in the lower forty-eight. He'd stayed here last summer, Leonidist said, soaking in the convent's hot sulfur springs, and was convinced he'd been miraculously healed of gout.

Pine logs dropped into the wood stove make the coals flare. The stove stands in an isolated hollow scooped from the mountain. The flue disappears into the rocky ceiling.

I milk the cows and the sullen goat, gather eggs from the hens, I slap the cows' haunches, urging them up and down the center aisle. They don't like the enforced exercise, but their shanks tend to develop abscesses. Sister Fiske, a paramedic and our only source of medical expertise during these frozen months, prescribed aerobics. The cows want only to stare into their food bins and meditate golden hay into existence. Their resistance makes the stroll hard work and I wonder about the medical benefits for any of us. After half an hour, I stop, panting. Their bony heads study me quietly, a pitying look which makes me smile.

I muck out the stalls and coop, spread down fresh straw, and rake the soiled material to the far entrance. I switch on the outdoor lights. This part gets tricky. If drifts have built up in the past hours, a path will have to be cleared. That means shoveling for two minutes, dashing into the warmth of the barn and scaring the heck out of the chickens, shoveling another two minutes, and so on.

To my delight, the door swings open easily and the path to the garden appears clear. I rake the straw outside and drag the mound a few yards when a snow-dusted rock catches my eye. A mound of black, a large stone that hadn't been there before . . . and with awful clarity the form resolves into that of a huddled person. My chest tenses with shock. I am kneeling next to the shape without memory of moving closer.

She is curled into the fetal position. The ebony veil, hard and shiny, has frozen into place, covering most of the profile, but there's enough exposed to see the broad jaw, the deep etch of lines from nose to mouth, the dark brown mole with its two stiff hairs stark against ashen flesh. Frost has made a mask of the features, smoothed out the web of wrinkles on her full cheeks, lessened the downward draw of persimmon lips. It is Sister Praxades, our cook, who refuses—refused— to bake white bread. In the kitchen with her black sleeves rolled up over dimpled forearms, she taught me to knead whole-grain dough. She smelled of flour and yeast and discontent.

With my right glove and liner off, I touch her throat where, in life, the carotid artery throbs. Her neck is frozen solid, hard and unyielding.

Her pudgy hands and feet are bare, pale as alabaster. How can this be? No one would willingly tromp barefoot in Alaska's winter.

My thoughts are slow lizards, too long in the cold.

My right hand signs the cross over her body. I mentally begin an Act of Contrition, but retreat to the barn when the air hurts my lungs. Chickens cackle and the goat bleats while I finish the prayer for Sister Praxades, an inadequate charity for a woman who had been more than tolerant of a newcomer.

Tears burn my cheeks. I, who have so little opportunity for love, loved her.

There had been seven of us.

Now there are six.

Reverend Mother thinks in German, a language I don't comprehend. Snatches of words, swirling in her mind-winds, fly out: *schnee, tot, unschuld, verlassen*. She is in her late forties, the youngest except for me, yet authority is a mantle she wears with ease. Her bearing is military, her oval face composed, her gray eyes sharp. Only now her gaze reveals disquiet upon my panicked report of Sister Praxades's death. Reverend Mother's face shutters down; her thoughts whirl. Rosary beads rattle within the folds of her black robes. Her pale lips shape the English words, "Jesus, Mary, Joseph," a favored indulgence of this order. Each nun says this prayer so often that the rhythm becomes one with each inhale and exhale. When the rare words seep from their minds, that is what I sense: JesusMaryJoseph.

Reverend Mother orients on me. Her lapse of control is over. Her fingers sign, *You—lead me—Praxades*. Even now Reverend Mother does not break the quiet meditation.

Her hand halts me as I turn. She shapes sentences fast, too fast, and I shake my head in confusion. She places a long index finger to her lips, then signs, *No tell—others*.

Why not tell the others? They'll know Sister Praxades is missing. I gesture for permission to speak, my sign language inept. Reverend Mother slices her hand in the negative, a command that reminds me of my position here. The shock of finding Sister Praxades has made me exceed my bounds. Flushing, I bow my head in apology, nod compliance, and we exit her office. It is up to Reverend Mother, not the distraught pseudo-novice "Sister" Ellen, to decide when to tell the nuns. If she waits until after the Angelus, before the noon meal when contemplation officially ends, Sister Praxades will not be any less dead for the delay.

In the hall Sister Leonidist, standing on a foot stool, scrapes tallow from a wall sconce. Candle glow highlights the postmenopausal down of her cheeks and chin. Thick red eyebrows shadow her sockets, making her pale blue eyes seem large and black. Leon the Lion, my pet name for her in my head, is the one I'd have gone to first to share the terrible discovery. She performs a modified curtsy from her perch in respect of Reverend Mother as we pass. I look longingly over my shoulder at Leon. She grins and winks, pretends to stick a finger up one wide nostril.

At the side door, before Reverend Mother dons her anorak, she removes her black headdress. Her hair is a flattened, short gray-brown, and its thinness somehow diminishes her authority. I focus on the splintered wood planks, embarrassed. It is disrespectful to see her so. After a moment, she nudges me, not unkindly. It is time to go out into the cold.

One voice: "*Dominus vobiscum.*" The Lord be with you.

Five voices: "*Et cum spiritu tuo.*" And with your spirit.

It is noon and the hours of silence end. Reverend Mother observes us from the lectern. Her hands clutch the frame on either side of the Bible. Her knuckles whiten. She is, I know, gathering strength to talk about Sister Praxades. The nuns do not speak. Their minds are suspended in a sea of expectation; no gleanings travel from their consciousness to mine, not even the Jesus, Mary, Joseph prayer. Leon catches my attention with a raised bushy eyebrow and looks pointedly at her lap. She signs: *Cook sick?*

The others may think that. We are not allowed in our cells except to sleep or to rest if we're ill. How I wish Sister Praxades were on her pallet, tucked under quilts, resting away a fever instead of curled miserably outside, the door of her mind forever frozen closed. I hope that whatever malady caused her to wander in the snow also prevented the cook from suffering.

My vision blurs and I drop my gaze to the pine table. In front of me and the four seated nuns are blue ceramic bowls of potato soup, our lunch. In the kitchen I simmered the potatoes in chicken stock—no wonder those fowl squawk with such alarm—and added cream, butter, salt, pepper, and a dash of crisp Chardonnay. As Sister Praxades taught, I tasted and added more butter, cream, tasted and added more spices, tasted and added more wine . . . and still the broth seemed bland.

Rich yellow butter dots the soup's surface, my poor attempt to duplicate the dead woman's craft. Only the bread, a thick, sweet rye, can be trusted. The large, round, crusty loaves were baked by the cook yesterday.

Reverend Mother's sharp inhale pulls my attention to the lectern. Her lips press together. "Sister Ellen found Sister Praxades outside this morning. Sister Praxades is dead." The bald statements straighten every spine, including my own.

"No," cries Sister Gabrielle, an old friend of the cook, eldest nun, knitter of woolens for the likes of me. Her misshapen hand fists, hits the table, and spoons jump. Her anguish bolts to my heart. She cries again: "No!"

"Sister Gabrielle," comes the cautioning, authoritative voice of Reverend Mother.

The old nun's mouth gapes, showing too-even dentures. Tears diffuse down cheeks as creased as parchment. She hunches over the table, gasping with hushed sobs, and a thread of saliva descends from her lips. Sister Fiske, the medic, sits next to the stricken woman. Her chin lifts, her eyes narrow behind magnified glasses. A sharp, disapproving line creases between her brows and her mouth thins, a compassionless look from a woman who frets about the abscesses of cows.

At a nod from Reverend Mother, Fiske rises, accompanies the crying Gabrielle into the stone corridor. The old woman's voice muffles in decrescendo. After a moment, the thin creak of the chapel door reveals their location. And in this room . . . silence. Leon stares at her lap. Sister Xavier, our housekeeper, an angular woman with a jaw as square as a box, fingers a soup spoon. She rarely speaks even when conversation is allowed.

Reverend Mother sighs deeply and bows her head. She says, "Why did you doubt?" Stress has made her German accent noticeable. Their shared emotion builds critical mass and penetrates my carefully erected barriers.

Each is deeply, piercingly ashamed.

Reverend Mother restricts me to the kitchen with my bowl of cooling soup while she conducts a private meeting with the others in the dining room. At the pine counter where Praxades taught me to shape loaves of whole wheat, I force myself to finish my lunch. Food is never wasted. Each tight swallow emphasizes my hurt: grief for the cook and, to my chagrin, the wound of being excluded from the nuns' discussion. I don't belong here, I chide myself. Why should Reverend Mother behave as though I'll stay beyond the spring thaw?

After I eat and feed more coal to the stove, the temptation to eavesdrop wins. I press my ear against the swinging door to the dining room. Not even hushed conversation seeps through the wood. Pushing the door open a crack—my toes still on the kitchen floor so there isn't technical disobedience—I see the five blue bowls on the table, still full. The nuns are gone.

Determined to be a help and to demonstrate a charity I'm not exactly feeling, I busy myself in the pantry, planning dinner. Surveying the shelves, my gaze touches opaque brown vials, medicines that Sister Praxades took on a complicated schedule. The names on the labels don't mean anything to me; once she showed me the collection on her chubby palm, pointing out one for blood pressure, another for cholesterol, and so on.

I pop the cap of one bottle and spill out beautiful azure capsules into my hand. Whatever her medications were supposed to do, they hadn't done their job last night. Sighing, I return the pills to their container and scoop the half-dozen prescriptions into my pocket. Fiske will want these returned to the infirmary.

I decide on tuna casserole, a dish I'm unlikely to ruin. I gather the canned fish, mushroom soup, noodles, and a stale bag of potato chips. The planks squeak under my tread and I see Praxades of last night, after dinner, sashaying and spinning her robes in exaggerated mockery of Sister Fiske, floorboards complaining under her weight. Mimicry was her gift and no one, myself included, was exempt, but Fiske was the cook's specialty.

At the sink I twist the crank of the opener around the tuna can and indulge the sweet sorrow of memories. Oddly enough, Praxades was liberal while the much younger Fiske was conservative. Praxades wanted a satellite dish and television so she could learn recipes from Julia Child; she wanted a subscription to *Gourmet* magazine, deliverable by bush pilot when weather allowed. In the common room, the arguments between Praxades and Fiske were high entertainment. Fiske struggled to control her indignation, I'll give her that. However, Praxades was a master of provocation. The cook's suggestions would become more and more extreme: The nuns should forgo habits and wear fleece slacks and shirts, the L.L. Bean catalogue had them in black.

Last night the cook's trump card, so to speak, enraged Fiske to unusual heights. Praxades suggested that evenings be passed by rousing games of stud poker, using holy cards as chips. The silent Sister Xavier grinned. Leon always looked happy, as though her features were incapable of any other expression. Fiske sprang to her feet, hands clenched by her sides, her complexion red; she'd flung her book to the floor. She sputtered, "You . . . you . . . you sacrilegious old fool, you disgusting—"

"Enough," interrupted Reverend Mother, a regal lift to her chin. "Sister Praxades, hold your tongue. Sister Fiske, you allow the cook to bait you every evening. Both of you must learn control and tolerance." However, Reverend Mother's eyes held a glitter of amusement; not, I'm sure, because of Fiske's fury but because of the cook's inane ideas.

Smug satisfaction brightened Praxades's plump face. Fiske retrieved *The Lives of the Saints*, touched the cover to her lips in apology—to the book, which must have been blessed—and returned to her chair, hands trembling. I felt the heat of her hate for the cook, an emotion as searing as any that had touched me in the cities. It is Lent, weeks of sacrifice in preparation for Easter, but she definitely wasn't offering up her aggravation to the Lord. Fiske even lacked the control to school her expression. She darted a withering, mean look at Reverend Mother, then dropped her gaze to her book. Her face was murderous.

The fork in my hand stops scooping out the tuna. An uneasy resonance jingles in my mind. Had Fiske looked surprised at Reverend Mother's dire announcement? I recall only Fiske's disapproving expression over Gabrielle's outburst.

Perhaps Fiske had nothing to be surprised about.

Fiske, while not a physician, plays the part of one by doling out medications. In my habit's pocket, my fingers clutch the containers of pills. No one would know if they had been tampered with. No one, that is, except for Fiske.

No, I think, please. Not here.

Not again.

Reverend Mother imposes an afternoon of silence in memory of the cook. When I enter her office and request permission to speak, she signs, "later." Minutes afterward, swaddled in my anorak, I tromp through the barn, chickens squawking in terror, and exit by the rear door. If Praxades was disoriented by medication, probably Fiske had to lead her outside. Snow squeaks like plastic pellets under my boots. Wind whips up millions of grains as fine as baby powder, shoving me nearly off my feet. My polarized lenses fog. I push the goggles above my eyes with awkward mittens and squint. The body is gone. While I was sequestered in the kitchen, the nuns moved the cook.

The day's dilute glow is muted by dark-bellied clouds, and though I search, crouching near the ground, crabwalking the path, there's no evidence that anyone has been here: not the dead cook, not the nuns, and—as I look at ground near my boots—not even Sister Ellen. The harsh land of winter has wiped away the traces. A spasm of shivering makes my jaw muscles tremble. I straighten. Abruptly a gale whites out the world and my name floats through the whirl: "*Ellen.*"

I pivot, pulse galloping, half-expecting to see Praxades levitating from the ground. That movement is a dangerous mistake. The wind increases, howling and spinning drifts, shoving so hard that I stagger. The mad swirl of snow is blinding. Panic shoots through my very core, more invasive than the cold. Which way is the barn? How long have I been out here? Two minutes? Three? Already my fingers are deadened, ice freezing together my eyelashes, narrowing my view to thin, blurry slits.

I must move. My feet stumble, forcing my body against the wind, and again I hear my name, swallowed by the squall, but definitely from my left. If I'm hallucinating, if hypothermia is creating a false call, then I'm dead. I fight, moving to my left for an eternity of seconds; finally arms grab and pull me into the thick smell and chicken cackles of the barn. Violent shivers drop me to my knees on the straw. The door latch clunks closed. My rescuer drags me to the heat of the wood stove.

My gloves are pulled off, then the liners, and my frozen fingers are clasped in hands so warm they burn my flesh. When the ice melts from my lashes, I'm staring into the kind, silent face of Sister Xavier. I know her the least, yet I know this: She will perform extra penance for the sin of breaking silence when she called my name.

In the infirmary, I proffer Sister Praxades's medicines. Fiske's cold fingers remove the bottles from my palm.

I speak, violating the imposed quiet. "Why would Sister Praxades go outside?"

The woman is still a moment, studying me, and the intensity of her stare and the knowledge of my scars makes my cheeks warm. Then she shrugs, a who-knows gesture. That motion is a lie. I feel her dissembling, controlling body language. She walks across the rough brick floor, twirling her robes in the way that Praxades mocked. For a moment the mirrored cabinet bounces her image at me, then her double swings away as she opens the cabinet. I follow. "The cook was fine last night. What would make her do such a thing?"

Fiske ignores me, reads the label on one vial, and places it on a shelf cabinet. In my cell, under my pallet, is a list of the prescriptions and one pill from each container. Feeble evidence. The thought strikes me that if Fiske decides to remove any other thorn in her side, by persisting like this, I'm making Sister Ellen the next likely target. Fiske's pinched face last night rises to mind, her seething fury at the cook . . . and, now I recall, toward Reverend Mother.

Anger, however, isn't an omen of murder. "What do you think caused her odd behavior?" I ask, observing her profile as she shelves the remaining vials. "The mix of drugs she'd been taking?"

Her lips curl slightly in contempt. This impugning of her medical care prompts her to talk. "Not at all."

During the next pause, I expect her to announce that Praxades was befuddled by a stroke or low blood sugar. Instead, she closes the wall cabinet. I'm careful not to look into the mirror. Fiske says, "Separation from God."

"What?"

"That's what killed your precious Sister Praxades."

She turns in a flare of robes and for a moment a silly picture forms, a ballet of nuns in long black habits. I catch her by the arm. With slow disdain, she rotates her head to fix a dark gaze on my hand. I don't let go. "She . . . you're saying she died from, what, weak faith? *That's* your clinical diagnosis?"

She raises her eyes to meet mine. Behind thick lenses her irises glint as though forged of hard, shiny metal. "No, Sister Ellen. That's my spiritual diagnosis."

Our gazes lock. I almost do the thing that I vowed never to do again under any circumstances: invade the mind of another.

If I forcibly examine her thoughts, she will know. They always knew. The last time I used this accursed ability, I destroyed everyone around me.

Fiske stares, a smirking, superior look. It strikes me that she knows all about me, but that's impossible. Her hands shape the words *Look, Files, Top, Ellen*. With a nod she indicates the tall file cabinet.

I release Fiske. She strides away, footfalls slapping the brick floor, and exits the infirmary. As I look at the file cabinet, my stomach clenches in sudden, inexplicable fear. I, of all people, understand that some things are better left alone. Yet minutes later I have scanned the thick files bearing my name. Everything is there: The *Journal of the American Medical Association* study about a woman with provable telepathy; the Duke University professor's interview in *People* magazine and a photo of me hooked to an EEG machine; the *Newsweek* and *Times* articles about my assisting with various murder investigations nationwide; the *New York Times* report about how Gardini the Magician, a debunker of so-called psychics, finally paid a quarter of a million dollars to a bona fide mind-reader.

Dozens of newspaper and magazine articles cover the famous psychic's last murder case: Psychic's Husband and Brother Guilty of Business Partner's Murder. Then the same grainy photograph shows up in report after report: my disfigured features after the men my brother hired attacked me with acid. Long before that, though, everyone I came into contact with was leery of me. And weeks before acid ate away my features, I decided never again to snare thoughts from another's mind. After plastic surgeons had done the best they could with flesh that scarred so badly, I sought anonymity, a location where my history and notoriety might be unknown, where I might find, if not peace, at least isolation.

I thought that the nuns hadn't questioned me about my past or my scars due to their otherworldliness. Now I see that they had no need to interview me.

I stand in front of the infirmary mirror, holding the heavy file and gazing at my wretched reflection.

During dinner, while heads bend over a surprisingly tasty tuna casserole, first Leon, then Reverend Mother read passages from the Bible. Dinners are a time to fortify our bodies and our spirits. Reverend Mother, now at the podium, chooses the verses describing Jesus walking on the sea. The expressions of Leon, Xavier, Reverend Mother, and Gabrielle—especially Gabrielle —are serious and downcast. Fiske, to my eye, appears artificially solemn. I swallow a second helping of casserole, eager for the meal to end so that I can interrogate Leon over the dishes. After a minute, the only sound of fork against plate is my own. I look up. Fiske, Xavier, Gabrielle, and Leon are rapt with attention on Reverend Mother. She reads:

> *"But when he saw that the wind was boisterous, he was afraid; and beginning to sink he cried out, saying, 'Lord, save me!'*

"And immediately Jesus stretched out His hand and caught him,
and said to him, 'O you of little faith, why did you doubt?'"

Reverend Mother closes the Bible, kisses the gold-embossed cover, and returns to her place at the table. Everyone resumes eating, but something has happened which I've missed. The heavy cloud of their mood has lifted. On a psychological level, the dim dining room is bright.

In the cavern, Leon and I wear headlamps to light our way to the spring. The earth-generated heat keeps the temperatures from dropping below fifty, yet the high humidity is chilling. The damp mist blurs her shape and when our buckets accidentally clang together as we walk, my pulse jumps. She appears comfortable with how the cook died. She explains that Sister Praxades was moved to a mining shaft north of the barn. After leaving the corpse, they barricaded the entrance. When the ground thaws and, with the approval of the medical examiner—from two-hundred-miles-away Lygon—and Praxades' relatives, a burial plot will be prepared. Until then, her body will remain frozen, and will be safe from the occasional arctic fox.

Her chipper tone nonpluses me. She might be discussing the disposal of the goat. We reach the pool and kneel down to draw water. I ask, "Why can't we have a memorial service now?"

"To mourn her would be to question God's will."

I set my full bucket down impatiently; water sloshes over the lip. "Leon, *talk* to me."

The desperation in my voice must have moved her. She sets her pail next to mine and says, "Of course I miss Sister Praxades. She brought this place alive. She made us laugh." Through the steam I see her grin. "Well, everyone except Sister Fiske," Leon amends. "Ellen, look at it this way. If you died, would you want those you love to feel grief, to suffer over losing you?"

I wouldn't. Still, I'm troubled by the acceptance of the cook's death. Even the elderly Gabrielle appears adjusted to her friend's absence, though perhaps that's not true. She might be numb with grief.

Leon places her hand on my shoulder. In the steam, her headlamp creates a bright halo. "Perhaps it's easier for us. Our beliefs treat death as a natural part of the soul's journey. It wouldn't make sense for us to behave as though Sister Praxades is gone forever."

I wish I believed in the immortality of the soul. "What if Fiske messed with Praxades's medication?"

Leon is quiet a moment. I know I've surprised her. "I guarantee that Sister Fiske is innocent of everything except anger. She's devoted to safeguarding our health, not endangering it."

Leon could probably find good in Judas. We trudge back through the tunnel toward the living quarters. An aura radiates from her, and in that aura three words ring over and over: JesusMaryJoseph.

I assume the duties of the cook, though joy has evaporated for me. The others appear inexplicably cheered, except for Reverend Mother, who wears a preoccupied expression as though straining to hear a faint voice just beyond the audible range. A snowstorm blankets the grounds with one foot, then two feet of powder. I watch Fiske, who ignores me. The weather rages and we turn inward; the times of silence are natural for them. This spiritual hibernation makes me edgy, though my bread-baking improves. Two days pass.

On the third morning, Gabrielle vanishes.

I sleep. I wake with a start, furious with my failed vigil. Today Leon, Xavier, and I searched outside for Gabrielle, but our efforts were thwarted by the storm's bluster. She disappeared in the night, like Praxades. The spirits of the nuns are visibly leadened, even Fiske's. My mind is groggy; confused speculations stick in my skull. Why is everyone so resigned about Praxades, now Gabrielle? Why does Reverend Mother appear fatigued? She walks hesitantly, as if movement is an effort. Is Fiske poisoning Reverend Mother? Has Fiske killed Gabrielle?

A distant sound travels from the corridor. I sit up. Was that the timbers creaking? I toss off the comforter; chill seeps through my habit, cold slipping like spiders under the thermal underwear. In a few seconds I light the hurricane lamp, pull on my insulated boots, and tiptoe into the dark hall. All but one of the cell doors are closed. I peer into that room and my candlelight glows on an empty pallet. Seeing the tidy vacant room is a blow. I run to the kitchen, the dining room, the infirmary, the sitting room, the chapel, my search as fruitless as I feared. At the entryway door, I yank on anorak, gloves, cap and let myself out into the clear, breezy night, the cold so sharp my lungs inhale reflexively with the shock. It is always like this after a storm, as though fierce weather hones winter to better express its nature. The northerly has swept the entryway clear of all but a half-foot of powder, though drifts smooth the side wall clear up to the eaves. I round the building and find wind and deep snow . . . and heartache.

A figure glows in the frosty moonlight, skin gleaming whitely, a wide sweep of back and jiggling buttocks. "Leon!" I cry. She turns, a statue of salt, merging into the colorless world except for dark thatches of hair at crotch and head. My boots sink deep into the fresh powder as I struggle to her side.

"Please don't worry," Leon said. "I have faith." Syllables slur from frozen lips. "I'm getting warmer. My feet—"

"Leon, for the love of God, *please*." Unshed tears chill my eyes. "You're not getting warmer. You're freezing."

My own face is ice. My stiff fingers won't grip. I loop my arm under hers and guide her toward the building. She resists; her red-lashed eyes blink sleepily under the narcotic of hypothermia.

"Damn you, Leon, *walk*."

Her pale mouth opens in a semblance of a smile, the muscles of her jaw stiff with cold. "I'm walking, Ellen," she mumbles. "I'll come back. Reverend Mother did." Her arm slips like mist from mine and she stumbles away, wading through fresh snow, moving with a speed I wouldn't have thought possible. But she is numb. My legs drag through thigh-deep drifts and, trailing her, I fall, flounder deep in powdery whiteness. My freezing arms thrash for purchase in a substance as unstable as flour. Snow blankets my vision. I regain my footing, breathing hard, brushing ice from my face. Every muscle trembles so violently, my body straining to produce heat, that I can barely stand. I am alone in a landscape as pale and barren as the moon, and I suddenly understand who the murderer is.

I race through the corridor to Reverend Mother's room and enter without knocking, throat parched from cold and panic. A single candle flickers from the floor. Reverend Mother lies on her bed in full habit, fingers laced at her waist, thick black socks on her feet. The down comforter and blankets have been kicked to the floor. I lean over her. "I don't know what rot you've been telling these women, but Leon's out there and you're going to help me get her inside. If she hears you calling, she'll come in." Part of me says it's already too late for Leon, but I can't listen to that.

Reverend Mother stares at me, eyes glittering as though a fire blazes inside her skull. "It's Lent. The Lord calls her. She's being tested."

I pull her to a sitting position and her heat radiates like a furnace. Fever has glossed her skin with perspiration. "This is not Christ asking the apostles to walk on water, damn it. This is Alaska and she'll die out there. No one can survive that cold."

Her hands clutch my shoulders with a frenzied strength. "I did."

An odor pierces my hysteria, a fetid smell. It isn't a chamberpot stink, but a scent of putrefaction and decay. With horror, I look at her feet, which she suddenly tucks under her skirts, a childlike gesture. I pull back the material. She isn't wearing thick, dark socks; frost-bitten toes and heels have swelled, rotted, and blackened. I slide up the polypro of her long underwear. Dark streaks on the calves disappear under the fabric, infection spreading toward her groin. Sickened, I cover her legs. Reverend Mother lies back against her pallet, and whispers a few words in German, the gist of which I understand. "Yes," I nod sadly, "you have faith."

The pilot and I haven't spoken. I'm his only passenger and wear heavy, insulated ear muffs to dull the engine noise; conversation is impossible. I'm also wearing a thin gauze mask that Sister Xavier fashioned at my request before I left the cloister. The pilot didn't ask about it. He probably thinks the mask is a religious garment. Below us is Anchorage, refreshingly green in its springtime mantle.

Xavier and I hunted but never found Leon's body. We speculated that she must have entered an abandoned mine shaft. After the start of the thaw, I found Gabrielle not far from the tunnel where the others had barricaded Praxades, and where we had entombed the corpse of Reverend Mother. I spent the last four months meditating on my own considerable responsibility in these terrible deaths. At first I raged at the twisted beliefs that corralled this small, insular society into suicidal behaviors. After talking awhile with Fiske and Xavier, though, I saw that I could have played a part in bringing a sort of heathen reasoning to their lives. However, my goal was self-protection and isolation, not involvement. Perversely, I managed to neither protect myself nor remain uninvolved. Guilt will always reside within me, a hard, frozen shard of northern Alaska.

After the pilot lands, I step down from the plane, pull the mask below my chin, and walk toward the terminal.

Travelers at the airport stare, but I've taken a gift—and a lesson— from my months in the cloister. In my soul spreads a vast emptiness, images and ideas bright stars with light-years of distance in between.

To write mystery stories well, one must understand characters. John Lutz knows characters, and more importantly, how to write about them so that they seem like they're going to step off the page and into real life. The protagonist of this story is a man with a plan to introduce a little more excitement into his life. Watch how the plot unfolds as only a master can write it.

Bingo

John Lutz

It wasn't as if Harry Archambault needed the money. Not that he and Gretta couldn't use it, as might anyone living in the sprawling retirement community of Sun Colony a few miles west of Phoenix. Retirement wasn't at all what most people imagined or wished for. If life's declining years were golden, that gold could melt fast in the searing Arizona sun.

Sun Colony comprised over nine hundred homes that seemed to have been created with a combination of half a dozen cookie cutters. That was the way developers built them nowadays; cost containment through duplication. All of the homes were single story, with decorative fireplaces, pale-shingled roofs to reflect the sun, two-car garages, and no basements. Each had been sold with a small Phoenix palm tree in the front yard; now many of those squat, indigenous trees were huge, some of them hacked and trimmed of low branches but left bushy on top so they resembled mutant, oversized pineapples. Individual houses were landscaped with saguaro cacti and citrus trees and were painted their own faded pastel colors, yet in Harry's eyes they were the same, wood and aluminum clones with only the slightest variation.

There was very little actual grass in Sun Colony; the neat, well-kept homes had yards made up of different-colored gravel, mostly reds and greens, the various hues separated by curving plastic or stone dividers laid low to the ground by skilled Mexican laborers. There were no children in Sun Colony, and no noise of any sort. It was illegal to park cars on the street. Trash was deposited in lidded underground containers in front of each house and collected three times a week. Though there were sidewalks, there was nowhere interesting to be reached on foot. There were only the neat rows of houses and the symmetrical, multicolored yards and the pale, sun-washed concrete. And beyond all that, like an extension of it, stretched the strange, stark beauty of the desert. It was like the landscape of the moon.

That was why Harry decided to break the law; he was tired of living on the moon.

"I don't see why you keep doing that," Gretta said. She seemed content since they'd moved to Sun Colony two years ago. She was in a book discussion club, did group aqua-aerobics in the community clubhouse swimming pool several times a week, and had just signed up for weaving classes. Most of these activities she did with her friend Wilma, a widow five years younger than Gretta, who lived in the next block. "We have too many cans of tuna now."

"This is Arizona," Harry said, "miles from the ocean. You can never have enough tuna."

He glanced over at his wife of forty years. She had evolved into a pleasant-featured but bland gray-haired woman who at times seemed like someone's grandmother rather than his wife. Did other seventy-year-old men think like that about their wives?

Of course Gretta *was* someone's grandmother—Harry's grandkids'. Gretta and Harry were grandparents five times over. But their children—and *their* children—were more than a thousand miles away. Ben, the nearest of Harry and Gretta's offspring, lived in Rockport, Illinois, with his wife and two sons. The daughter, Vera, lived with her husband and three children in Morristown, Tennessee. The other boy, Freddy, was single and worked in what he described as "various creative enterprises" in New York City.

Harry shrugged off these musings and concentrated on setting up the printing calculator so the tape looked like a genuine receipt for the purchase of two cans of Fish Ahoy chunk white tuna. If the labels of two cans with proof of purchase were mailed to Fish Ahoy headquarters in Maine, the company would return a free can of tuna plus two dollars. At Norton's supermarket, a twelve-ounce can of Fish Ahoy tuna sold for $1.59 including tax. Which meant Harry could buy two cans of tuna, send in their labels, receive a free can with a check for two dollars, purchase a third can of tuna, send in its label with the free can's label (and a Harry-generated receipt falsely signifying the purchase of two cans), and so on, each time making a profit of forty-one cents. Gretta didn't seem to understand this.

"You're a driven, wacky old man," she told him, "sitting there counterfeiting grocery store receipts so you can swindle a company out of free cans of tuna. Shameful!"

"It isn't the tuna," he said in exasperation. "It's the profit."

"You're not an entrepreneur, Harry, you're a retiree."

"So I should sit in the sun and die?"

"No, you should play boccie ball or go to aquatic exercises with me or play bingo at the recreation hall Saturday nights."

"Sitting in the sun and dying sounds better."

She glared at him with cold blue eyes behind thick prescription lenses. "Did you ever stop and think what your time is worth? Figure that in your calculations and you're probably hundreds of dollars in the hole."

"That's why I'm doing this," Harry said glumly, "because of what my time is worth."

Gretta, preferring not to think or talk in the abstract, began to read a glossy magazine about weaving. Harry noticed a free-offer coupon on the back cover and decided he'd examine the magazine later.

A week later Freddy, on his way home from Las Vegas, drove up in a rental car for a short visit. He suggested that there were people who might be looking for him in Vegas and in New York, so it was a rare opportunity to spend quality time with his folks.

Freddy was the son most like Harry, only with a certain additional ability to overcome moral inhibitions. Harry looked at his son's permed and styled hair and obviously expensive suit and speculated that Freddy was doing very well in New York.

The third evening of his visit, Freddy sauntered outside and sat down next to Harry on the vinyl-padded glider on the patio, facing a lemon tree.

"Quiet out here," he observed.

"Always is," Harry said. "Like the grave."

"Hot too."

"But it's a dry heat."

"So's an oven. You and Mom ever drive out to Vegas or Laughlin and gamble?"

"No. Too expensive, your mother says, and no gambler wins in the long run. Your mother can quote the odds to back up that statement."

Freddy gazed for a while at the lemon tree, along with Harry, then grinned. "Something supposed to happen in that tree, Pop?"

"Something does happen. Lemons get larger, riper, then they drop on the ground and I have to pick them up or they rot."

"Why don't you pick them from the tree before they drop and eat them?"

"Don't like lemons. Useless, bitter fruit from useless trees."

"Mom's worried about you. She told me about your sales receipt-coupon scam. That very profitable?"

"Not really," Harry said. "It's just something to do so I feel useful."

"Kind of clever, though," Freddy said.

"Enough so that it works. Paid for that beer you're drinking."

Freddy sipped beer and continued contemplating the lemon tree with his father.

"Your mother worries too much," Harry said.

"Yep," Freddy agreed. He sighed loudly, stretched, then stood up. "You ever think about planting a different kind of tree, Pop?"

"All the time," Harry said.

The day before he left for New York, Freddy ushered Harry into the den. "Bought you a little gift," he said, "for putting me up here when I needed a place to go."

Harry stared dumbfounded at what was on the table near the window. "A copy machine," he said.

"The latest Mitziguchi-Nagasaki model. Copies anything, in shades of gray or in vivid color."

"I don't know a thing about copiers."

"You will, though," Freddy said. "I know you."

"Copiers got something to do with your business in New York, Freddy?"

"Sorta."

Harry felt like questioning Freddy about New York, about why he'd needed a place to stay and who might be looking for him, but he knew when not to pry. "Not that I don't appreciate your generosity," he said, "but I've got no use for a copier."

"You won't feel that way for long," Freddy said. "It comes with instructions, and it's not as hard to operate as you might imagine. Have fun with it."

He walked into the kitchen and told his mother goodbye, then went out to the garage to get in the rental car and drive it to the airport to catch his flight to New York.

"You be careful in that city," Gretta called, as he was backing the car down the driveway. "I mean, with the crime and all."

"There's crime here in Sun Colony too, Mom," Freddy said, and winked at Harry.

Harry and Gretta stood on the porch and watched their son's car until it was out of sight, a glimmering fragment of their past retreating into memory like all the rest of their lives.

"He must mean muggers," Harry said, and turned to go back in the house.

Freddy was right. Within a few days Harry could work the copy machine without a problem. Within a week he felt he had it mastered.

"I wish you'd get tired of that thing," Gretta told him. "Seems there's at least two of every piece of paper in the house."

Which got Harry thinking. Just fooling around, mind you, he bought some very thin paper and ran copies of a twenty-dollar bill. Astoundingly accurate and precise as they were, he knew they would hardly fool anyone. Besides, counterfeiting was against the law.

But he soon found that coupons were different. It was relatively easy to find copy paper the approximate thickness and glossiness of magazine pages and run off very impressive duplicates of coupons.

The next day—just as a kind of test—Harry copied half a dozen two-for-one coupons for a brand-name athlete's foot spray. He spent the afternoon and part of the evening going to drugstores and supermarkets and passing the bogus coupons. Not one store clerk gave the slightest indication that the coupons might be copies.

"What did all that gain you?" Gretta asked after breakfast the next morning. "Now we've got a dozen aerosol cans of fungus spray we don't need."

"Half of them were free," Harry pointed out. "And don't forget the money we saved on magazines."

"And don't you forget that neither of us has athlete's foot."

Gretta's trouble, as Harry had long known, was that she lacked imagination.

Soon Harry was duplicating scores of coupons. Half off this, a free one of that, a dollar refund with this and proof of purchase. Then he learned to alter dates and figures on genuine sales receipts and run copies of them to send in with his phony coupons. By the end of the month, Harry was turning a tidy profit.

Harry never thought of what he was doing as counterfeiting; it was more like simple and harmless duplicating. He even referred to his duplicates as doppelgängers, a German word meaning "double . . . a shadow self." All he was doing was creating doppelgänger cereal coupons. So what if an old man, a doppelgänger shadow of his old self, made a few dollars in his spare time? Where was the harm?

He did most of his work while Gretta and the widow Wilma played bingo Wednesday and Saturday evenings at the Sun Colony recreation hall.

"I know what you're up to while I'm away," Gretta told him one Sunday morning several weeks later.

"What I'm up to?" Harry said guiltily.

"You're going to bring the FBI down on us, Harry!"

"The FBI doesn't care about an old retired codger like me with a hobby."

"Your hobby's illegal, Harry!"

"You copy rental videos," he pointed out. "That's illegal too."

She sniffed irritably and showed him the twenty-dollar bill she'd won the night before at bingo.

Two days later, Billy, the checkout clerk at the supermarket, paused as he was bagging tuna and said, "Fella was around here asking questions, Mr. Archambault."

"Questions?" Harry said. "Like what aisle's the cereal in?"

Billy smiled. He was too old to be thought of as a boy, really, probably in his mid twenties, but his frail build, blond hair, and poor complexion made him seem like a teenager. "Like he was asking if anybody knew Mr. Archambault, and directions out to your house."

"Anybody tell him?"

"Sure. You ain't got nothing to hide, do you, Mr. Archambault?"

Harry shook his head no, watching Billy begin stuffing a second plastic bag with tuna. "Fella say who he was with?"

"With?"

"You know . . . an insurance company, the Internal Revenue Service, that kind of thing."

"Nope. Barry, the store manager, said the guy was probably a relative of yours, needing directions to pay you a visit. I didn't see him that way, though."

"Oh? Why not?"

"He was a big fella dressed all wrong for Arizona—had dark clothes and wore a tie. Spoke with a slight accent I couldn't quite place. But more than that, he didn't seem, well, friendly. Seemed more . . ."

"Official?"

"Sort of. But with a meanness about him."

Harry's heart began slamming against his ribs. "Like a cop?"

"No, nothing like a cop."

The manager's voice came over the store's speaker system: "Billy, help out on register one."

"He seen us talking," Billy said with a smile. "Barry don't like conversations with the customers on company time."

Harry gathered up his bulging plastic sacks. "Thanks for the information, Billy. If the man turns up, I'll let you know who he is."

"Do that, Mr. Archambault." Billy scurried around the counter and started toward an end register. Then he turned, wiping his hands on his white apron. "One other thing, Mr. Archambault. I figured the guy wasn't a relative because he didn't know your name. Called you Fred."

Freddy, who wrote that his business in New York was doing well, sent Harry a small notebook computer, again with thanks for providing safe haven between Las Vegas and New York. "I'm sure you'll think of something to use it for," Freddy's accompanying note read. "It's in the genes."

Harry wasn't quite sure what his son meant by that. It was as if Freddy knew something about him and was toying with him, providing opportunities and opening doors to see if Harry would step through. Harry had always been scrupulously honest and in fact a bit of a prig, in Freddy's view. Freddy had said so more than once. Now it seemed the amoral Freddy was deriving some sort of pleasure from exploring his father's capacity for corruption. And oddly enough, Harry didn't mind. He'd always been closer to Freddy than to the other kids, and now he felt that only Freddy understood how stultifying life was here in Sun Colony. It was as if Freddy wanted to rescue dear old dad from the tragic and seemingly inevitable trajectory of his remaining years on the moon. Maybe in repayment for all those Cub Scout meetings and horrendous PTA spaghetti dinners.

Harry considered writing or calling Freddy to tell him about the man who'd inquired about him at the supermarket, then decided it wasn't necessary. Freddy had known people were searching for him, and he'd already left, so what was the point?

But he did call Freddy after the man appeared at the front door. It had to be the same man, large, dressed in dark clothing, even a tightly knotted tie that made his thick neck bulge.

"Had a helluva time finding this place," the man said. His features were thickened, as if he'd had an unsuccessful boxing career. The smile he attempted only made him uglier." All the houses look alike."

"They do at that," Harry said.

"I'm looking for a Fred Archambault," the man said, in what Harry knew right away was a New York accent.

"I'm Harry Archambault."

"Yeah, I knew you wasn't him. You know him?"

Harry thought about his answer. Freddy's rental car had been parked out of sight in the garage during his visit, and as far as Harry knew, no one had seen him. One of the advantages of living on the moon. "I've got a son named Fred," Harry said, "but he lives in New York and I haven't set eyes on him in over a year."

"Long way between here and New York," the man said, staring hard at Harry.

"I guess it is," Harry said. "I never made the trip."

"Fred ever made it? To pay you a visit, I mean."

"Let's see . . . Last time he was out here was three Christmases ago."

The big man wiped his forehead with the back of his wrist. "Sure is hot out here."

"But it's a dry heat."

"Mind if I step in outa the sun?"

"Guess not." Harry moved back and let him enter. He felt small next to the man, and old. And slightly sickened by the overpowering scent of stale sweat and cheap deodorant.

With his ugly smile spread wide on his face, the man idly began walking about, gazing through doors and down halls. "Nice place," he commented.

Harry thanked him, glad Gretta was at weaving class.

"Mind if I use the bathroom?" the man asked.

Harry told him where it was.

He listened while the toilet flushed. While the man roamed around the back of the house, making sure all the rooms were unoccupied.

After a few minutes the man returned to the living room, his hands lingering near his belt buckle as if he'd just zipped up his fly. "Thanks," he said.

"I doubt my son's the Fred Archambault you're looking for," Harry told him. "Archambault's a more common name than you might think."

"I suppose you're right." The big man lumbered toward the door.

"Want me to give him your name if he calls? Just in case?" Harry asked.

"Naw, you just be a good senior citizen and don't mention I was here." The smile dropped away from his face, as if it had been too much of a strain for him to hold it there. He nodded goodbye to Harry and walked out the door.

Harry heard a car start and went to the window in time to see the man drive away in a dark-blue Chrysler, probably a rental. He stood watching the car until it was out of sight, feeling angry, not liking that "senior citizen" remark.

After a while, he went to the phone and called Freddy to tell him about the man's visit.

The computer was more difficult than the copier, but Harry soon caught on to it and became quite proficient. About that time, Freddy called from New York and said not to worry about the man who'd visited Harry, that everything had been taken care of and Freddy was sending Harry some new software to go with the computer. Out of gratitude. Freddy had rarely shown gratitude in the past.

Strangely enough, Harry felt a kind of gratitude toward Freddy. He realized that he'd enjoyed the visit from the big man, uneasy though it had made him at the time. It was as if something from the outside world had made it through space to the moon, as if for a change something real had happened in Sun Colony.

A month later Harry surprised Gretta by saying, "I think I'll tag along when you go to play bingo tonight."

"Stay out of my way, then," Gretta said, when she'd lowered her eyebrows. "The other girls and I take our bingo seriously."

"Wilma gonna be there?"

"No, she hasn't been going lately. Got in an argument with Marge about how much pineapple juice was in the punch. Marge punched her. Just stay out of our way."

Harry took her at her word and sat in a corner by himself, near where sweaters, shawls, and light jackets were hung, listening to the bingo caller sing out the numbers, playing with quiet intensity.

★　　★　　★

Sun Colony buzzed for weeks about the string of winning bingo cards Harry had played. It was a run of luck worth a write-up in the *Sun Colony Bugle* under the heading LUCKY SUN COLONY RESIDENT WINS $1000'S AT BINGO.

Harry knew it hadn't exactly been luck. He'd worked out a program on his little computer that enabled him to create an index system for the bingo cards he'd duplicated and kept next to him while he held the computer in his lap. When the computer showed a string of numbers corresponding to a winning card in Harry's file, he quickly and unobtrusively eased the appropriate card up onto the table, covered the necessary numbers with bingo chips, and raised his hand to signify that he'd won.

Easy money. Harry had heard about it all his life, and now here it was, when he was too old to really enjoy it.

Between coupon money and his bingo winnings, Harry had over five thousand dollars: $5,021.26, to be exact. Gretta pointed this out to him when she discovered the money in a coffee can in the garage.

The dollar amount seemed to assuage her guilt, so that she stopped harping at him to quit occupying himself with his high-tech toys. Harry had reached her price.

"What we're going to do with the money," she told him, "is to buy up to a bigger house right here in Sun Colony."

"We don't need a bigger house," Harry pointed out.

"I suppose," Gretta said, frowning, "that you'd rather buy a second house exactly like this one. You've developed a fixation on duplication that's a real irritation."

"That rhymes," Harry said, "like a rap song."

"You're too old for rap music."

"Not as old as you think. Not too old to live."

"You're as old as you *are*, Harry, even though you've developed a foolish streak of vanity and begun to dye your hair."

"You noticed?"

"I found the bottle in the trash. What are you going to do about it?"

"Keep dyeing it, I suppose."

"I mean the larger house. What are you going to do with the money?"

"I'm going to drive to Las Vegas and gamble," Harry said.

She appeared startled, then she smiled. "My, my, you are full of surprises." She rose from where she was sitting on the sofa and began to stalk about the room. Her feet in her practical rubber-soled shoes made no sound on the thick carpet. "It's time you came to your senses, Harry. You've had fun and made money with your electronic toys, but there's a limit. You're going to stop now with your doppelgänger nonsense and—"

But it was Gretta who'd stopped. Her pacing had taken her near a window, and she'd glanced out at the front yard and driveway. Her voice was, for the first time, frightened.

"Harry, who is that woman sitting in our car?"

Harry and Wilma loved Vegas. The system was simple there. You gave a casino cashier money and the cashier gave you chips. Later, if you were lucky, you gave the cashier chips in exchange for more money than you started out with.

Harry didn't see why luck had to have anything to do with it.

J. Michael Straczynski is famous for being the creative spark behind Babylon 5, *the critically and publicly acclaimed science fiction television series. Like many creative people, he works in more than one medium, and we are very happy to bring you this original story by him. "We Killed Them in the Ratings" is a dark look at the dirty tricks of the television industry, and how some people will do anything to get ahead.*

We Killed Them in the Ratings

J. Michael Straczynski

Carl Sarotkin was getting desperate. He tried to hide it from every-one else at the station, carried on with a Business As Usual smile stamped firmly on his face, but he could feel the stress building every day. He was losing weight, his thinning hair was looking even greyer than before, and his eyes felt pinched behind his wide-frame glasses.

StreetScene was slipping in the ratings.

It had started out as a terrific idea. Competition between the Los Angeles independent stations had kicked into high gear, and the general manager was leaning on everyone to develop something snazzy to bring up the seven-thirty to eight P.M. time-slot, before the network feed at eight. Scuttlebutt said the station managers and owners wanted to sell it to one of the new mini-networks, but they needed to boost the ratings first. This would increase the ad revenues and therefore the going price of the station. The other local affiliates filled the 7:30 slot with syndicated "info-tainment" strips, talk shows or magazine format shows covering local sto-ries, elections, whatever made the front pages of the Metro or Style sections in either of the local daily papers. It was good business, low-cost, and gave the news anchors another venue for getting their faces out in front of the public, which in turn kept them from jumping stations.

That's what it all came down to, after all. Business.

Just business.

That was all Carl had in mind when he created *StreetScene*.

⋆   ⋆   ⋆

StreetScene: a mobile minicam unit dispatched to a different neighborhood every day, from the high-priced enclaves of the rich, to the theater district, Chinatown and (during sweeps) the high-crime, hooker infested tenderloin areas, combining interviews with hidden camera shots taped through the mobile unit's rear window. The idea was to show the contrasts of Los Angeles, portray it as a vibrant city in transition, showing the highs and the lows and the in-betweens, the glamour and the gutter, the pimps and the powerful (when you could tell them apart, which was becoming increasingly difficult.) As icing on the cake, the show would be broadcast live, adding an element of immediacy to the show.

Given his background producing other live shows for the station, Carl took the helm of *StreetScene*. It was his idea, after all, and he wanted to see what was happening out there for himself. *Thou shalt know thy audience*. It was the second rule of television.

The first rule being, *Thou shalt make a profit*.

When it came time to present the concept to the news department, he pitched it as The Man On The Street meets *Our Town*. To the advertising department he pitched it on its local angle, and to the program director he pitched it as sleazy and sexy and timely, with a slightly illicit edge (but never going over the line) that would appeal to concerned citizens and busybodies and voyeurs, the same people who had turned *Cops* into a license to print money.

That had sold it immediately. That, and the fact that it would be cheap to produce. They almost always had a spare minicam left out on the streets after the local news, no sets were required, and the only on-screen talent they needed was the local citizenry . . . and they were always camera ready.

The first three weeks of *StreetScene* did solid numbers. Not spectacular—it would have to grow, find its audience, and the PR department would have to get off its butt and actually promote something for a change—but there was real potential. Viewers were curious: which neighborhood would show up next? It seemed to Carl that people had an endless capacity for fascination when it came to watching ordinary people doing ordinary things that suddenly became not so ordinary because they were being done on *television*. That was one of the things that fascinated Carl about television: its ability to elevate the mundane simply by pointing a camera at it and hitting the ON switch in a TV news control room.

A few years before, Carl had been invited to speak before a class of telecommunications students at San Diego State University. Because the proceedings were being taped for the campus library, monitors were positioned at strategic locations throughout the hall, allowing those who were further back to see what was going on at the front of the room.

After a few minutes, he noticed again what he'd seen a hundred times before: even the students close enough for a good view of him and the stage preferred to watch the monitors, to watch the phosphor-dot image rather than the person, even though he was *right there*. At accident and murder locations, when the TV cameras arrived and lit up red at broadcast, onlookers watched the stand-up reporter's TV monitor of the scene rather than looking at the crime scene itself, only five or ten feet away.

Same ground, same yellow tape, same dead body covered by the same rubber coroner's sheet, but the crowd looked at the monitor rather than the real thing.

Because it was on television.

Carl had been willing to take a chance that the rule would obtain with *StreetScene*. His gamble paid off: ratings for the seven-thirty to eight time-slot continued to improve. He was able to move into a better office, with a view of the hillside behind the station. His phone calls were returned more quickly. There were even rumors that the show was being watched closely by the network, which was thinking of adapting the format and putting it on nationally, if it continued to prove itself locally.

He would, of course, become the producer for that show as well. It was, after all, his idea.

And it was clear he knew what the people wanted.

The only nagging question, the one he couldn't answer, was how *long* would they want it?

The ratings began to slip just as the station was gearing up for sweeps. Focus groups confirmed what Carl had dreaded: the immediacy was wearing thin, local curiosity was turning into apathy. Seen one hooker hanging her butt out of the passenger window of a too-small Toyota at midnight, seen 'em all. They had gone from a twenty share, to a seventeen share, to a twelve share. People stopped returning his calls. A new station executive brought in from out of town was sizing up Carl's office every time he walked past.

Carl couldn't deny it any longer. *StreetScene* was fading fast, and taking him with it. He sat in his office, looking out at the hillside that was rapidly turning brown, and closed his eyes, hoping it would all just go away.

He started forward again at a knock at the door. "Yes?"

The door opened slightly, and Margie stuck her head inside. "Andrea says there's a call for you, but said *you* told her you didn't want to be disturbed. I told her I'd check and see if you really meant it."

Carl nodded. "I did, and I do." As his personal assistant and associate producer, Margie was the only one he allowed into his office when he was in a Blue Funk. She had also been much more. But that was history. Six months worth of history. Breaking off their affair had been hard, but he knew that if he didn't, his wife would find out about it sooner or later. Better to cut it short than extend the error and eventually find the affair exposed to gossip, his wife, and her attorneys. Margie had understood, or seemed to. Either way, for six months she had continued to work as efficiently as ever, though now that work consisted mainly of bailing water out of *StreetScene*'s sinking ship.

"What's the call?"

Margie shrugged. "He wouldn't say. But he insisted on speaking only to you. Said it was important."

"I've heard that before." He reached for the phone that, as always, was lit with calls. "Which line?"

"Six." She turned and stepped back into the other office, closing the door behind her.

He pushed the blinking button and sat back. "Carl Sarotkin speaking."

The voice at the other end of the line was quiet, soft-spoken. Carl had to strain a bit to hear the words. "Is this the man in charge of *StreetScene*?"

"You got him. What can I do for you?"

"Monica Fairburn's eyelids were nicked. Two small vertical slashes and a line across."

The sentence took a moment to register. Then Carl's chest tightened and the room suddenly seemed to tilt. Monica Fairburn's body had been found three nights ago, the third victim of the Angel killer. That was the name signed to several postcards sent to the police. The stations had agreed to cooperate with the District Attorney's office and not release some of the physical details, to avoid compromising the investigation. The nicks were one of the things they had not released.

"You still there?"

Carl cleared his throat. "Yeah," he said, "I'm still here." He gripped the receiver tightly, wishing he'd left the door open so he could signal Margie. If they could somehow flag the call and trace it. . . .

"I won't be on very long," the caller said, as if anticipating his thoughts. "So you better get this right the first time. Do you have a pencil?"

"Yeah, sure." Carl grabbed a pencil and notepad. "Shoot."

"Never. A knife is so much more elegant, don't you think?" Angel laughed. Carl's stomach tightened but he said nothing. Somehow he hadn't thought serial killers could have a sense of humor. Granted, it wasn't *that* terrific a joke, but being a serial killer means never having to listen to someone tell you your jokes aren't funny.

"Seven-fifty tonight," Angel said. "Corner of Aberdeen and Fourteenth. You got that? Read it back."

Carl read back the time and address. As if from a great distance he noticed that his hand was shaking. "Is that your address? I mean, if you're going to surrender we can have—"

There was a snort of disgust from the other end. "Not on your life, asshole. Think about it."

He looked at the time. Seven-fifty. If he wasn't going to surrender at that time, then what—

Suddenly, he understood. "Oh, shit. . . ."

"Then you understand," Angel said, and Carl heard a smile in his voice. "That's good. But get this straight: no one comes near me, no one tries to talk to me, no one does anything. You tell your people to stay in their van and do their job or there'll be four more people meeting the Angel tonight."

"Why are you doing this?" Carl asked.

"People have to understand. They have to listen to the message of the Angel. Seeing is understanding. Seeing is *believing*. They must believe. In time, they'll understand what I'm doing. Once that happens, I'll stop. You're doing them a *favor*. So think it over. But don't take too long."

Click and disconnect.

Carl racked the phone and for two minutes did absolutely nothing, allowing himself two minutes of panic as he decided what to do.

His first impulse was to call the police. But his hand didn't reach for the rolodex, where the pager number for the lead detective investigating the Angel murders was two cards down, just past Domino's

Pizza. He was a producer of a news/information show, not a cop. Catching murderers wasn't his job.

The relationship between police and reporters was a delicate and constantly changing one. TV stations were frequently subpoenaed for tapes to be used as evidence in trials. Those subpoenas had been successfully fought, but always with great difficulty. At the Atlanta Olympic pipe bombing, camera crews had recorded the blast, the panic, the crush of people falling over one another in a blind rush for the open streets, the wounded bleeding onto the cobblestones, but hadn't moved to help, to bind up, to resuscitate, to hold hands or staunch bleeding.

Because that wasn't their job.

Reporters weren't supposed to take sides, they were to be uninvolved observers. The reporters who'd covered Vietnam weren't there to fight for their country, they were there to report the news. Reporters traveling with Central American guerrilla troops fighting American-backed government forces had to refrain from passing back intelligence to "our" side, always for the same reason: to report, not make, the news.

Reporters in the Midwest had even stood by, tape rolling, as a man immolated himself on the lawn of City Hall. It had been a terrible thing. But the report made national news, got constant airplay, and the networks paid good money for the rebroadcast rights. Carl was reasonably certain that, whatever moral concerns had been running through the mind of that cameraman, he did his job, and had been rewarded for it with a big new office . . . maybe even one overlooking a hillside.

Terrorists, hostage takers, snipers, bombers, kidnappers, they had all realized the McLuhanesque dream of brief fame on television courtesy of the all-seeing Eye that does not blink, does not judge, and does not turn away.

Was this really any different?

If he notified the police, they'd send out a SWAT team and probably spook the Angel into going underground. Then when he emerged, he'd be even more dangerous than before. And somewhere on the list of victims-to-come, Carl suspected, would be his own name. If Angel were telling the truth, they'd lose their chance to help people understand why he was doing this, which in the final analysis was all the guy wanted, and then he'd go away. They'd lose a chance to *save* lives.

Besides, if a minicam crew just happened to be at the scene of the crime moments before it *became* the scene of the crime, they might be able to get the first pictures of the Angel . . . pictures that could be critical in bringing him to justice.

There was one more factor to be considered: no one else knew that the call had come. He could choose to keep this to himself for now, and send out the *StreetScene* crew the same way he sent it out every weeknight. No one else needed to know. Afterward, if there were any questions or suspicions, Carl could plead coincidence. Like the man who got a photograph of a falling PSA Airline jet that was so clear that you could almost see the faces through the windows, or the Rodney King case, or the amateur photographer who shot ten minutes of tornado on his home video camera, it would simply be a case of synchronicity. The right camera in the right place at the right time.

"Margie!"

The door swung open a second later. "Yeah, boss?"

"Which location are we slated for tonight? The street fair or the Boy's Club Olympics?"

"Street fair. News division found out the Mayor's going to make a surprise visit, so we scrubbed the boy's club. They were pretty mad. I didn't think they allowed that kind of language in the boy's club."

Carl nodded, wondering if the Angel had planned it this way. Strike when the mayor would be across town, taking with him a substantial number of cops and tying them up with the need for crowd control and Hizzoner's personal protection.

Carl chewed his lip, hesitating.

"Something up, Carl?"

He nodded. "Scrub the street fair. Reroute the van to the corner of Aberdeen and Fourteenth. Then get hold of research, see if they have any interesting historical stuff on the neighborhood: colorful residents, crime rate, has anybody big come from there, anything and everything. Just give us something for voice-over, okay?"

"Yeah, I guess." Margie's face was unreadable, a mask. "It's a grungy neighborhood; I doubt research will find much. You sure you want to do this?"

"Nope. But let's do it anyway."

Margie threw up her hands and headed out into her office. "Okay," she said doubtfully, "it's your neck."

As the door closed, Carl added, "Not necessarily."

Seven-thirty P.M.

They were on the air.

It was the longest twenty minutes Carl Sarotkin had ever known. Research had done their usual good job, and had come up with a few

useful facts with seconds to spare before they hit broadcast. The neighborhood featured some of the oldest homes in the city, and many of them
were faced with demolition, barring an effort by the Historical Society to
stop the redevelopment, or at least relocate the structures to another location. Covering that part took them to the first commercial break.

Carl ran through it in his head. The audience would still be with
him to this point. They wouldn't start channel surfing until they got
closer to the top of the hour. And people always go for the little-guy vs.
the big bad developers story. But it wouldn't hold for a full half-hour.

Not unless something happened.

After the commercial break came the man-on-the-street segment.
One of the news crew stood outside the van, soliciting comments. The
first few passers-by declined to be interviewed, which was standard for
this sort of thing. Others were content to stop and answer a few questions about the upcoming mayoral election, and the gun-control initia-
tive on the ballot this year. In the background, a handful of kids waved
at the camera, while a few adults further back studiously avoided the
camera's glare. Carl guessed they were drug dealers, but studied them
closely, wondering if any of them might be *him*.

They were running out of story.

"This is gonna kill us," Margie said from behind him. The control
room was just big enough for the director, himself and Margie. It was
always tense, but now the frustration in the air was almost palpable. "A ten
share tops, mark my word. Shit." She sat back, lit up another cigarette.

Carl glanced up at the clock as the sweep-second hand passed
7:48. Just how punctual *was* this guy, anyway? On the monitor, he could
see the number of people on the street starting to thin out. That always
happened once they pulled the cameras back inside the van for the next
segment, a taped background piece they'd put together earlier. A few
people walked by, but most were inside the two-story walkups on either
side of the street, eating dinner, or—most likely, he thought with some
discomfort—watching the other channel.

Carl had to admit that by now he'd have switched channels himself. If they could hold on just a minute longer. . . .

Then a scream came through the monitor.

Even filtered through the walls of the van it sounded horrible,
barely human. The director sat up at his console, all attention now,
shouting instructions. "What the hell's going on out there?" He listened
for the frantic response from the van on the closed-circuit audio feed.
Carl could hear the shouting from the director's headset even several

seats down. "Get the camera around! Two, go two! God damn it, get it around!"

The image on the screen cut to a shot of the street from camera two, positioned at the van's side window.

There. A flash of movement in an alley barely lit by a street lamp. A man. Long coat. Hat. His face concealed behind something dark, maybe cloth. He had her up against the alley wall, forearm against her neck, pinning her back, hard, and forcing her face up. Her eyes glittered in the lamplight.

He's playing to the camera, Carl thought, distantly. *He wants us to see her face.*

"Oh my god," Margie said. "Oh, god, look!"

It happened in an instant. Another flash. Something bright glittered in his hand, then disappeared in the gap between them. She screamed again. Briefly. Then slumped to the ground. He stood over her, his back to the van.

The director shouted over his shoulder. "Camera crew's asking to go outside. They want to—"

"No! Tell them to stay put!" Carl was almost frantic now. "Margie, get the police, fast!" Not that it was necessary; by now there were probably half a dozen squad cars en route to the scene. But it would help keep them off the track.

Keep them from finding out what Carl knew.

He looked up at the monitor again. The killer was still there. Taking his time. The dark figure bent over the smaller one, and did something the camera couldn't pick up. *Probably nicking the eyes,* Carl thought, surprised at his ability to look at this objectively. Then the Angel ran off down the alley, never turning back, never allowing the camera a clear shot of him. He made it out of sight around a corner, the sound of his footfalls replaced a moment later by the roar of a car racing away into the gathering dark.

The Angel's newest victim did not move.

The police arrived within minutes, too late to do anything but cordon off the area, and expel the camera crew and van after questioning them thoroughly and getting statements.

No one even thought to question Carl. Everyone assumed that it was coincidence, nothing more. If anything, the police seemed grateful, though they'd never admit it. For the first time they had something to go on, could at least add the basics of height and weight and build to the Angel APBs. They compared relative heights to points in the alley, examined the position of the van and its angle relative to the assault, and worked out a whole series of measurements.

They would not be the only important measurements made that night.

The overnight ratings said that the last ten minutes of *StreetScene* shot up to a thirty share, the highest rating anybody could remember for a long time. Carl knew it would drop a little over the next few weeks, but they could keep it at a good level by holding the exclusive rights to the segment and rebroadcasting it on a twice-weekly basis, ostensibly to help capture the Angel. But it was simply good business . . . provided he could keep the station manager from selling the footage to competing stations in order to make a few short-term dollars.

The program director had been sickened by what he saw that night, horrified when he reran the raw footage, but eminently satisfied with the numbers. It was at least as good as the SLA shootout and the Reagan near-assassination combined, and when the footage went out on their proprietary feed, NBC jumped in fast, picking up the details for overnight and national news the next day. Even Ted Koppel mentioned it, though he couldn't show any of it. Wrong network.

With that kind of exposure, viewers who had left the show came back out of curiosity, and those who had never previously watched *StreetScene* tuned in to see the segment that had made history, when the crew happened to be in the right place at exactly the right time. Suddenly the station was looking even better to both the mini-nets and the big boys at the three-letter networks.

Carl was determined to hold onto that audience. He sent minicam units back into the neighborhood for follow-up reports: interviews with neighbors and those who saw the attack, statements from police officials and Neighborhood Watch advocates. Were there sightseers at the scene of the murder? Did local tourism go up, or down? What was the impact of the murder, and what was the impact of their coverage of the murder?

Carl loved it when a story lent itself to them doing a story on themselves. What was the responsibility of journalists in a situation like this? How did it affect the news team? Would the coverage have effects on the community? There was a parade of consultants, psychologists, councilmen, attorneys and ministers. It was a TeeVee Mobius loop, feeding from viewer to reporter and back again, and because he was in control of it, he could play out one aspect after another.

And, of course, they ran the tape of the attack endlessly. For the public good. Strictly to help find the Angel killer.

But as rich a gold mine as he'd struck, he knew he could only mine it for so long. Sooner or later, they'd have to go back to their normal programming.

The question then was, what next? How do you top something like this?

Having built up momentum for the series, he had to find ways to keep that momentum going when the sensationalism died down. Over the following weeks, he tried out several of them. He tried changing the thrust of StreetScene, so it would no longer focus on street fairs, festivals, tanning salons for rich, or the all-too-frequent hundredth birthday of some local citizen who—just to piss off the doctors who had poked and prodded and prescribed foul-tasting medications for a full century— would ascribe that longevity to four cigars and a glass of gin every day.

StreetScene dedicated itself to examining the underbelly of the city it served. They began with a series of stories about the city's growing porn industry, setting up shop in front of a motel known for renting out rooms to producers of x-rated videos, leaving only when threatened by a lawsuit by the manager, citing interference with his trade. Which was true and not-true. The minicam didn't violate the letter of the law, which required that they present a physical obstacle to those wishing to enter the motel. But who wanted their face broadcast all over the city as they went inside to star in the Hi-Eight production of "Twins In Love"?

They got a few good pieces of film out of that one. Audiences loved sidewalk spats and people driving off with coats over their heads to hide from the media. But the ratings still dropped two points.

So they moved the minicam into progressively seedier parts of town. They broadcast drug deals going down, followed hookers as they plied their trade along dark streets. Mid-week they caught a break and managed to spot a mugging in-progress, the story going out live and continuing as police—alerted by the broadcast—sped to the scene in time to apprehend the muggers.

Ratings jumped back four points that night, and stayed there through Friday, bolstered by the realization that the police were watching this show too, and might respond if things got hot. That would increase the potential for action.

At this point, Carl decided to go to tape-delay. The feed would come in to the station, be processed, and go out to the viewers five minutes later. As far as the audience ever knew, it was a live broadcast.

And technically, it was. They just fudged a bit, to make sure the police didn't arrive on the scene too early.

After all, they had half an hour to fill.

"Carl?"

Carl rolled over, half asleep, and pulled the covers up over his head. Why did Grace always wait until he was ready for sleep before she would bring up Matters Of Importance? He could tell that this was going to be one of those. She had that sound in her voice. "Hmph?" he said.

"When are you going back to the old format?"

"I dunno. Soon, maybe."

A moment passed. "I just don't like it. The way you've got it now."

"I've noticed."

"It's so, I don't know—so seedy. I always feel like I need a bath afterward."

"We're performing a public service."

She shook her head. "You're going for the numbers."

"Same thing."

Another silence. "How's the show doing?"

"Okay. But I'm not. I need some sleep, okay?"

He closed his eyes, knowing sleep would be denied him now that the wheels had started turning again, now that The Problem had flagged down his attention.

The ratings were slipping again.

Carl's intercom buzzed as he was going over the schedule for the coming week. Andrea's voice came through a moment later. "Line five, Carl."

Carl didn't look up from his schedule. "Who is it?"

"He wouldn't say. Just said to tell you it was an old friend."

Carl reached for the phone, his gut tightening. Even before he heard the voice on the other end, he suspected—no, *knew*—it would be him.

"You did real well," the voice said, a voice like dry leaves rustling down a sidewalk.

"I did my job, that's all."

"Yeah, right. We all got our jobs to do, don't we? You got yours, and I got mine. We're both in the education business. We just have different ways of going about it."

"Look, what's this—"

The voice cut him off. "Pencil and paper."

Carl rubbed at his face. "I don't know. . . ."

"Paper and pencil or I hang up."

Lips thin, Carl reached for a pen. *If I don't take it, he'll just call some other station.* "Go ahead."

The voice on the other end supplied a time, and a place. Carl recognized the address as a slightly better district than the Angel had previously hit. It wouldn't be difficult to divert the minicam team there, wouldn't seem too much a break in format.

Carl stopped short. Was he really going to do this? Give the Angel another broadcast? Send his crew into a possibly dangerous situation? What was he *thinking* of?

"They must be there," the voice said, anticipating him again. "They must carry my message."

"We can't give you air-time for a statement. No way."

"No statement. The mission *is* the message." He hung up.

Carl cradled the phone. "Margie!"

She appeared in the doorway a moment later. "Yeah?"

"A change tonight. Here's the address. Have research—"

"I'll get them," Margie said. She took the slip of paper, looked at it, lingered longer than she had to. Then she reached behind her and shut the door, lingering inside.

"First a phone call comes. Then you turn several shades of pale, and now this. Same as the last time you changed the schedule on me. The night we ran into the Angel."

Carl said nothing. He never could hide anything from women. Not her. Not Grace. Which was why there was only Grace now and not her in his bed.

"You've got a pipeline to this guy, don't you?" she said.

"That's pure speculation."

"Which whenever a politician says it, always means yes. Relax. Nobody'll know but us. Nobody'll even suspect. Things are so disorganized around here that I don't give anyone the schedule for the evening shoot until a couple of hours before they leave anyway."

"I don't know what you're talking about."

"Okay, then let me try this on you for size." She held up the sheet of paper. "If—just if—anyone should ask me when you gave me the address for tonight's shoot, I'll tell them that we arrived at this by mutual consensus as early as last week. Do you have a problem with that?"

Carl looked away, said quietly, "No."

Margie nodded, turned back toward the door, then hesitated. "What's he . . . I mean, what does he sound like?"

"Like death," Carl said, looking at her hard. "What the hell did you expect?"

The Angel's next attack was almost a carbon-copy of the one before. Except this time the victim was a man, a harmless looking little fellow wearing a Dodgers baseball cap who was yanked into an alley as he passed it on his way home. The camera caught it all. The cry of surprise, then the bludgeon—a claw hammer, the police would later determine—coming down, once, twice, again and again. Then the speedy retreat, pausing only to nick the victim's eyes.

The ratings skyrocketed.

This time, though, there *were* questions to be answered. The police noted the coincidence, but went in the wrong direction. They assumed the Angel was following the mobile unit around in hopes of finding the right moment to get on television. This possibility did little to comfort the minicam team, who were far from mollified by the offer of police protection for the next week or so, just until it could be determined if the van was, indeed, being followed.

After they left, Margie stepped back into the office and closed the door behind her again. "We've got the standard offer from the networks for the piece, although they want this one edited down a little better than the last one. Seems some folks out in DuBuque got a bit nauseous last time."

Carl nodded numbly. It would be a difficult editing job. There had been blood everywhere. . . .

"Did you hear the latest?" She waited until he shook his head. "Rumor from upstairs has it that the NBC owned-and-operateds are willing to commit to a weekly national series if we can keep an average rating of a twenty share for the rest of the month. They'll make some changes, broaden the appeal a little, but that's to be expected. They buy you for what makes you different, then take away whatever made you different and interesting so you'll fit their format. That means you lose the whole point of the show and, over time, the viewers. But what the hell, by then we're in at a network and we can write our own ticket."

She came over, sat on the edge of his desk. "Who knows? Maybe we'll turn it into The Crime of the Week. Make it into a game show.

Thieves! Robbers! Rapists! C'mon down! Show us your stuff! Call early for reservations, and don't forget the home game version. What do you think?"

"Charming."

She nodded. "Yeah, it does have a certain *je ne sais quoi*, doesn't it?" Smiling down at him, she brushed his hair back from his forehead, letting her hand linger for a moment. "We're going places together, aren't we? I always said we made quite a team."

"You're forgetting someone, aren't you?" he asked, tapping his ring finger with his thumb.

"Not one bit," she said, and leaned over. She kissed him gently, and to his surprise Carl found himself returning it. She sat back, nodded as if satisfied with something he'd said—or, more precisely, hadn't said—and swept out of the room, looking quietly pleased with herself.

As she walked out, Carl remembered reading somewhere that the Chinese ideogram for trouble was a symbol showing two women under one roof.

"Trouble," Carl muttered, "on top of trouble."

Two weeks later Carl was coming back from a lunch that went later than he had planned. The ratings were still fairly solid. They generally petered out a little in the last quarter hour, once it became apparent that nothing major was going to happen, but they were sticking around long enough to give the sponsors the overall half-hour rating they needed. As he headed past Andrea at the front desk, the mannequin-pretty receptionist flagged him down and handed him a number of pink sheets. "Your messages."

"Thanks," he said, pressing on.

"Oh, and while you were out, your friend called again."

Carl turned back toward the desk. "What friend?"

"I don't know, I'm just repeating what he said. He told me he had some information for you, but he wouldn't say what it was. He was very upset that you weren't here, and said he'd try to get hold of you at home."

Carl felt the blood rushing in his ears. "He had my home number?"

"Yes," she said, but he was already past her and heading for his office. *Grace,* he thought. *Oh, shit.*

He slammed through the office door and was dialing before he even sat down. One ring. Three. Seven.

He held the receiver to his ear, panic squeezing his heart.

A knock, and Margie popped in. "Oh, good, you're back."

Carl racked the phone. "We've got to do something, he knows my—"

She pressed a finger to her lips, and nodded toward the waiting room. "Your wife's here, and she doesn't look happy. You don't think she's found out about us now, after all this time, do you?"

Carl racked the phone, relief flooding in. "That's the least of my worries right now. Send her in."

Margie stepped out. A moment later the door reopened, and Grace entered, shutting the door behind her.

Doesn't look happy doesn't begin to describe her, he thought.

"Carl," she said, "I want you to tell me what's going on. I want you to *talk* to me."

"About what?"

"Don't lie to me, Carl. This isn't the time, and I'm not in the mood. I got a call at the house an hour ago from a man who said he was a friend of yours. He wouldn't give his name. He kept trying to give me an address, but when I asked him what this was about, he got . . . strange, angry. And his voice. . . ." Her own voice tapered off. Carl knew all too well what she must have heard.

"I asked him how he knew you. He said he'd only spoken to you over the phone, and you'd never met in person. Then he asked if I'd seen the broadcasts on the days those two people were killed. I said how could I not see them, they were all over the place. Then he asked me what I'd *learned* from watching them."

"What did you say?"

"That it proved there are a lot of sick people out there who ought to be locked up for the rest of their lives. That's when he got really angry, that kind of angry that comes out cold and hard and quiet. He said to never mind, and he'd call you here, later."

Carl nodded, said nothing. He felt the trap closing around him.

"For the last time, Carl, what have you gotten yourself *into*? How did this man get our phone number?"

"Grace, I'll explain it all later. Honest. But right now, I just can't."

Grace's jaw worked, the cheeks tightened. "It's him, isn't it? That . . . that *monster*. I felt something was wrong, something inside you. I just didn't know what it was. But as soon as I picked up the phone, as soon as I heard him, I got a chill. I was *afraid*. I just want you to look me in the face and tell me that it isn't him."

He looked up at her, knowing that the truth was in his eyes, and knowing that she would see it, as she always did. "And if it is?"

"Then I want you to cancel the show. I want it *over*! I won't tell anyone about this if it stops now, because it could ruin both of us. But if it happens again, I'm going to the police. I love you, but I won't let you get involved in this madness. For your own sake."

She stepped closer to him, but stopped halfway across the room, hesitant to touch him. "If there's no killing tonight, maybe I'll believe you, that it isn't him. But if there is, I'll know, and one of us will have to do something about it."

With that, she turned and, without looking back, stepped quickly out of the office.

The click-clack of Grace's heels was no sooner gone than Margie stepped into the office. "Boy, it's a good thing you have me here to save your ass."

Carl groaned quietly, wishing the ground would open up and swallow him. "Too late."

"No, it's not," she said, and for the first time he noticed the slip of paper in her hands. "*He* called while you were talking to Grace. Lucky for you I was here to take the call. Your friend is getting loonier every day."

"He's not my friend."

"I know. But he sure takes rejection personally. He gave me the time and place, said if the team's not there, he'll go on a real rampage, double the killings. Of course, we'll say we were planning to be there all along, as soon as we. . . ."

"Forget it." He stood, taking the sheaf of papers with the week's schedule and dumping them into a drawer. "Grace knows. She threatened to go to the police if there's another killing."

"Well, that's too bad, because we don't have any control over what he does. We can't even get hold of him."

"No, we can't," Carl admitted, "but we can at least not put it on the air. That'll count for something."

She made a sound of disgust. "What a waste."

"Yeah, and it happens every day. Remember, there was a time when every casual murder didn't show up in your front room in living color."

Margie shook her head. "You're really going to do it, aren't you? You're knuckling under." Her tone verged on amazement. "Unbelievable. This is the best chance we've ever had to get out of here, go network, and you're pissing it away because you don't want wifey getting all shook up. This has been *good* for us, damn it!"

"Swell choice of words."

"All we need is one last good show, one more good ratings night and we're out of here anyway. The Nielsen people think we can hit a forty share or better, Carl. *Forty*. Christ, we haven't had a forty since the networks were blown off the air during the fires five years ago. You want to drop it then, walk away, fine. We'll be on our way and away from all this anyway. Wifey'll get her wish. You'll be free and clear. Everybody gets what they want."

"And if Grace doesn't see it that way, and goes to the police?"

"She won't. She's not the type. She only wants you out of this. She doesn't really care about what's going on out there. She can't relate to it. As long as you're not involved, as far as she's concerned, that's the end of it. And that'll happen after tonight."

"You don't know her like I do. At the very least she'll leave me."

"So? You once told me that wouldn't be such a bad thing."

"Different circumstances." He sat back heavily. "I'm sorry, Margie, I don't see any way around it. We're going back to our old format, starting tonight. If he calls after that, we'll figure out some way to put him off. Tell him the station manager overrode us, that we had technical difficulties, anything. If he gets abusive we'll just stop taking his calls."

"And then what?"

"I don't know, but we'll figure out something. Now I suggest you get hold of the crew and give them their schedule. Pick anything, I don't care." He thought for a moment. "Isn't there a block-party going on in Little Italy tonight?"

Margie winced, nodded. "Yeah."

"Then that's it," Carl said. "We'll go with that. As of now, it's over. Clear?"

She shrugged and headed out. "Whatever you say, boss."

There was a tone in her voice he didn't like, but then, he could understand her feelings. This was their chance, and he was cutting them off at the knees on the last lap of the race. But he couldn't risk losing Grace, or going to jail, or both.

It was the right thing. She'd see that in time.

Stu, the director, glanced up as Carl entered the control room. "You're late." The clock read 7:26.

Carl ignored him, found Margie, asked if she'd told the station manager they were changing tonight's format. She nodded. "What'd he say?" Carl asked.

"'Whatever it is, just make it good.'" She shrugged. "Well, we'll try, but the way things are right now, I have my doubts."

Carl nodded, looked back at the clock. 7:29. There was nothing on the console. "Shouldn't we be receiving the feed by now?" he asked. The time delay was usually five minutes, sometimes seven.

"No point to it now," Margie said, "there's nothing to delay. Just endless shots of pasta and pizza and overweight grandfathers dancing with little girls standing on the tops of their shoes."

There was a knock on the door, and Andrea stuck her head in. "Call for you on seven, Carl."

"I don't think you should take it," Margie said quietly, giving him that look that said trouble might be at the other end. He knew exactly what kind of trouble she meant.

"Tell whoever it is that we're about to go on the air and I can't be disturbed, all right? Just that and no more."

Andrea shrugged, looked as if she had a question, but chose not to voice it. She said only "Okay," and stepped back out of the control room.

Stu glanced over at both of them. "Is there something going on here I should know about?"

"No comment," Carl said, smiling as winningly as he could.

Stu shrugged resignedly, then turned back to the control board, fingers hovering over the rows upon rows of switches, faders, levers and illuminated buttons with easy familiarity.

The sweep second hand on the wall clock hit 7:30 exactly. The station ID flashed on the on-air monitor.

"It's showtime," Stu said, and his fingers flew over the board. "Cue open," he said.

The monitor went from the ID to true black. Held for a beat. Then two. Then the music, low but building. Under the music, the sounds of conversations, laughter, snatches of street-talk; car horns, heels clicking on sidewalks, trucks rumbling down streets, each sound cross-fading over the next, an audio-montage designed to suggest a busy, active, vibrant street life. Then, on the black screen, jagged white lines began to appear, slicing down the screen, forming letters that became words that became

StreetScene.

"Hi, baby," Carl whispered to the monitor. "Bye, baby."

Margie said nothing, only sat and smoked in stony silence, watching the credits flicker by.

Produced by Carl Sarotkin.
Associate Producer Margaret Whitmore.

Then: a fade to black, dissolving into scenes shot by the van as it traveled to its latest destination. This was the only pre-taped part of the show. The voice-over provided background on what landmarks they were passing, what the neighborhoods were like. . . .

Carl barely heard it. "We *might* get a thirty share for a block party," he said, trying to be positive. "We have a large Italian population here. And there might be enough of an audience hanging on from the last broadcast to carry us through."

Margie's eyes reflected the same sure doubt he held in his own mind. "Only if it's one hell of a block party. Or if *all* of them are Nielsen or Arbitron families, or if they get abducted by aliens. . . ."

"Skip it," Carl said, and sat back to watch his baby go down in flames.

"Okay, ready two," Stu said into the closed-circuit mike that kept him in touch with the van. He paused, then: "Go two." The image on the monitor shifted, stabilized. The camera crew had arrived at their destination and were cruising slowly through the streets, shooting out through the window.

"Give me a follow shot," Stu said quietly as the van passed a few kids playing on a corner, and another few further down who were trying without much success to open a fire hydrant. A couple of cars passed the van going in the opposite direction.

Odd, Carl thought. *When they have a block party they usually cut off the street to thru-traffic.* "Must be a smaller party than we thought," he said.

He swiveled at the sound of the door opening. Andrea stood in the doorway again. "That was your wife on the phone, Carl. She said to tell you she understands, she accepts your offer, and she's waiting. Oh, and she wants to know why you picked such a crummy neighborhood for dinner." Andrea stepped back out to the sound of the switchboard ringing in the other room.

"Go one," Stu said. A long, darkened street appeared on the monitor. The street lamps had come on nearly half an hour ago, but they didn't seem to do much good.

Carl swiveled back, looked at Margie. "What the hell was *that* all about?"

Margie hesitated before answering, appearing inordinately interested in the burning tip of her cigarette. "I just thought I'd call her and let her know your decision. She seemed very relieved." She kept glancing furtively at the clock.

"Zoom in," the director said. On the screen: deserted shops, a few still open, bars on their windows. A liquor store. "Pan along."

"But dinner—"

"It just seemed like a good idea, get the rapprochement off on the right foot," she said. Then she looked at him . . . and something in her expression froze him to the spot.

She said I picked a crummy neighborhood. . . .

He glanced at the monitor. "Where did you tell her to meet me, Marge?"

Silence.

"Goddamn it Marge, where did you—"

"Go two."

"*Jesus Christ, Margie!*" But she was looking at the monitor.

Not looking at him. At the monitor. Where a lone woman stood outside a questionable looking restaurant. She checked her watch, visibly impatient. He couldn't see her face yet, but he didn't need to.

In a second Carl was on his feet, grabbing for the control room phone.

"What're you doing?" Stu asked, then glanced up sharply. "Oh, shit!"

Carl spun about.

He was there. He glided out of the shadows with practiced ease. The camera had found him, but Grace hadn't. She stood with her back to the darkness. *Look around, god, please look around!*

He was on her in a second. Fast. Christ, how fast! The flash of a steel blade, almost too quick to see. They fell to the ground.

"Oh god oh god ogod. . . ." Carl's knees went out from under him. He fell into the chair, horror squeezing at his heart. He couldn't breathe.

Suddenly a spotlight pierced the night from above. The blue-white light illuminated what he hadn't seen until now, had hoped he wouldn't see, knew he would never stop seeing whenever he closed his eyes.

There was so much blood, an impossible amount.

"Pull back!" Stu shouted. He was frantic, trying to follow the action, unmindful of what was going on behind him. "There!"

Three squad cars screeched up at both ends of the street. Police jumped out, guns drawn. The spotlight danced crazily, lancing down from the helicopter hovering above.

"Freeze!" someone shouted. "Drop the knife!"

The Angel turned from the still body, and in the fierce light Carl could see every detail of his face; the madness, the anger, the determination. The eyes so wide, so full of hate and frustration.

He ran forward, reaching into his long coat as he screamed something so garbled and throaty that Carl couldn't catch it, could only make out: *have to understand!*

They opened fire.

A spray of bullets, more than Carl had ever seen, splattered the wall behind the Angel, wave after wave of them, splintering brick, shattering wood, opening flesh, exploding bones into shards.

For a moment the Angel stood under the onslaught, body suspended by the force of the bullets driving into him, holding him up against the wall by sheer momentum. Then he fell.

Everything *right there*. On the monitor.

Now there were two bodies on the sidewalk.

The firing stopped.

"Go in! Go in!" Stu was screaming now, ordering the crew out of the van, to take the hand-held cameras, get on-the-spot interviews. Reactions.

Close-ups.

"We got it!" Stu cried. "Jesus, we got it! The cops must've been watching, went in as soon as they saw it go down. Thank god we weren't on tape delay." Then he was back on line with the minicam crew.

The camera moved in for a better view of the bodies. In a second, Stu and everyone else would know that the wife of the producer of *StreetScene* had become the last victim of the Angel, that fate had closed the case with a final, cruel irony.

Margie stubbed out her cigarette, exhaled slowly, and nodded to herself.

"A forty share, at least," she said.

Marlys Millhiser is a popular author whose series character, Hollywood agent Charlie Green, has appeared in several novels, with more (hopefully) on the way. She has also written excellent stand-alone books, Willing Hostage *being a fine example. She takes ordinary occurrences and slowly turns them on end until the result is quite different from what's expected. In "Cara's Turn," the simple act of buying a house sets loose all sorts of trouble.*

Cara's Turn

Marlys Millhiser

Ed Hornsby could smell the closing before he and his client stepped out of his car. This property had certainly been good to him.

The house sat up close to the street, an updated Victorian on the outside with clear-stained cedar siding and bay windows, teal colored trim, and picket fence. Inside it was modern, quality all the way, and unique even for Boulder. Ed should know: he'd built it for himself.

But Cara Williams pulled up short before she reached the tiny front porch. "You're beginning to remind me of a used car salesman, Mr. Hornsby." She'd called him Ed until he'd sold her house out from under her. "You promised to show me only houses in my price range. I told you we can't afford much debt right now with Jay due to retire. And he's not going to move twice."

Cara was middle-aged, plump, and taking on that vagueness older married women use to fight stress. Ed had noticed how divorce or widowhood resharpened them fast. His ex, Sharon, for one. She'd turned into a veritable stiletto after only a few months of shock.

"This is in your price range. And notice it has a small yard so your husband won't have to spend all his time mowing. And the double garage he wanted."

"It's almost sitting in the street." But she rolled her head back to look up at the peaked roof above the porch that matched the peaked roof of the house above the upstairs bays.

"Hey, you don't have to mow street." Ed had talked the Williamses into putting their house up for sale because it was on an acre with a buildable lot behind it. Well, he'd talked Cara into it. That was the only house the couple had ever owned, an old fifties ranch. They'd raised a family and now had extra rooms in a rundown seventies decor, but in an upscale Boulder where deserting Californians were infilling the little available space left. Ed had set the price low and turned that sucker over before Jay Williams had the chance to pout and scowl long enough to make his wife give up the idea.

"So what's wrong with it?" The sky was gray, her hair was gray, her eyes were gray, and so was the lone snowflake that glided down to rest on the top edge of her rimless glasses. Why didn't she take hormones, color her hair, lose weight, fix herself up? Sharon had, but not until he'd dumped her. Bitch.

"You said you wanted a change at this point in your life." He rang the bell and waited until it appeared Custler wasn't home before he went to the lock box attached to the garage door handle, spun the combination, and extracted the house key.

Ed had planned all along to move the Williamses out of town. Boulder was getting too upscale for them and they were afraid of debt. They could afford a real upgrade out in the county with the money he'd sold their property for. But they refused to budge and on that he hadn't been able to out-maneuver them, even with the closing date on their house days away.

This house was, frankly, the only choice they had unless they wanted to risk renting until something else turned up. California money was driving everything sky high and Real Realty was raking it in. And the Williamses were definitely not risk takers. He reached for the front door hoping she wouldn't notice the scratches where a workman had been careless the last time the locks were changed. And he remembered to turn off the alarm system just inside the front door without her noticing it. It was embarrassing to have the police arrive while you were showing a house.

"Well, welcome home, Cara."

Cara Williams had heard those words before and from the same mouth. She'd seen other doors open with the same flourish by the same hand. She wasn't impressed. But she was panicked. Jay was going to be hell to live with for being forced to move at all. He wouldn't stand for it twice if they had to rent. He did not appreciate anything ruffling his routine. Flat and placid is how he liked his life and made hers. Sometimes she appreciated that and sometimes it suffocated her.

At first glance, Cara couldn't tell what was wrong with the house.

The door opened to stairs climbing the wall to the second floor. Next to them was a long room serving as both living and dining room. The carpet was a lighter teal than the trim and the picket fence outside, rather than the cheap sterile neutral color that coated every other house Ed Hornsby had shown her. The small kitchen and family room combination had golden hardwood flooring Jay would never have allowed in their huge country kitchen. The two combination main-floor rooms formed an L around the attached garage.

A grand piano. An elegant glass-topped dining-room table. Shiny gas fireplaces with marble hearths in living and family rooms. Small sculptures and large paintings of hunting scenes or couples copulating. Jenn-Air appliances and ceramic tile counter tops in the kitchen.

Everything was of a fineness Jay would consider ostentatious and nonessential. Pipes and insulation and furnaces and wiring were what mattered.

"So what's wrong with this place, Mr. Hornsby?" But Cara, once she figured out all the locking mechanisms and lifted the floor bar, opened the sliding glass doors to step out onto a back deck and discovered what was wrong with this place for herself.

A deck crowded with a covered hot tub Jay would never pay to keep heated. Tiny backyard with a circle of grass around a circle of sandstone with a charming fluted-edged birdbath at its center. Two little wrought-iron chairs on the sandstone suggested morning coffee in your bathrobe in summer, watching a frisky robin bathe.

But what was wrong with this place was what put the front porch almost on the street, not unusual in Boston and San Francisco maybe but damn strange in Boulder, Colorado. An eight-foot (at least) solid wood fence, not at all in keeping with the ornamental teal picket decorating the tiny front and side yards, enclosed the one in back. Great slashes of white and gray and bluish bird droppings streaked the upper portions of the inside of the fence in spite of rows of barbed wire affixed to its top edge. And right up next to it was a low roof with heat fumes rising out of a pipe chimney.

Ed Hornsby took her elbow and walked her down the steps of the deck to the birdbath, gesturing around him at the incredible barrier. "Keep the deer out, that fence."

Boulder's resident deer population would soon outnumber its human.

Ed reminded Cara of a rotund and balding Elvis (whom she'd personally dubbed "old blubber lips" when she and Jay and Ed and Elvis were young.) She pulled her elbow out of the realtor's hand and swallowed back a lurch of distaste. From down here you couldn't see the roof. "So who lives on the other side of the fence? I didn't know zoning would allow that kind of thing."

"Nice people. Keep to themselves. You can get variances if you know how to go about it. But what I wanted you to see was the upstairs."

Upstairs were a lavish master bathroom and bedroom of equal size. A guest room and another full bath. Cara had wanted to look down from the back windows at the house behind the fence but Ed Hornsby whisked her into the remaining upstairs room and she forgot all about the other house.

Bookshelves lining two walls. A desk twice the size of her crowded one at home. A padded window seat with a view of the mountains.

Mountain views were fast becoming the prerogative of doctors, lawyers, drug dealers, CEOs, Arab sheiks, university administrators, and other wealthy life forms. But this house was situated directly across from a side street that would never grow trees or houses to block the view. The window faced south and sparse gray snowflakes still fell. The flatiron-shaped mountains on the edge of town were lost in weather murk halfway to their knees. But the winter sun, slanting low at this time of year, stabbed a hole through the gloom to light a swath through Boulder. It spread gold across the window seat. It was like a religious experience. Cara sat down in the desk chair. She could see the view from there, too.

"Merry Christmas, Cara Williams," Ed Hornsby said as if he were Santa Claus himself. He had her and he knew it. "Know who's selling this house? Warwick Custler, the writer. He sits right there where you are now and looks at that view and gets his inspirations. And in the basement there's a laundry room, three more finished rooms, and plenty of storage."

Cara caressed the desk top in front of her. She'd raised four children and then worked low-paying jobs to help educate them. Jay was about to retire from work that had interested him. Now it was her turn. Cara'd written some articles for the local newspaper. She'd always wanted to write novels. She wasn't interested in the basement.

She should have been.

The sun rays caressing Cara and her fantasies did not reach Wilma in the house behind the fence. The only light piercing the gloom in that house came from the television in the living-dining-kitchen-family room which was also her father's bedroom. He moved grudgingly from the daybed to the tiny bathroom next to Wilma's equally tiny bedroom to the La-Z-Boy lounge in front of the mammoth television where Wilma brought his food.

He ordered it over the telephone and had Wilma store most of it in a freezer that took up half the kitchen space and made nearly as much noise as the television. He selected it from a catalog sent to them each month. Food (mostly beefsteak even Wilma could fry and frozen pies she could pop in the oven), but also toilet paper and things anybody would normally need. Unless they were fancy folk who lived in the house that blocked Wilma's sun. Or Wilma's friends who came to visit.

Wilma was "retarded," her father never tired of telling her. She'd come to know it meant there were many things she didn't know that other people did. But Wilma knew she knew things other people didn't.

She knew critters—deer, squirrel, raccoon, skunk, and all the lovely whimsical birds. Wilma especially liked the birds. She had been to a special school as a child, before her mother died, and could read some, if laboriously. She found a flier from a wild bird store in the house in her front yard once. Wilma discovered that deer, squirrel, skunk, and coon liked the black oil sunflower seeds as much as the birds. She stole money from her father's secret horde in the root cellar. Then she convinced whoever lived in the front yard at the time to fetch the bags home for her.

Raymond Jorgenson would have her bring him a handful of bills out of which he'd pay their expenses by mail, wrapping the money in plain paper before putting it in the envelope and sending Wilma with it out along the pretty blue-green fence to the mailbox on the street.

Raymond rarely left the house these days. The old Chevy sat on flattened tires in the shed by the back door. His joints were knotting up on him. The knuckles in his skinny fingers looked like unshelled walnuts Wilma had found in the house in the front yard last year at this time. That was when her enemy had brought her a box of chocolates and wished her a Merry Christmas.

It had been a long while since her father had called for a cab and taken Wilma on an excursion for some new item they needed. But Wilma had a way of convincing the people in her front yard to run errands for them, so the Jorgensons and Wilma's friends didn't do without for long.

Wilma knew lots of things. One of them was how to bide her time.

Wilma stepped outside to rest from the television/freezer noise and to check the feeders. She found a patch of sunlight on the side of the house that wasn't facing the fence. High privacy fences surrounded the little house and its shed. But, like a cat, Wilma knew every spot of warm sunlight left to her and where it would move with the seasons. She could remember when the farmhouse was surrounded by orchard and pasture land and she could roam for sunspots. Little by little, as her father sold off the land to build the horde in the fruit cellar, bulldozers had destroyed Wilma's world and fenced her freedom.

But, like the deer and raccoons and birds, she'd learned to cope with change and turn it to her advantage. The city deer had learned to look both ways before crossing streets and to turn around and kick the crap out of loose dogs instead of running. Wilma had learned to use the people in her front yard.

And, like her critter friends, she sensed things she couldn't verbalize. Wilma sensed, for instance, that the one thing her enemy would hate more than death would be the loss of his own flamboyant freedom.

The Real Realty sign had gone up next to the mailboxes again. Wilma saw the man who'd persuaded her father to sell off the last piece of house yard talking to Mr. Custler while he pounded the sign into the dirt edging the road. He'd used a mallet that was the same color as the sign. They were yelling at each other, he and Mr. Custler, and had become so engrossed in their mean words that the Real Realty man left the mallet leaning against the picket fence when he drove off.

Mr. Custler was not a good neighbor. He didn't leave the house to go off to work like the others. Wilma liked to sit on the upstairs window seats in the sun and look at the pretty mountains and sky.

Wilma decided she'd bided her time long enough.

"This is one hell of a time in our lives to start having to deal with stairs," Jay Williams said the minute Ed Hornsby opened the front door on the house Cara had decided was to be their new home. Jay was a Republican and knew there was no purpose in change for its own sake. But the older the woman got the less she would listen to reason.

He'd made the mistake of taking off work early and met the two in his driveway. Instead of a cold beer and a warm dinner, he had to look at another goddamned house. Jay was an engineer at a government research lab where he'd spent his entire working life and would soon be forced into early retirement. Too many changes coming at him too fast.

But his wife took his arm and pulled him up the stairs to a room with a massive desk and with bookshelves reaching to a ceiling that sported one of those silly fans. A bay window with a seat in it. His wife looked at him expectantly.

"What the hell am I going to need with all this?"

"This is for me, Jay. This is where I'm going to write my novel. This is where Warwick Custler writes his."

"Aw Jesus, not that again." He stalked out to inspect bed and bathrooms. Hornsby followed him.

The master bathroom was huge, carpeted, with a skylight, mirrored walls so you could watch yourself pee, a glass chandelier to bang your head on in the middle of the night, and two sinks for chrissake.

"You can damn near trade even up for this one, Jay," Hornsby said. "You have to go some place and fast. Everything's quality here."

"This isn't a house. It's a pad." Jay had signed the Real Realty contract, thinking their property wouldn't bring enough to replace itself now that all the rich were moving in to jack up prices and that his wife would get over this latest whim when she realized that. He'd made the mistake of assuming the sale was contingent on finding a replacement home first, could have sworn Hornsby had assured him of that. He was so pissed off at the whole idea he hadn't read through the contract carefully enough. Jay would love to wring Hornsby's neck.

Instead, he looked out one of the three bathroom windows. A giant of a woman, wearing overalls and with a thin spot at the crown of stringy gray-yellow hair, bent down in the drive of a tiny house built hard up against the solid back fence of this one. A magpie ate something from her hand, a deer licked at a pile of something on the ground, and behind her a squirrel impatiently scratched his ass.

"Only in Boulder, huh?" Ed stood next to Jay. "You're right, though. This was going to be a bachelor pad. I built it myself after my divorce. But you know realtors. Got such good offers I was forced to sell it."

No, Jay didn't know realtors but he was fascinated with the size of the woman below and the fence enclosing the nothing backyard his wife was about to sentence him to in retirement. The fence was well decorated with bird excrement. This was a hell of a strange house and he'd seen only the top floor.

"I don't think 'only in Boulder' is going to cover this one, Ed. I can handle Bambi and the birdshit, but why is that tiny house slap up to the fence? I can handle you manipulating my wife into all this glamor stuff, but who's that down there and why is this yuppie finery so cheap? Tell me that, Ed." It was then Jay realized his wife had joined them.

She watched him in the mirrored walls that were really sliding closet doors. The disappointed tears spoke all she'd probably have to say to him for awhile. Why couldn't she ever be satisfied with what they had?

Jay passed her to walk into the master bedroom, which also sported a bay window and seat. He could already tell by the furniture that their comfortable, lived-in trappings would be out of place here. How could Cara have lived with him all these years and learned nothing about the built-in waste of extravagant living? "Where in hell would we put the kids when they come home to visit?"

Hornsby led him down the stairs to the living-dining room, replete with costly furnishings, pornographic art, two tall narrow windows on either side of the fireplace that looked onto the side yard, and another bay window with a view to the front. Jay thought he saw a movement or shadow edging out of one of the side windows but Hornsby drew him into the tiniest kitchen he'd ever seen and he forgot all about movement or shadows.

Great. Just great. Cara was going to start being a novelist and stop being a cook.

There was even that icon of yuppiedom, a hot tub, on the deck. And an intricate set of locks on the sliding-glass door leading to it, wires from a security system along its edge.

Ed Hornsby shrugged. "California people can't sleep at night without security systems. You know how they are."

"I still want to know who lives on the other side of the fence. Is it a rental? Who's the monster?"

"Owner. Nice quiet people. She's the owner's daughter. But what I wanted to show you was the space for a workshop in the garage. And the full finished basement where you can stick the kids when they come home to visit. Cara barely glanced at it but I knew you'd want to inspect the furnace, pipes, washer-dryer hookups, storage, hot-water heater." He closed the door to the garage and opened the one to the basement stairs.

★   ★   ★

Ed Hornsby had given up trying to figure out how the huge vacant Wilma Jorgenson managed to get in and out of the house at will no matter what kind of locks and security devices various owners had tried. Why they rarely called the police on her he couldn't figure out either. One had resorted to trained guard dogs but Wilma tamed them to feed out of her hand in a few days. One owner explained she'd felt sorry for the retarded woman. But by the time she put the house up for sale a month later she'd looked more frightened than sorry.

Custler had actually called the cops when he first moved in but they took one look at Wilma and decided no way could she outsmart that security system. Besides, her father claimed she'd been watching a football game on TV with him at the time. Boulder police were getting fed up with paranoid refugees.

Jay Williams studied the floor drain in front of the washer and dryer, the insulation behind the water heater and furnace. "Forced air. Isn't as good as the hot-water heat we got."

"You don't got it anymore," Ed reminded him. Jay Williams's house belonged to the Baggleys, who would gut it, build on top of it and around it. And Jay's kids were all planning to come home from three states to help the folks move over the holidays. Ed had been in sales most of his life and he knew a man like Jay Williams would have a tough time passing up a freebee like that. Moving costs, like everything else in Boulder, had gone ballistic.

Cara wandered down the hall and peered into rooms without entering as she'd done earlier that afternoon and with about as much interest. She did straighten up, blink, furrow her brow, and step inside the game room this time though. Custler had installed a wet bar and a fancy pool table. A big stuffed Santa'd been lying on it and a partially decorated tree stood in the corner when they'd glanced in before. The writer was apparently getting ready for some Christmas entertaining despite his angst at having to list with Real Realty.

Whenever this house was listed with another realtor weird Wilma would make herself too apparent and scare off the customers. So old Warwick had been forced to call Ed, like all the rest. But he sure hadn't been happy about it. Ed didn't know why Wilma favored him, but he was thinking he ought to give her another box of candy this Christmas, when Cara Williams shot out of the game room with her hand over her mouth. She didn't make it to the floor drain before she lost her cookies.

*   *   *

"That's what all them sirens was about," Raymond Jorgenson repeated with a particular glee, struggling to sit up in his La-Z-Boy. "I'll be damned." He gave his old-man cackle. His daughter had grown fond of it. Which was fortunate for him. This is exactly what he'd said when the nice policemen left. Now he and Wilma sat enraptured by the ten o'clock news, watching the stretcher being carried out to the ambulance past the Real Realty sign.

"There's our mailbox." Raymond raised gnarled fists. "See? See?"

The voice on the television explained that famed Boulder novelist, Warwick Custler, had been found murdered on his pool table in the basement of his home, stuffed into a Santa Claus suit and bludgeoned with a mallet striped in red, white, and blue with Real Realty written across it. The camera zoomed in on the For Sale sign again.

"Witnesses report the novelist and his realtor, Edward B. Hornsby, had a shouting match in the street. Custler's head and face were almost totally destroyed. The bloodied mallet was found in the trunk of Hornsby's automobile. He is the president of Real Realty in Boulder. When asked why the alleged murderer would dress his victim in a Santa Claus suit, his ex-wife, Sharon, said she wasn't surprised, that she'd always thought of him as Weird Ed."

Next, the man talked to a graying couple who had found the body while Weird Ed was showing them the house. He tall and thin and scowling, she short and plump and bewildered. Wilma took a closer look at "she" and decided she'd be a lot easier to handle than the previous tenant.

So when the "he" came to the door to check out the Jorgensons, Wilma was on her best behavior. She was repaid by seeing the couple move in. It was like a present.

But it wasn't until after Easter that the man on television told Wilma that the president of Real Realty had been convicted of the murder of Boulder author, Warwick Custler. His were the only fingerprints on the death mallet. His ex-wife, Sharon, testified to his violent nature. Passing walkers, runners, cyclists, and homeless had come forward to recount witnessing the ferocity of the argument he'd had with Custler out on the street. The murder weapon had been found in his car.

Defense lawyers argued that Hornsby wouldn't have shown the house if he'd killed the victim and left him on the pool table.

The prosecution, however, pointed out that he'd have done exactly that to avert suspicion. And the jury brought in a guilty verdict.

"Merry Christmas, Mr. Real Realty," Wilma said softly and left her father napping in front of the giant flickering screen. She slipped out the back door and around the shed where she hoisted up the doors to the root cellar.

She flicked on the switch to the overhead lights—two bare bulbs, one at the front of the cellar and one in the middle—and picked her way through the debris of her father's treasures, mostly old papers and tools. He was sure they were safe from thieves down here. They weren't safe from raccoons and damp, but Wilma didn't bother him with that, couldn't remember the last time he'd been to the cellar.

The ghost smells of the fruits, jellies, and vegetables her mother had stored here years ago when there'd been more on the table than beefsteak and pie always saddened her.

To protect the metal boxes filled with money from the masked bandits, Wilma had devised a grid over a ledge at the back of the cellar. The mischievous critters didn't mean any harm, had in fact shown her how to reclaim her front yard.

It was a long, narrow cellar and when she found the raccoons had pulled out loose bricks and then dug the dirt away to try to reach Raymond Jorgenson's money from behind, Wilma began to think the cellar of the new house wasn't all that far from hers. It was still in the process of being built and she could hear the building sounds. And, since her father dozed off more than he didn't, she had ample time to use his tools to continue the digging once the builders left. Hammering through the hard wall of the other cellar took longer. But behind it had been a piece of wooden paneling Wilma pushed out now and, slipping through the hole it left, replaced it. If you didn't know what to look for you couldn't see where she'd come in.

Once inside, Wilma brushed off the seat of her overalls and went up to see how Mrs. Williams's writing was coming along. She sure hoped the woman wasn't going to be any trouble.

Brian Garfield has been writing novels and short fiction for over thirty-five years, although one would never know it by reading his latest works. His voice is always fresh and engaging, keeping up with current events and social mores while still bearing his unmistakable style. "Scrimshaw," a finalist for the Edgar Award for best short fiction, is a short tale with a surprise ending we defy you to guess.

Scrimshaw

Brian Garfield

She suggested liquid undulation: a lei-draped girl in a grass skirt under a windblown palm tree, her hands and hips expressive of the flow of the hula. Behind her, beyond the surf, a whaling ship was poised to approach the shore, its square-rigged sails bold against a polished white sky.

The scene was depicted meticulously upon ivory: a white fragment of tusk the size of a dollar bill. The etched detail was exquisite: the scrimshaw engraving was carved of thousands of thread-like lines and the artist's knife hadn't slipped once.

The price tag may have been designed to persuade tourists of the seriousness of the art form: it was in four figures. But Brenda was unimpressed. She put the piece back on the display cabinet and left the shop.

The hot Lahaina sun beat against her face and she went across Front Street to the Sea Wall, thrust her hands into the pockets of her dress and brooded upon the anchorage.

Boats were moored around the harbor—catamarans, glass-bottom tourist boats, marlin fishermen, pleasure sailboats, outrigger canoes, yachts. Playthings. It's the wrong place for me, she thought.

Beyond the wide channel the islands of Lanai and Kahoolawe made lovely horizons under their umbrellas of delicate cloud, but Brenda had lost her eye for that sort of thing; she noticed the stagnant heat, the shabbiness of the town, and the offensiveness of the tourists who trudged from shop to shop in their silly hats, their sunburnt flab, their hapless T-shirts emblazoned with local graffiti: "Here Today, Gone to Maui."

A leggy young girl went by, drawing Brenda's brief attention: one of those taut tan sunbleached creatures of the surfboards—gorgeous and luscious and vacuous. Filled with youth and hedonism, equipped with all the optional accessories of pleasure. Brenda watched gloomily, her eyes following the girl as far as the end of the Sea Wall, where the girl turned to cross the street. Brenda then noticed two men in conversation there.

One of them was the wino who always seemed to be there: a stringy unshaven tattered character who spent the days huddling in the shade sucking from a bottle in a brown bag and begging coins from tourists. At night he seemed to prowl the alleys behind the seafood restaurants, living off scraps like a stray dog: she had seen him once, from the window of her flyspecked room, scrounging in the can behind the hotel's kitchen; and then two nights ago near a garbage bin she had taken a shortcut home after a dissatisfying lonely dinner and she'd nearly tripped over him.

The man talking with the wino seemed familiar and yet she could not place the man. He had the lean bearded look of one who had gone native; but not really, for he was set apart by his fastidiousness. He wore sandals, yet his feet seemed clean, the toenails glimmering; he wore a sandy beard but it was neatly trimmed and his hair was expensively cut, not at all shaggy; he wore a blue denim short-sleeved shirt, fashionably faded but it had sleeve pockets and epaulets and had come from a designer shop; and his white sailor's trousers fit perfectly.

I know him, Brenda thought, but she couldn't summon the energy to stir from her spot when the bearded man and the wino walked away into the town. Vaguely and without real interest she wondered idly what those two could possibly have to talk about together.

She found shade on the harbor front. Inertia held her there for hours while she recounted the litany of her misfortunes. Finally hunger bestirred her and she slouched back to her miserable little third-class hotel.

The next day, half drunk in the afternoon and wilting in the heat, Brenda noticed vaguely that the wino was no longer in his usual place. In fact, she hadn't seen the wino at all, not last night and not today.

The headache was painful and she boarded the jitney bus to go up-island a few miles. She got off near the Kapalua headland and trudged down to the public beach. It was cooler here because the northwest end of the island was open to the fresh trade winds; she settled under a palm tree, pulled off her ragged sneakers, and dug her toes into the cool sand. The toes weren't very clean. She was going too long between baths these days. The bathroom in the hotel was at the end of the corridor and she went there as infrequently as possible because she couldn't be sure who she might encounter and anyhow, the tub was filthy and there was no shower.

Across the channel loomed the craggy mountains of Molokai, infamous island, leper colony, its dark volcanic mass shadowed by perpetual sinister rain clouds, and Brenda lost herself in gruesome speculations about exile, isolation, loneliness, and wretched despair, none of which seemed at all foreign to her.

The sun moved and took the shade with it and she moved round to the other side of the palm tree, tucking the fabric of the cheap dress under her when she sat down. The dress was gone—frayed, faded, the material ready to disintegrate. She only had two others left. Then it would be jeans and the boatneck. It didn't matter, really. There was no one to dress up for.

It wasn't that she was altogether ugly; she wasn't ugly; she wasn't even plain, really; she had studied photographs of herself over the years and she had gazed in the mirror and tried to understand, but it had eluded her. All right, perhaps she was too bony, her shoulders too big, flat in front, not enough flesh on her—but there were men who liked their women bony; that didn't explain it. She had the proper features in the proper places and, after all, Modigliani hadn't found that sort of face abominable to behold, had he?

But ever since puberty there'd been something about her gangly gracelessness that had isolated her. Invitations to go out had been infrequent. At parties no one ever initiated conversations with her. No one, in any case, until Briggs had appeared in her life.

. . . She noticed the man again: the well-dressed one with the neatly trimmed beard. A droopy brown Hawaiian youth was picking up litter on the beach and depositing it in a burlap sack he dragged along; the bearded man ambled beside the youth, talking to him. The Hawaiian said something; the bearded man nodded with evident disappointment and turned to leave the beach. His path brought him close by Brenda's palm tree and Brenda sat up abruptly. "Eric?"

The bearded man squinted into the shade, trying to recognize her. Brenda removed her sunglasses. She said, "Eric? Eric Morelius?"

"Brenda?" The man came closer and she contrived a wan smile. "Brenda Briggs? What the devil are you doing here? You look like a beachcomber gone to seed."

Over a drink in Kimo's she tried to put on a front. "Well, I thought I'd come out here on a sabbatical and, you know, loaf around the islands, recharge my batteries, take stock."

She saw that Eric wasn't buying it. She tried to smile. "And what about you?"

"Well, I live here, you know. Came out to Hawaii nine years ago on vacation and never went back." Eric had an easy relaxed attitude of confident assurance. "Come off it, duckie, you look like hell. What's happened to you?"

She contrived a shrug of indifference. "The world fell down around my ankles. Happens to most everybody sometimes, I suppose. It doesn't matter."

"Just like that? It must have been something terrible. You had more promise than anyone in the department."

"Well, we were kids then, weren't we. We were all promising young scholars. But what happens after you've broken all the promises?"

"Good Lord. The last I saw of you, you and Briggs were off to revitalize the University of what, New Mexico?"

"Arizona." She tipped her head back with the glass to her mouth; ice clinked against her teeth. "And after that a state college in Minnesota. And then a dinky jerkwater diploma mill in California. The world," she said in a quiet voice, "has little further need of second-rate Greek and Roman literature scholars—or for any sort of non-tenured Ph.D.'s in the humanities. I spent last year waiting on tables in Modesto."

"Duckie," Eric said, "there's one thing you haven't mentioned. Where's Briggs?"

She hesitated. Then—what did it matter?—she told him: "He left me. Four years ago. Divorced me and married a buxom life-of-the-party girl fifteen years younger than me. She was writing advertising copy for defective radial tires or carcinogenic deodorants or something like that. We had a kid, you know. Cute little guy, we named him Geoff, with a G—you know how Briggs used to love reading Chaucer. In the original. In retrospect, you know, Briggs was a prig and a snob."

"Where's the kid, then?"

"I managed to get custody and then six months ago he went to visit his father for the weekend and all three of them, Briggs and the copy-writer and my kid Geoff—well, there was a six-car pileup on the Santa Monica Freeway and I had to pay for the funerals and it wiped me out."

Eric brought another pair of drinks and there was a properly responsive sympathy in his eyes and it had been so long since she'd talked about it that she covered her face with the table napkin and sobbed.

"God help me, Eric. Briggs was the only man who ever gave me a second look."

He walked her along the Sea Wall. "You'll get over it, duckie. Takes time."

"Sure," she said listlessly. "I know."

"Sure, it can be tough. Especially when you haven't got anybody. You don't have any family left, do you?"

"No. Only child. My parents died young. Why not? The old man was on the assembly line in Dearborn. We're all on the assembly line in Dearborn. What have we got to aim for? A condominium in some anthill and a bag full of golf clubs? Let's change the subject, all right? What about you, then? You look prosperous enough. Did you drop out or were you pushed too?"

"Dropped out. Saw the light and made it to the end of the tunnel. I'm a free man, duckie."

"What do you do?"

"I'm a scrimshander."

"A what?"

"A bone-ivory artist. I do scrimshaw engravings. You've probably seen my work in the shop windows around town."

Eric's studio, high under the eaves in the vintage whaler's house that looked more New Englandish than tropical, revealed its owner's compulsion for orderly neatness.

She had never liked him much. He and Briggs had got along all right, but she'd always found Eric an unpleasant sort. It wasn't that he was boorish; hardly anything like that. But she thought him pretentious and totally insincere. He'd always had that air of arrogant self-assurance. And the polish was all on the surface; he had the right manners but once you got to know him a little you realized he had no real understanding of courtesy or compassion. Those qualities were meaningless to people like Eric. She'd always thought him self-absorbed and egotistical to the point of solipsism; she'd felt he had cultivated Briggs's friendship simply because Eric felt Briggs could help him advance in the department.

Eric had been good at toadying up to anyone who could help him learn the arts of politics and ambition. Eric had always been very actorish: he wasn't real—everything was a role, a part, a performance: everything Eric did was done with his audience in mind. If you couldn't be any help to him he could, without a second thought, cut you dead.

He wasn't really handsome. He had a small round head and ordinary features. But he'd always kept himself trim and he'd always been a natty dresser. And the beard sharpened his face, made it longer, added polish to his appearance. Back on the mainland, she remembered, he'd tended to favor three-piece suits.

Eric's studio was spartan, dominated by a scrubbed-clean workbench under the dormer window's north light. An array of carving tools filled a wooden rack, each tool seated in its proper niche, and there were four tidy wooden bins containing pieces of white bone of graduated sizes. Antique inkwells and jars were arranged beside a tray of paintbrushes and other slender implements. In three glass display cases, each overhung by a museum light, lay examples of Eric's art. One piece, especially striking, was a large ivory cribbage board in the shape of a Polynesian outrigger canoe with intricate black-and-white scenes engraved upon its faceted surfaces.

"That's a sort of frieze," Eric explained. "If you follow those little scenes around the board, they illustrate the whole mythology of the Polynesian emigration that led to the original settlement of Hawaii a thousand years ago. I'm negotiating to sell it to the museum over in Honolulu."

"It must be pretty lucrative, this stuff."

"It can be. Do you know anything about scrimshaw?"

"No," she said, and she didn't particularly care to; but Eric had paid for the bottle and was pouring a drink for her, and she was desperate for company—anyone's, even Eric's—and so she stayed and pretended interest.

"It's a genuine American folk art. It was originated in the early 1800s by the Yankee whalers who came out to the Pacific with endless time on their hands on shipboard. They got into the habit of scrimshanding to pass the time. The early stuff was crude, of course, but pretty quickly some of them started doing quite sophisticated work-manship. They used sail needles to carve the fine lines of the engraving and then they'd trace India ink or lampblack into the carvings for con-trast. About the only materials they had were whalebone and whales' teeth, so that's what they carved at first.

"The art became very popular for a while, about a century ago, and there was a period when scrimshanding became a profession in its own right. That was when they ran short of whalebone and teeth and started illustrating elephant ivory and other white bone materials. Then it all went out of fashion. But it's been coming back into favor the past few years. We've got several scrimshanders here now. The main problem today, of course, is the scarcity of ivory."

At intervals Brenda sipped his whiskey and vocalized sounds indicative of her attentiveness to his monologue. Mainly she was think-ing morosely of the pointlessness of it all. Was Eric going to ask her to stay the night? If he did, would she accept? In either case, did it matter?

Watching her with bemused eyes, Eric went on, "The Endangered Species laws have made it impossible for us to obtain whalebone or ele-phant ivory in any quantities any more. It's a real problem."

"You seem to have a fair supply in those bins there."

"Well, some of us have been buying mastodon ivory and other fos-silized bones from the Eskimos—they dig for it in the tundra up in Alaska. But that stuff's in short supply too, and the price has gone through the ceiling."

Eric took her glass and filled it from the bottle, extracting ice cubes from the half-size fridge under the workbench. She rolled the cold glass against her forehead and returned to the wicker chair, balancing herself with care. Eric smiled with the appearance of sympathy and pushed a little box across the bench. It was the size of a matchbox. The lid fit snugly. Etched into its ivory surface was a drawing of a humpback whale.

"Like it?"

"It's lovely." She tried to summon enthusiasm in her voice.

"It's nearly the real thing," he said. "Not real ivory, of course, but real bone at least. We've been experimenting with chemical processes to bleach and harden it."

She studied the tiny box and suddenly looked away. Something about it had put her in mind of little Geoff's casket.

"The bones of most animals are too rough and porous," Eric was saying. "They tend to decompose, of course, being organic. But we've had some success with chemical hardening agents. Still, there aren't many types of bone that are suitable. Of course, there are some people who're willing to make do with vegetable ivory or hard plastics, but those really aren't acceptable if you care about the artistry of the thing. The phony stuff has no grain, and anybody with a good eye can always tell."

She was thinking she really had to pull herself together. You couldn't get by indefinitely on self-pity and the liquid largess of old acquaintances, met by chance, whom you didn't even like. She'd reached a point-of-no-return: the end of this week her room rent would be due again and she had no money to cover it; the time to make up her mind was now, right now, because either she got a job or she'd end up like that whiskered wino begging for pennies and eating out of refuse bins.

Eric went on prattling about his silly hobby or whatever it was: something about the larger bones of primates—thigh bone, collarbone. "Young enough to be in good health of course—bone grows uselessly brittle as we get older . . ." But she wasn't really listening; she stood beside the workbench looking out through the dormer window at the dozens of boats in the anchorage, wondering if she could face walking into one of the tourist dives and begging for a job waiting on tables.

The drink had made her unsteady. She returned to the chair, resolving to explore the town first thing in the morning in search of employment. She *had* to snap out of it. It was time to come back to life and perhaps these beautiful islands were the place to do it: the proper setting for the resurrection of a jaded soul.

Eric's voice paused interrogatively and it made her look up. "What? Sorry."

"These two here," Eric said. She looked down at the two etched pendants. He said, "Can you tell the difference?"

"They look pretty much the same to me."

"There, see that? That one, on the left, that's a piece of whale's tooth. This other one's ordinary bone, chemically hardened and bleached to the consistency and color of true ivory. It's got the proper grain, everything."

"Fine." She set the glass down and endeavored to smile pleasantly. "That's fine, Eric. Thank you so much for the drinks. I'd better go now—" She aimed herself woozily toward the door.

"No need to rush off, is there? Here, have one more and then we'll get a bite to eat. There's a terrific little place back on the inland side of town."

"Thanks, really, but—"

"I won't take no for an answer, duckie. How often do we see each other, after all? Come on—look, I'm sorry, I've been boring you to tears with all this talk about scrimshaw and dead bones, and we haven't said a word yet about the really important things."

"What important things?"

"Well, what are we going to do about you, duckie? You seem to have a crucial problem with your life right now and I think, if you let me, maybe I can help sort it out. Sometimes all it takes is the counsel of a sympathetic old friend, you know."

By then the drink had been poured and she saw no plausible reason to refuse it. She settled back in the cane chair. Eric's smile was avuncular. "What are friends for, after all? Relax a while, duckie. You know, when I first came out here I felt a lot the way you're feeling. I guess in a way I was lucky not to've been as good a scholar as you and Briggs were. I got through the Ph.D program by the skin of my teeth but it wasn't enough. I applied for teaching jobs all over the country, you know. Not one nibble."

Then the quick smile flashed behind the neat beard. "I ran away, you see—as far as I could get without a passport. These islands are full of losers like you and me, you know. Scratch any charter-boat skipper in that marina and you'll find a bankrupt or a failed writer who couldn't get his epic novel published."

Then he lifted his glass in a gesture of toast. "But it's possible to find an antidote for our failure, you see. Sometimes it may take a certain ruthlessness, of course—a willingness to suspend the stupid values we were brought up on. So-called civilized principles are the enemies of any true individualist—you have to learn that or you're doomed to be a loser for all time. The kings and robber barons we've honored through-out history—none of them was the kind to let himself be pushed around by the imbecilic bureaucratic whims of college deans or tenure systems.

"Establishments and institutions and laws are designed by winners to keep losers in their place, that's all. You're only free when you learn there's no reason to play the game by their rules. Hell, duckie, the fun of life only comes when you discover how to make your own rules and laugh at the fools around you. Look—consider your own situation. Is there any single living soul right now who truly gives a damn whether you, Brenda Briggs, are alive or dead?"

Put that starkly it made her gape. Eric leaned forward, brandishing his glass as if it were a searchlight aimed at her face. "Well?"

"No. Nobody," she murmured reluctantly.

"There you are, then." He seemed to relax; he leaned back. "There's not a soul you need to please or impress or support, right? If you went right up Front Street here and walked into the Bank of Hawaii and robbed the place of a fortune and got killed making your escape, you'd be hurting no one but yourself. Am I right, duckie?"

"I suppose so."

"Then why not give it a try?"

"Give what a try?"

"Robbing a bank. Kidnapping a rich infant. Hijacking a yacht. Stealing a million in diamonds. Whatever you feel like, duckie—whatever appeals to you. Why not? What have you got to lose?"

She twisted her mouth into an uneven smile. "You remind me of the sophomoric sophistry we used to spout when we were undergraduates. Existentialism and nihilism galore." She put her glass down. "Well, I guess not, Eric. I don't think I'll start robbing banks just yet."

"And why not?"

"Maybe I'm just not gaited that way."

"Morality? Is that it? What's morality ever done for *you*?"

She steadied herself with a hand against the workbench, set her feet with care, and turned toward the door. "It's a drink too late for morbid philosophical dialectics. Thanks for the booze, though. I'll see you. . . ."

"You'd better sit down, duckie. You're a little unsteady there."

"No, I—"

"Sit down." The words came out in a harsher voice. "The door's locked anyway, duckie—you're not going anywhere."

She scowled, befuddled. "What?"

He showed her the key; then he put it away in his pocket. She looked blankly at the door, the keyhole, and—again—his face. It had gone hard; the polite mask was gone.

"I wish you'd taken the bait," he said. "Around here all they ever talk about is sunsets and surfing and the size of the marlin some fool caught. At least you've got a bigger vocabulary than that. I really wish you'd jumped at it, duckie. It would have made things easier. But you didn't, so that's that."

"What on earth are you talking about?"

She stumbled to the door then—and heard Eric's quiet laughter when she tried the knob.

She put her back to the door. Her head swam. "I don't understand. . . ."

"It's the ivory, duckie. The best material is fresh human bone. The consistency, the hardness—it takes a fine polish if it's young and healthy enough. . . ."

She stared at him and the understanding seeped into her slowly and she said, "That's where the wino went."

"Well, I have to pick and choose, don't I? I mean, I can't very well use people whose absence would be noticed."

She flattened herself against the door. She was beginning to pass out; she tried to fight it but she couldn't; in the distance, fading, she heard Eric say, "You'll make fine bones, duckie. Absolutely first-rate scrimshaw."

R. L. Stevens is the pseudonym for Edward Hoch, probably the most prolific short story writer today. No matter what the genre, mystery, western, or any other, he has written so many stories under this name that they could comprise a book of their own. Whatever byline the story appears over, it's a sure bet that it will be an exciting tale, with the trademark Stevens (or Hoch) twist.

Bull and Bear

R. L. Stevens

I raised the rifle to my shoulder and took careful aim. The great lumbering grizzly, with a beautiful deep brown coat and the familiar hump on its shoulders, came out from behind the shelter of the tree and started across the rocky slope to the nearby woods. There would be time for only one clean shot and I made it count. The grizzly reared up on its hind legs in anger, took a few steps and then collapsed.

I approached the big bear cautiously until I was certain it wasn't moving. At nearly five hundred pounds, grizzlies can be deadly even when they're not up to full strength, and I hadn't driven up from Idaho Falls and spent two nights in the woods to be mauled by an angry bear. I put down my rifle and unstrapped the backpack from my shoulders.

That was when I saw the bearded stranger come out from behind a boulder and start down the slope toward me. He was carrying an old 30-30 deer rifle, which wouldn't have been much good against the grizzly. "That was nice shootin', mister. Brought him down with one shot, huh?"

"Lucky shot," I answered, not liking the looks of the man. I'd heard stories of poachers who followed hunters through the woods to hijack their kills.

"What kind of rifle you use?"

I was about to reply when his jacket fell open and I saw the butt of a revolver protruding from a shoulder holster under his left arm. Some hunters carry sidearms to finish off a wounded animal at close range, but I'd never known one to wear a revolver in a shoulder holster like that. I suddenly realized who this man was. "You're Bull Marlin, aren't you?"

The bearded man threw back his head and laughed. "God, I didn't know my fame had spread this far!"

Bull Marlin had operated a garage in Boise until a year ago when he went a little crazy and pumped six bullets into his wife and another man. Rather than take his chances in a court of law he'd run off into the hills, making his way east through the Sawtooth National Forest with the police on his tail and search helicopters circling overhead. They hadn't found him, and after a few months the press more or less forgot about Bull Marlin.

But then he'd killed again, breaking into a cabin where a Vietnam vet with mental problems was hiding out from the world. This killing lost him whatever sympathy he might have had, and when he attacked and raped a girl hiker a few weeks later the law came after him in force.

They didn't find him. Bull Marlin just kept moving east, like a wandering grizzly bear, slapping down anyone that got in his way. Most lawmen figured he'd crossed into Wyoming by now, possibly heading for Yellowstone National Park, but somehow I wasn't too surprised to find him here, in the mountains near the Bear Gulch Ski Area.

"Your picture's in every government office," I told him. "I figured you were still in Idaho somewhere."

He'd come down level with me, stepping around the bear's body to get a clear shot at me with the 30-30. I knew I had to do some fast talking or I'd be a dead man very soon. "What's your name?" he asked.

"Ron Halliday."

"You a lawman?"

"No, just a hunter."

"Grizzly hunter, eh?"

"It's the biggest thing around."

"But not the smartest, Ron. I'm the smartest thing around. You shoulda come huntin' for me."

"This where you been hiding out?" I asked.

"For the summer. I figured a ski area don't attract too much attention in the summertime. Come winter I'll head over to Yellowstone."

"The bears didn't bother you?"

"Didn't know they was here. Figured Bear Gulch was just a name."

I sat down on a log. The rifle jerked but he didn't fire. Maybe after all those months alone he felt like talking to someone. "They say back in Idaho Falls that you killed three people." I didn't mention the rape.

He laughed, loud enough to echo off the hills across the gulch. Maybe he was crazy like some people said. "Four people. They ain't found the last one yet."

"I hope that's not me."

He laughed even louder. "No, you'd be number five if I decide to kill you."

"Why do they call you Bull?" I asked, trying any ploy to keep the conversation—and myself—alive.

"'Cause I got a bull neck and I'm bullheaded. Them's good enough reasons."

"Where'd you get the revolver and shoulder holster?"

"Off number four. He was a private dick my wife's family hired to track me down. God, he was good at followin' a trail. But he wasn't as good as old Bull. I got him from behind with my 30-30, and dumped his body in Mud Lake."

He was telling me too much. I knew there wasn't a chance in the world that I'd be walking away from him alive, not unless I came up with something quick. "A regular Mountain Man, aren't you?"

"I'm gettin' to be," he agreed. "Livin' off the land, takin' what I want." That reminded him of something. "You must have a car with you, Ron boy."

"I parked it at the ski area and hiked in," I told him truthfully. "I've been camped up here two nights waiting for a grizzly."

"Them's a threatened species, you know. I think it's against the law to shoot 'em except in Alaska."

"Then we've got something in common, Bull, with our law-breaking. Tell you what—neither of us can turn the other in without getting in trouble ourselves, so why don't we make a deal? We just separate and forget we even saw each other."

Bull Marlin laughed again. "You take me for a sucker, Ron? I know you're just waitin' to get back to Idaho Falls and tell the cops I'm up here. Maybe there's even a reward for me."

"I don't know. I'm not interested in any reward."

Bull glanced down along the trail. "You're alone, aren't you? Didn't bring a partner along?"

"I'm alone."

"Well, we'd better get on with it, then." He pumped a cartridge into the chamber of his rifle. "This is nothin' personal, you understand. Not like with my wife and Gregory. When I shot them, *that* was personal! I enjoyed every bullet."

"Can't we talk about this?"

"Hell, seems like we been talking the better part of an hour already!"

"Why don't you just leave me tied to a tree?"

"You might starve to death." He chuckled. "This way's more humane."

I stood up, wiping my sweaty palms against the sides of my pants. He was about eight feet in front of me. I wondered if I could cover that distance in one leap before he squeezed the trigger. Probably not, I decided.

"At least give me a minute to pray."

He raised the rifle. "One minute, buddy."

I lowered my head and said a silent prayer that the big old grizzly bear would come back to life.

"Thirty seconds."

"Just give me—"

"Time's up!"

The bear gave a startling roar as it raised itself from the dead. Bull Marlin whirled around, his terrified face twisted into a scream. The bear made a half-hearted swipe with its massive paw before I yanked him back by the collar, out of harm's way. Then I knocked the rifle from his trembling hands and pulled the revolver from his shoulder holster.

"What in hell? That bear's dead!"

"Only a little sleepy," I said, twisting his arms behind him so I could tie them with a leather thong. "I'm with the Department of Wildlife. We shoot the grizzlies with tranquilizer guns so we can attach collars with little radio transmitters. They're a threatened species, like you said, and we have to keep track of their wanderings."

"You tricked me! You kept me talkin' till that damn bear woke up."

"He'll still be groggy for an hour or two. By that time I should have you back to civilization and inside a jail cell."

Clark Howard is another writer whose popularity rests mainly on his body of short fiction, including the Edgar-winning story "Horn Man" and the Edgar-nominated "All the Heroes Are Dead." This is not to say he isn't proficient at longer works. His nonfiction crime books detailing events at the infamous prison Alcatraz and the Zebra killings that terrorized San Francisco are recognized as among the best of their kind. In "Wild Things," he returns to the roots of his work, the quiet, incredibly effective suspense tale.

Wild Things

Clark Howard

Tree O'Hara lay prone on the ground and peered down at a little crossroads settlement through twelve-power binoculars. He was in a stand of tall pines six hundred yards or so up the mountain. The settlement, which did not even have a name, consisted of a Conoco gas station, a general store, and a roadhouse restaurant, each occupying a corner where the two mountain highways intersected. The fourth corner was unimproved and stood vacant except for a roadsign which read BUTTE 112.

It was Sunday afternoon and both the Conoco station and the general store were closed. The roadhouse restaurant was open but there was only one car parked in front of it: a five-year-old Cadillac with California plates.

Tree lowered the binoculars and got to his feet. He was a tall, once lean man, now beginning to flesh out with his age approaching forty; but still muscular, still quick. His most striking feature was his eyes—they were cold, and so black and flat they could have passed as sightless. He wore denim jeans and a Levi jacket over a faded work shirt; on his feet were lace-up lumberjack boots.

Leaving the edge of the pines, Tree walked briskly another hundred yards into the forest where he had left his horse. It was an Appaloosa, the horse—its foreparts white as a perfect cloud, its loin and shank spotted with round black markings. A mare, she stood just under fifteen hands high. When Tree had caught her, wild, in the Nez Perce National Forest four years earlier she had been a fast and trim thousand or so pounds. Now he reckoned she weighed around twelve hundred. She had fattened out from their inactive life in the upper forest. Tree rode her on a regular basis only twice a month, when he came down to the settlement for supplies. But she was a happy animal—she loved the man who had captured her, and Tree guessed that if he ever had to do any hard riding, she would run her heart out for him.

The mare snorted and dug at the ground with one hoof as Tree approached. "Easy, Elk," he said quietly. Elk City, west of the Bitterroot Range, was where he had roped her, so he had named her Elk. He rubbed her throat now to calm her, then stepped back to the saddle and put his binoculars in a case hanging from the horn. From a blanket roll behind the saddle he removed a pair of telephone-pole climbers and buckled them to the inside of his legs. From one saddlebag, he took a telephone lineman's intercept set—a receiver with a dial built into it and two magnesium clips for tapping into a wire—and hooked it onto his belt. "Keep still," he said to Elk, rubbing her throat again.

Walking fifty feet to a string of telephone poles that went up and over the mountain, Tree put on gloves and climbed one of them to its crossbeam. He hooked one arm around the beam to steady himself. With his free hand he laid the intercept set on the beam, attached the magnesium clips to one of the telephone wires, and got a dial tone in the receiver. He dialed the number of the restaurant at the crossroads. John Grey Sky, the Shoshone owner, answered.

"John," said Tree without preliminary, "who's the Caddy belong to?"

"Oh, Tree, it's you. The Caddy? Nobody, man. A couple of sharpies and some bimbo passing through. They're slopping down beer and arguing about which route to take to Chicago."

"What do they look like?" Tree asked. "The men, I mean."

"Losers," said John. "Small-timers, punks."

"You're sure? They're not just pulling an act?"

"Listen, brother, I know rabble when I see it," John assured him. "You're safe. Come on down. I got your supplies."

"Okay," Tree said. He had hesitated just a beat before answering. He hoped John Grey Sky had not noticed. He and John had been friends for twenty-five years, since attending Caribou Indian School together as young boys. It would never do to insult a friend of such long standing by doubting his judgment. If Grey Sky said he would be safe, Tree had to assume he would be. All the same, when he got back to Elk and put his equipment away, he took a loaded forty-five automatic from the saddle-bag, jacked a round into the chamber, thumbed the safety on, and stuck it in his waistband under the Levi jacket where it could not be seen.

Tree led the Appaloosa to the edge of the pines and tied her reins to a buffalobur shrub. The bush had just enough prickly spines on it to discourage Elk from nibbling the reins untied and following him, as she liked to do. "Be a good girl," he said, scratching her ears. "I'll bring you an apple."

Tree made his way down the slope and came onto the highway around the bend from the roadhouse. He approached the crossroads from behind the closed Conoco station, aware with every step of the gun in his waistband. From the side of the station he studied the car with the California plates. The tires were fairly worn, there was some rust on the chrome, and a small dent in the right rear fender had been left unrepaired. It looked like a loser's car, all right, just as Grey Sky had said. All the same, Tree was glad he had the gun.

Hurrying across to the rear of the roadhouse, Tree slipped through the open back door into the kitchen. John Grey Sky was scraping down his fry grill. "Hey, bro," he said.

"Hey, John." Tree's eyes swept the room, looking for anything out of the ordinary. Through the service window he could hear the voices of Grey Sky's three customers.

"Your supplies are there on the meat table," Grey Sky said.

Tree stepped over to a butcher block and examined the contents of a burlap bag: cheese, coffee, tins of meat, dry cereal, powdered milk, beef jerky, magazines, a dozen fresh apples for Elk. "You get my animal food?" he asked the roadhouse owner.

"Under the table."

Tree pulled out a twenty-pound sack of processed dry animal food pellets. Similar to the food sold commercially to feed dogs and cats, it differed in that it contained flavors attractive to wild as opposed to domestic animals.

"You must be feeding half the wild things on that mountain," Grey Sky commented. "They're going to have to learn to scavenge all over again after you're gone."

Tree felt himself tense. "After I'm gone where?"

John Grey Sky shrugged. "Wherever."

Tree stared at his friend's back. Grey Sky could get a lot of money for betraying Tree O'Hara. Tree wondered if his friend was ever tempted.

The voices from the front of the restaurant grew louder. "You're getting a free lift to Chicago," a man's voice said. "Least you could do is be a little more friendly."

"Drop dead," a woman's throaty voice replied. There was a loud cracking noise then—the unmistakable sound of a face being slapped.

Frowning at each other, Tree and Grey Sky walked out from the kitchen. One of the men was standing, half bent over the table. The woman, seated, was staring up at him defiantly, one side of her face turning an angry red.

"You kick dogs, too?" she asked.

He hit her again, backhanded, on the other side of her face.

"Hey, man, no rough stuff in here!" Grey Sky said.

The man raised his hand again.

"Don't do it," Tree said. His voice, like his eyes, was flat and hard. It was clearly an order.

The man at the table turned around, one hand reaching for an empty beer bottle. "Who the hell are you?"

"Don't matter who I am," Tree said. He pulled back one side of his Levi jacket to expose the gun. "Don't hit her again."

"You gonna kill me if I do?" the man challenged with a sneer.

"No, just cripple you," Tree replied matter-of-factly. "I'll put one in your left instep. Blow your foot all to pieces."

The other man at the table intervened. "Hold it, chief," he said with a forced smile. "We don't want no hassle." He took the bottle from his friend's hand and put it down. "Come on, Lou, forget it. It's their patch." Picking up the check Grey Sky had given them, he looked at it and put some money on the table. "You coming?" he asked the woman.

"Not on your life," she said. Both sides of her face were now violently red.

"Please yourself. Come on, Lou."

The two men started to leave.

"Wait a minute, I've got a suitcase in that car!" the woman said urgently.

"Come on," Tree said. He went outside and stood with her while Lou opened the trunk and set her suitcase on the ground. Then the two men got in the Caddy and drove off.

The woman picked up her suitcase and followed Tree back inside. "Thanks," she said.

"Forget it," Tree told her. He studied her for a moment. She was, he guessed, an old twenty-five. There was no telling what her true hair color was—bottle blonde with black roots was what he could see. Too much makeup. A well used but still good body. A bimbo, he thought. Like Grey Sky had said. The kind who'd take a free ride with two losers in a five-year-old Caddy.

"What time's the next bus through here?" she asked uncomfortable under Tree's scrutiny.

"Friday," said Grey Sky.

"*Friday!* This is only Sunday. Are you kidding me?"

"I never kid about anything as serious as bus service. Just once a week the bus comes over the mountain. Rest of the time it follows the Interstate around the mountain." Grey Sky looked over at his friend. Tree was staring at him, the realization having just dawned on him that the roadhouse owner was right. "Didn't think about that, did you, Galahad?" asked Grey Sky.

"Where the hell am I going to stay until Friday?" the woman asked in a half whine. "I don't have money for a motel."

"That works out just fine," Grey Sky said, "cause there's no motel anyway."

"Well, what am I gonna do!" she shrieked.

Tree looked at his friend. Grey Sky held both hands up, palms out.

"Not me, bro. I got my wife, four kids, my wife's mother, my unemployed brother-in-law and *his* wife and two kids—all in a two-bedroom, one-bath house. Sorry."

"Could you let her sleep here, put a cot in the kitchen—?"

Grey Sky shook his head. "My insurance don't allow overnight occupation of the premises. If she accidentally burned the place down, I couldn't collect a nickel. You're going to have to handle this good deed yourself, Galahad."

Tree glared at his friend. Grey Sky was obviously enjoying himself.

He could hear the woman panting as she trudged along behind him, lugging her suitcase with both hands. "How—much farther—is it?" she gasped.

"Not far." Carrying the burlap bag of supplies on one shoulder, the sack of animal food on the other, Tree deliberately kept his pace slow to allow her to keep up with him. But when he saw that she was falling too far behind anyway, he stopped to let her rest.

"How come you live up in the mountains anyway?" she demanded. "You antisocial? Don't you like people?"

"As a matter of fact, I don't," he said, "very much."

Now it was her turn to study him. She was not sure whether she liked what she saw. Those eyes of his didn't seem to have even a degree of warmth in them. "What'd that fellow down there say your name was? Galahad?"

"He was just trying to be funny. My name's Tree O'Hara."

"Tree? How'd you get a name like that?"

"My mother's family name. She was Indian. I'm one-quarter Minnetonka."

"Oh. Well, my name's Violet. I was named after a flower. You can call me Vi."

He nodded. "Come on," he said, "let's go on."

After one more rest stop, they came to the edge of the pines where Elk waited. As they approached, the mare snorted and pawed the ground edgily. "She smells you," Tree said. "She knows you're a woman. She's jealous.—Come on—easy, baby," he said to Elk, putting an arm under her neck.

"Sure is a funny-looking horse," Vi said. "Looks like the front of one and the back of another, stuck together."

Tree threw her an irritated glance. "This happens to be an Appaloosa. It's one of the most intelligent breeds of horse in the world, as well as one of the fastest. This horse has more stamina and endurance than any other breed you can name. It is the best stock horse, the best show horse—"

"All's I said was it was funny-looking," she interrupted. "I'm sorry, but that's my opinion. Personally, I like Palaminos. Like Trigger, you know?"

Tree turned away in disgust. *Trigger!* A Hollywood horse. Great spirits!

Tree lashed the two sacks one on top of each other just behind the blanket roll, then helped Vi into the saddle. She had to hike her skirt far up on her thighs in order to straddle the horse's back, but it didn't seem to bother her. Tree noticed that her legs were well rounded, fleshy—in fact, all of her was well rounded and fleshy; she wasn't skinny anywhere, a fact that Tree approved of. He didn't care for overly slim women—they always looked too fragile, like stickwood. Elk was of a different mind, however; the mare did not like the woman at all, and showed it by shuffling around skittishly and snorting loudly through flared nostrils. Tree finally had to cut up an apple and feed it to her so they could be on their way.

The trip to the cabin took another two hours, Tree leading the horse and rider while carrying Vi's suitcase in his free hand. He didn't mind the walk—in fact, he was glad to get the exercise because he knew he was about ten pounds overweight. For the first couple of years after he had gone into hiding he had made a point of exercising five days a week—calisthenics, weight-lifting, jogging through the woods. That, along with chopping wood and pumping water out of his cistern, had kept him nicely in shape. But for the past three or four years he had grown lazy: sleeping late, not watching his diet, lying around like a much older man. He had become complacent in his mountain hide-away. He felt safe there; only rarely did he feel threatened any more. After six years, he figured they had stopped looking for him.

Probably.

Maybe.

Tree and the woman arrived at the cabin just at twilight. It sat on a small clearing at the six-thousand-foot level in the Beaverhead Forest, just east of the Continental Divide. When the clouds were high, Chief Joseph Pass could be seen from the porch. If they were very high, one could regularly see the moon and the sun at the same time, in different parts of the sky. The natural beauty of the place was indelible. The woman didn't notice the scenery, however—she was too acutely aware of how isolated it was.

"Look, before we go in," Vi said, "I think we ought to get something straight. I had a falling-out with those other two guys because they had some weird ideas about how I should pay for my ride. I hope you're not thinking along those same lines as far as room-and-board goes."

"I'm not," Tree told her.

He said it a little too quickly to suit her. With a little too much determination. She hesitated on the porch, not following him into the cabin.

"Listen, no offense, you understand," she said, "but you're not— well, *peculiar* or anything, are you? I mean, living up here all alone—"

Tree returned to the doorway and faced her. "Why don't you lighten up?" he said. "You'll be safe here. But if you don't believe me, hike on back down the mountain and make other arrangements."

"A girl can't be too careful, is all I mean. I have this problem in that men usually find me very attractive—"

"I don't," Tree assured her. "My taste runs to darker women. When I get lonely, I ride down to the Salmon River Reservation. Lots of nice Nez Perce and Shoshone women down there. They like me because my skin's light. I stay for a few days and then come back home. I was just down to the reservation last week, so I'm settled for about a month now. Like I said, you're safe."

Turning, he walked away. When she finally came into the cabin several minutes later, she found her suitcase on the bed in the tiny bedroom. Tree had decided, he told her, to sleep on the couch. Not because he was such a gentleman—he just didn't like the idea of leaving her out in the main room alone all night. The main room—which was a kitchen-living room—was where he had the television, shortwave receiver, his books, magazines, guns, ammunition: things he didn't want her fooling with. Sleeping on the couch, he could keep an eye on everything.

After Tree took care of Elk, rubbing her down briskly and putting her in the one-horse lean-to stable he had built onto the rear of the cabin, he came back into the cabin just in time to hear Vi, in the bedroom, say, "Damn!"

"What's the trouble?" he asked.

"My cosmetics bag! It was in the back seat of the car! I don't have any makeup!"

"Tough break," he said indifferently.

He went into the kitchen, unpacked his supplies, and began preparing supper. Presently Vi came in.

"Listen, I can cook," she said. "Why don't you let me fix supper?"

"I'll do it," he replied. "I know how I like things."

Vi shrugged. Strolling, she looked the place over. "You've got enough books," she commented. "All the comforts of home, too—radio, TV, everything. How do you manage it way up here?"

"I manage," Tree said. He was not about to share any confidences with her. For electrical power he had illegally tapped into a main power line running across the mountain. For water he had a cistern next to the cabin. For television, a microwave dish he had assembled on the roof, which stole signals from the sky. For shortwave, a simple antenna wire strung up a high tree. For backup, a battery-operated generator, constantly charging off the tapped electricity.

"Okay if I look at these old magazines?" she asked, standing in front of the bookcase where he kept them.

"Sure. But do me a favor first. Step around back and make sure I closed the lean-to door, will you? I don't want Elk to be in a draft."

While she was out of the cabin, he went quickly to the bookcase, took a small scrapbook from one of the shelves, and put it on top of the bookcase out of her sight and reach. Then he returned to the kitchen.

They shared an uneasy supper, both telling whatever lies they felt necessary to project or protect their respective images. Tree told Vi he had originally come to live in the mountains to avoid the Vietnam draft, and had not gone back because he didn't relish the idea of steady employment. He said he worked down at the roadhouse restaurant during tourist season to earn enough to live on the rest of the year. Vi told Tree that she was a model on her way to Chicago for a job at Marshall Field's. Because she wasn't due there for another week, she had accepted a ride with the two guys in the Cadillac. She had thought, she said, that they were legitimate businessmen, traveling salesmen or something, and had been very surprised to learn they were just a couple of petty hustlers.

Because each of them was lying, neither Tree or the woman asked any questions of the other. They kept conversation to a minimum. After supper, Vi found that she was extremely tired. It was the climb and the altitude, Tree told her. "Your blood's thinned out. Better go to bed." She did, and fell into an immediate deep sleep.

When he was sure she was sleeping soundly, Tree slipped into the bedroom and got her purse. He brought it into the main room and searched it. There was an expired Illinois driver's license, a faded Social Security card, an address book containing no names that Tree recognized, a blank, unmailed postcard with a photo on it of Harold's Club in Reno, and twelve dollars.

A loser's purse for sure, Tree thought. He put it back in the bedroom.

Later, Tree fed Elk, opened his nightly bottle of beer, chewed a little peyote, and watched an old John Garfield movie on some channel he was pulling in from a satellite. When the movie was over, he spread his sleeping bag on the couch, stripped, climbed in, and went to sleep, the forty-five lying loaded and cocked on the floor just inches away.

The next morning, Vi found him out back of the cabin with his wild things. She stood out of sight around a corner of the cabin and watched him feed them from the sack of pellet food he had brought back. She was amazed at the number and variety of the animals. Some of them she couldn't even identify—others, like the rabbits, squirrels, and small deer she knew. Tree knelt right in their midst and fed them from his open hand. The sight of it was a wonder to her.

"You can come around and watch if you want to," he told her without looking around. "Just don't make any sudden moves."

Vi eased around the corner but stayed well back from the menagerie. "How'd you know I was there?" she asked curiously.

"This little mule deer told me," he said, scratching the middle forehead of a somewhat scroungy, unattractive deer. "I saw its nostrils flare—that meant a new scent was close by. Mule deer have very poor eyesight; they have to depend on their sense of smell for survival." He looked at her over his shoulder and grinned. "Plus which, I saw your shadow."

"Oh, you!" She moved a little closer. "What in the world are all of them? What's that reddish one with the yellow belly?"

"Ermine weasel. Turns pure white in the winter. That's when the trappers go after them."

"And that one, by the deer?"

"Pronghorn. It's a kind of bastard antelope." He stood up and started pointing. "That's a wolverine over there: baby wolf. This big guy with the white mark on his forehead is a badger. My mother's people named him. They called the white mark a badge. I bet you didn't know 'badge' was an Indian word."

She shook her head. "No."

Tree smiled. "Most cops don't, either."

"What's that one, with the partly webbed feet?"

"That's the one the ladies like: she's a mink. Next to her there— that big shiny grey animal—that's a marten."

From a nearby limb came a clipped, scolding bird call. Tree looked over at a long-tailed black-and-white bird chattering noisily.

"All right," he said. He stepped out of the center of the wild things, closing the bag, and came over to where Vi stood. From a wooden storage box, he removed another bag and scooped out a hand-ful of its contents. "Bird seed," he said. He took her hand. It felt good. "Come on."

She let him lead her over to a low aspen and watched him hold out his open hand to feed the bird. "It's a magpie," he told her. "Biggest nag in the woods. Never gives you a minute's peace if he's hungry."

After a couple of minutes, he closed his hand. "That's enough, Porky. I named him Porky 'cause he's such a pig."

He bobbed his chin toward another tree, a spruce. "Want to see an owl?" They walked over to a low, heavily leafed limb where a small, unpleasant-looking owl was hunched. Its oversized head seemed to comprise half of its body, and its big direct eyes and hooked beak gave it a definite aura of hostility.

"Is it mad?" Vi asked, holding back tentatively.

"No," said Tree, "just sleepy. He'll burrow down into the leaves and go to sleep in a bit." Tree fed the owl, as he had the magpie, from his palm. "Mostly he eats forest mice, but he likes these seeds, too." With the last of the seed, he led Vi to a small flat boulder jutting up from the ground like a fist. He sprinkled the rest of the seed on the flat of the rock and drew Vi a few feet away from it. "Now you'll see my favorite wild thing," he said quietly.

As they watched, a glossy black bird with wild yellow eyes swooped gracefully onto the rock and, after a cautious look around, began eating. As it ate, it honed its already razor-sharp talons on the rock.

"That's Midnight," Tree told her. "A raven."

"Won't it eat out of your hand like the others?"

"Not yet. He doesn't trust me enough yet. Someday he will. In another few years."

They walked back to the rear of the cabin. A few of the wild things were still there. Vi shook her head in wonder. "I didn't know animals were that friendly."

"They aren't, as a rule," Tree said. "That wolverine there, she's a natural enemy to the mink, the rabbit, and the marten. They're usually her prey. And the badger generally goes after the ermine weasel when he sees one. But they know I don't allow any fighting here in the clearing. I chase them off if they start fighting. It doesn't take long for them to learn that not fighting is best. Animals are a lot smarter than people."

"You really love them, don't you? These animals?"

"Yeah, I guess I do," Tree admitted. "It makes me feel good when I bring two natural enemies together and get them both to eat out of my hand at the same time."

"Too bad that can't be done with people," Vi remarked. "It would stop all the war and killing in the world."

"No, it wouldn't," Tree said quietly. "People would still kill, for sport. Man is the only animal that kills for sport. You'd never stop that. Man will always have to kill. It's his nature."

Vi stared at him. As he spoke, his eyes seemed to grow colder.

The next morning when Vi came out of the bedroom, Tree was at his shortwave set listening to an English-language broadcast from Moscow. "Don't look at me," she said. "I'm totally out of makeup and I look *awful.*"

Tree did look at her, and liked what he saw. "You look fine to me," he said.

"Nice and scrubbed." He switched off the radio. "Want to go fishing with me?" he asked. He didn't want to leave her alone in the cabin.

"I don't know how to fish."

"I'll teach you. Or you can just watch. We can take some food and have a picnic."

Vi consented and together they packed a knapsack with lunch. Tree got his lines and bait, and they trudged up-mountain several hundred yards toward a narrow stream of cold snow-water coming from high up.

"How come everything's always *up*hill?" Vi complained, taking his hand so he could help her. "Isn't anything ever downhill?"

"Nothing worthwhile," Tree replied matter-of-factly.

They walked along the stream and Tree showed her how to set fish lines without poles or other apparatus. "Poles scare fish off," he explained. "They cast a shadow over the water."

When he had the lines set, they walked on to a point where the stream bed dropped six feet, creating a low waterfall. There the water rushed and formed whitecaps, and occasionally they could see a mountain trout swimming upstream, actually jumping up the falling water. They found a place to open the knapsack and eat. While they were there, Vi told him about herself.

"I was one of those young girls with stars in her eyes who went out to California to get into the movies. Or TV. Or modeling—*anything*, you know, except the nine-to-five office bit. It took me a while to realize I wasn't the only one with big ideas. There were hundreds of others just like me. We were all pilgrims who made it to Mecca—only Mecca turned out to be Hustle City. I was lucky—I ended up waiting tables at a Hamburger Hamlet. A lot of others weren't lucky. They ended up on drugs or selling themselves on Hollywood Boulevard for some pimp, or even worse. That's why when the two sports in the Cadillac asked if I wanted a ride east, I took it."

"No modeling job at Marshall Field's?"

Vi shook her head. "The most I've got to look forward to is a monotonous job in some dull office."

"That's more than some people have got," Tree commented darkly.

That night, her third night at the cabin, Tree let her cook for him. She made breaded pork chops from his freezer and managed to whip up some decent mashed potatoes from his dehydrated food stock.

"Not bad," he said. "Where'd you learn to cook?"

"Marshall High School, on the west side of Chicago. Home Ec was required. Where'd you go to school?"

"A reservation in Idaho."

"What was it like living on a reservation?"

"Poor," he said quietly. "Cold poor. Hungry poor. Hard-knock poor."

"How'd you get away from it?"

"I joined the Army." He realized the slip at once.

"You told me you came up here to evade the draft," she reminded him.

Tree looked down at the table for a long, silent moment. Finally he met her eyes. "That was a lie. But I can't tell you the truth. Let's just leave it alone for the rest of the time you're here, okay?"

They resumed eating, with no further conversation for several minutes. Finally Vi put her fork down and rose.

"I told you the truth about me," she said. It was clearly an accusation. She left the table and went outside.

Tree finished his supper, cleared off the table, and washed the dishes. Then he got an apple out of the food locker for Elk and went outside. Vi was sitting on the porch looking up at a sky full of stars that looked close enough to touch.

"Want to feed this apple to Elk?" Tree asked.

"Elk doesn't like me," Vi said.

"She's just not used to you. Come, you can feed her." Vi did not move. Tree coaxed her. "Come on. I'll show you how. It's easy. Come on."

Finally Vi got up and went with him around to the lean-to. Tree cut the apple into sixths and showed Vi how to hold her hand out straight, palm up, so that the horse could take the food with its lips and not hurt Vi's hand with its powerful teeth. Vi was nervous, but Elk, whose affections could always be bought with fresh apples, played the perfect lady and ate properly.

"Go ahead, scratch her neck," Tree said. "She likes that."

"Don't we all," Vi replied mostly to herself.

Vi petted the Appaloosa for awhile, then Tree closed the stall and they returned to the porch.

"I'll let you help me feed the wild things in the morning if you like," he offered.

"You don't have to."

"I don't want you to be mad."

"I'm not. I don't blame you for not trusting me."

"It's not that I don't trust you. It's just something I don't talk about. Not to anybody."

She was sitting in a shaft of light from the window and Tree saw her shrug. "Okay," she said.

"I'm sorry."

Another shrug. "Sure."

They sat without speaking for ten minutes, listening to the night sounds of the cool, high-mountain evening. Finally Vi stood up. "I think I'll go to bed. Goodnight."

"Goodnight."

Tree remained on the porch for a long time, thinking about things—the vivid dangerous past, the nebulous, unsure future, and the clear, demanding present. He admitted to himself that he wanted the woman, then told himself in definite, forceful language that he could not have her. Alone is safest, he reminded himself. Alone is smartest. Alone is best.

He grunted softly. Alone was also loneliest.

It was midnight when he finally went inside, stripped down, and slid into his sleeping bag. But he couldn't sleep. It was as if he was waiting for something.

He was still awake when she came to him in the darkness.

At first they were skittish about her, made nervous by the sight and scent of her so close. But because they trusted Tree so completely they gradually eased their way up to her. Soon she was kneeling in their midst just as Tree did, and they were nuzzling her hands, putting front paws up on her legs, making their individual little noises to get her attention. She learned that the mule deer and the pronghorn would nibble at her ears with their lips if she paid too much attention to the ground animals and not enough to them. Feeding the wild things was a decided thrill for Vi—she couldn't wait for the next day to feed them again.

"I want to feed them every morning!" she said with delight. Tree looked curiously at her and Vi's smile faded. "I forgot," she said. "I've only got two more mornings, haven't I? The bus comes over the mountain on Friday."

Tree nodded. "Yes. On Friday."

They went swimming that afternoon, in the same stream in which they'd fished the previous day. Vi thought she was going to freeze.

"It's like ice water!" she shrieked.

"It *is* ice water," Tree said, laughing. "It's melted snow from way up. Move around—you'll get warm."

She did move around, but she did not warm up. After five minutes she had to get out. Tree wrapped her in a blanket and left her on the bank while he swam for another quarter hour. When he came out, his tan body shone like the coats of the wild things who were his friends.

After their swim, they walked arm-in-arm back to the cabin and Tree built a fire. They stretched out on a Navajo blanket in front of the fireplace, chewed some peyote, slept, woke up and made love, and slept again.

That night, Tree said, "You don't want to leave, do you?"

Vi shrugged. "I don't want to mess with your life, Tree. You've got everything you want up here. The one thing you haven't got—well, it's available down on the Salmon River Reservation when you want it, and you don't have to bring it home with you." She looked away from him. "I think it would be bad for both of us if I stayed."

They didn't discuss it any further that night, each retreating into silence.

On Thursday morning, Tree was sick.

"My cooking," Vi said lightly. "Now you know why I've never married."

"Probably the peyote," he told her. "It gives you a great feeling but sometimes it raises hell with the digestive system. How's your stomach?"

"Fine. Let me mix you some cold powdered milk—that'll probably settle it."

The milk helped some, but later in the day he had severe nausea and a bad headache.

"Do you have any medicine up here at all?" Vi asked. He directed her to a cabinet in the kitchen where he had aspirin, codeine, and Valium tablets. She gave him two of each and made him take a nap in the bedroom.

While he was sleeping, she went to the bookcase and took down the scrapbook he had hidden on top of it. She had watched through the window the night he had put it there. Opening it on the table, she read the newspaper clippings he had saved. The stories they told were different, but they all had common headlines:

LABOR LEADER SLAIN, one read.

GANGLAND BOSS FOUND DEAD, read another.

WITNESS MURDERED IN HOTEL.

RACKETS INFORMER EXECUTED.

GAMBLER KILLED IN MIAMI.

The clippings had datelines covering a five-year period. The last one was dated six years earlier.

Tree came out of the bedroom while she still had the scrapbook open in front of her. He was very pale, but his eyes were still dark and dangerous. He was fully dressed and Vi couldn't tell whether he had his gun or not.

He sat down heavily across from her.

"You enjoy my press notices?" he asked.

Vi closed the scrapbook. "They ended six years ago. That was when you came to live up here. What happened?"

"They wanted me to hit a woman," he said. "A young woman with a brace on one leg, who was going into a convent of handicapped nuns who taught handicapped children. She was heir to a lot of money, but she was going to take a vow of poverty and give it all to the order she was joining. A cousin who was her only living relative bought the hit. Prior to then, I had never hit anybody but gangsters and punks—a stoolie now and then, a gambler who welshed on somebody. Now they wanted me to do a crippled young woman who never hurt nobody. They wanted me to run her down in the street so it'd look like a hit-and-run, an accident." Tree shook his head. "I couldn't do it. So I took off."

"And now there's a contract on *you*," Vi concluded.

"A big one," Tree confirmed. "And it keeps getting bigger every year." Suddenly he buried his face in his hands. "I'm sick, Vi—" he said weakly.

She helped him back to bed, mixed him some more powdered milk and made him eat a few soda crackers to see if that would help calm his stomach.

Sitting on the bed beside him, she felt his forehead. "No fever," she reported.

"Maybe it's the flu," he said. "My muscles and joints ache like hell."

After he ate, she massaged him where he hurt and gave him more aspirin and Valium. Then she tucked him in and stroked his cheek.

"How'd you get to be a—you know," she asked curiously.

"A paid killer?" Tree smiled wanly. "In the Army. I was a P.O.W. I did time with a Ranger captain who had mob connections. When we were exchanged and went home, he asked me to work for him. It sounded better than going back to the reservation." He reached up and touched her hand. "You won't go tomorrow, will you?"

"No. I won't leave you while you're sick."

He had a miserable night. Between bouts of diarrhea and vomiting, he was left weak and shaky. She helped him to and from bed, gave him more medication, more milk, more crackers. His muscle and joint aches agonized him all through the night—even codeine tablets failed to curb the pain.

Toward morning he still had no fever, but his pulse had become very weak and his eyes no longer looked threatening. When Vi took his gun from under his pillow where she had noticed it, he didn't complain—he knew he did not have the strength to fire it, anyway. Still, he was relieved to see her merely lay it on the nearby bureau and leave it there.

Two hours after sunup, he was breathing very lightly and was extremely pale. She was holding his head up, feeding him a little warm oatmeal.

"Feed them," he said feebly.

"I will," she assured him. "After I feed you. You're sick, they're not."

When he had eaten as much as she thought he could, she let his head back down and wiped his face with a damp cloth. She opened a window for him to get some fresh air and cleaned up the dishes they had used during the night. When she came back in to check on him he was barely awake. Just enough to say faintly, "The wild things—"

"All right," she said. "I'll do it right now."

He gave her a faint smile. She bent and kissed him lightly on the lips.

Out back, Vi got a bucket of pellet food from the storage locker and went over to where the animals waited. She held out her hand to them, but they would not come. They merely stared at her. She tossed a handful of food to them, but they didn't touch it. Maybe they smell the arsenic on my hands, she thought.

She shrugged, poured the bucket of food on the ground, and went back inside to see if Tree was in a coma yet.

Joyce Carol Oates is widely regarded as one of America's premier authors. Her novels and short stories deconstruct modern life as we know it, magnifying seemingly inconsequential events and showing the motives and rationalizations behind it all. She can make everyday life seem horrifying, and when she writes suspense fiction, there are few authors who are her equal. In "Craps," she tells a familiar story with her own spin: never put your trust in luck.

Craps

Joyce Carol Oates

Just when I thought he'd drifted off to sleep, his head heavy and warm on my shoulder, Hughie says, What's that story you were going to tell me about Vegas? And I tell him quickly, There's lots of stories about Vegas.

Late Sunday morning I'm lying on top of the bed half dressed with Hughie, my ex-husband, sort of cradled in my arms—he'd dropped by earlier just wanting to talk, he said, in one of his moods where he needs consolation and some signs of affection—and lying together like this, just lying still and drowsy, is an old habit of ours but it's Hughie who always requires it, these days. We fit together like a hand and a glove—Hughie's head on my right shoulder and my arm under his neck (where, sometimes, it goes to sleep, gets so numb I can't feel it there), his right arm cradling my breasts from beneath, and his right foot tucked between mine. There are these old habits you slip into no matter how you actually feel about each other, or anything else. Or where your mind drifts, late Sunday morning.

I was seventeen when I met Hughie, who is twenty-two years older than me. I was twenty-seven when I asked him please to leave. The divorce came through in about eighteen months but we're still friends; you could say we are like brother and sister if it was qualified to mean not always getting along with each other but always there; in a small town like this where's there to go? After the divorce, last year, we have actually gotten along better. Hughie is always changing jobs and changing woman friends and stopping drinking (and starting again) and none of what he does is my problem now, though naturally, being the way I am, I take an interest. But I don't let it hurt me, now.

He's away for months and doesn't call and I'm busy with my own life; then suddenly he'll drop by, lonely, depressed, three days' beard and bloodshot eyes and I won't lend him money if that's what he wants (sometimes I think he's just testing me, anyway) but I'll make him supper, or sometimes he has brought something special to eat, or a bottle of wine, sometimes even flowers. Flowers! I can't help laughing when he holds them out to me like a guilty little boy. He was always ready to spend our money on things we didn't need and I saw through that long ago but here's the same Hughie; they don't change. All other things change but they don't change, men like him.

So what's this story about Vegas? Hughie says. I'm waiting.

It isn't any story, I tell him. What's Lynn been telling you behind my back?

Some guy you met at craps. Some millionaire Texan.

I didn't meet him at craps and he wasn't any millionaire Texan and why don't you stay quiet, if you're going to stay here at all. You said you just wanted to nap.

So Hughie draws this long deep breath and burrows his face in my neck and lies very still. You've been to Vegas yourself, I say, you know what it's like. Hughie doesn't answer but I can tell he's waiting for me to go on. Of course it was a real surprise to *me*, I say, walking into the casino with Lynn and already at 9 A.M. there's so many people gambling, at these machines that look like video games. Almost the first people I saw, I swear they looked like your parents: this elderly couple playing the slots side by side, and she's winning some, a few quarters, and he doesn't care to be interrupted, just keeps on playing, leaning real close to the machine like he can't see too well, dropping in a quarter and pulling the lever, dropping in a quarter and pulling the lever, over and over the way they do, and it *is* fascinating, sort of, you can see how people get hooked. Lynn and I spent the morning on the machines and won some, lost some, the way you do. We saw some people Lynn said were probably retired to Vegas just for the slots and some of them, their right hands were actually deformed, like with arthritis, shaped like claws, pulling the lever a thousand times a day. But you could see they were happy, doing what they want to do.

There's lots of Vegas stories we heard just in the brief time we were there, and new ones every day. A man drives across the desert with two suitcases in the car, one empty and one filled with five-hundred-dollar bills; he's got five hundred thousand dollars and places a bet on some heavyweight boxer that the odds are six to one against—and he wins! And they fill the second suitcase for him with thousand-dollar bills and he drives off again and nobody even knows his name. That's a true story, supposed to have happened just a few weeks before. Then there are these millionaire, I mean billionaire, Arab sheiks that fly in for the poker games, these special poker games at some club not open to the general public where there's no limit on bets. I saw some of them, I think, just caught a glimpse. Up at the Sands some man died at black-jack, he'd been at the table for a long time they said and had a coronary for no special reason—I mean, not because he'd won a lot of money, or lost. We were in Vegas at the time but not in that casino, thank God! One thing that did occur, in the Rainbow Casino, it's sort of disgusting, a woman lost control of her bladder, playing the slots and not wanting to take time off, I suppose; people all started walking away fast, as Lynn and I did. Can you imagine! And she wasn't all that old either, around fifty, but a drinker—they must be the worst kind, hooked in with the slots on top of drinking.

Lynn's crazy about the slots but she said we should set ourselves a limit, make it seventy-five apiece, and see how far that would go, which is the only sensible way to approach gambling, and I wasn't playing ten minutes before I won a hundred and sixty dollars, which was one third of a jackpot for that machine. I was excited as a kid, jumping up and down; if it'd been me alone I would have quit right there and gone off and celebrated with a drink and something rich and fancy like a chocolate eclair, but Lynn just laughed and kissed me and said to calm down. Wait till you win a real jackpot, she said. That'll be time to cele-brate, then.

I forgot to mention all the conventions being held in the big hotels, and people drinking too much and acting like kids: the National Association of Morticians was one of them, the Fred Astaire Dance Association was another, a bunch of hypnotists, veterinarians—you name it! A lot of them fattish bald guys wearing badges with a look like they're running loose, no wives to crimp their style. I mean *a lot.*

I did see one sight that scared me, a little: that night, late, we were walking with these guys we'd met through Caesar's Palace—you know what that place is like, my God!—and there's this nice-looking woman about my age playing the slots, all alone evidently, with her cigarettes and her drink and one of those waxy paper buckets half filled with coins, and all of a sudden she hits the jackpot and it's one of the big jackpots, one thousand silver dollars, and the machine lights up, you know, the way they do, and plays some honkeytonk music, and people come over to watch, especially tourists who've never seen a big jackpot, and all she does is light up a cigarette, her hands are shaking and she doesn't even look at the coins spilling out, she's half turned away from the machine, her face so sad you'd think she was about to cry, and all the while the silver coins are tumbling out and filling the trough and spilling onto the floor and on and on and on! I mean, it keeps *on*, one thousand coins! It's just such a happy sight, the machine lighting up, and the silly music like cartoon music, but she isn't taking the least bit of happiness from it—just tired-looking and so sad it was painful to look at her. This man I was with, Sonny, he said, She's waiting for the jackpot to finish so she can keep on playing. That's all she wants, to keep on playing. A jackpot like that gets in the way.

And that turned out to be the case. At least with that woman—we stood off a ways and watched.

OK, Hughie says. Now tell me about Sonny.

What I was needing, I thought, was a new life. Not a new *life*, that sounds sort of extreme, but some new outlook on *this* life. Some new surprise, a set of new feelings. I want a baby but that's not it; I been wanting a baby for a long time. (Which was one of the reasons Hughie and I broke up. He has kids from his first marriage and definitely doesn't want any more.) That might be part of it but that's not it. Some nights, after work, thinking how there's nobody prominent in my affections any longer and nobody I even know of I'd like to be prominent, not in this town at least, where everybody knows everybody else's business and some of them, the men, have the idea I'm still married to Hughie or belong to him at least—some nights I'd start in crying for no reason I could name. Or, not even crying, just my throat closing up, that feeling of some old hurt returning.

So Lynn, my crazy friend Lynn, she comes over and shows me this charter-airline stuff, these brochures about Vegas, how cheap it is to fly there and how the hotels, some of them, aren't really that expensive, considering where you are—the big-name stars playing out there, the quality entertainment. Lynn has been to Vegas a half-dozen times and always enjoyed herself, and she told me if I was feeling bad this was the time to go—mid-January and the holiday season dead and gone and anybody's spirits just naturally need picking up. It didn't matter whether you were sad or not, Lynn said, this time of year would do it.

So I said no, then I heard myself say yes—you know how Lynn is with me. She just winds me around her little finger.

Hughie stirs and says, Oh, yes? And who wants to be wound?

I give him a pinch and tell him to be quiet. Does he want to hear this or doesn't he?

Go on, he says. I'm waiting for Sonny, the millionaire Texan.

Anyway, as you know, it was my first time in Vegas. The first time flying over the Rockies like that, and the Grand Canyon—my God, that's beautiful; the whole time in the air was beautiful, sort of like a dream—Lynn hates window seats so I was sitting next to the window and we're flying at thirty thousand feet or whatever the pilot said, over these mountains, these snowy peaks, then over clouds like snow crust— miles and miles of it, I mean *hundreds* of miles of it—and I guess I got sort of hypnotized looking out. It's a funny feeling you have, flying over a big stretch of cloud, like a field piled with snow, but there are people living below it not able to guess how big the field is and how there's other people flying above it. How they're down there hidden and you're up above, flying over.

Hughie is lying heavy against me with his chin sort of sharp on my shoulder. He's breathing hard and steady so I think he might be dropping off to sleep. But he says, a little too loud in my ear to suit me, OK, OK, I'm waiting for the high roller. So I tell *him* OK: this guy, Sonny Drexel as he introduced himself, from Oklahoma City, a rancher he said he was, him and his buddy were watching Lynn and me at blackjack, where we hadn't any luck—all those damn games go fast, the serious ones; you put your chip down and Christ it's gone before you know what happened. (Which is why some people prefer the slots— you go at your own speed and never lose much.) So these two, Sonny and Brady, said they'd stake us just to keep us in the game, and we all played for a while and got along pretty well, though Lynn and I never did get any luck, me especially. The strange thing is, Sonny said I was luck for him, wearing my turquoise dress, you know that one, and a black velvet ribbon in my hair, that makes me look ten years younger than I am—that's what caught his eye, he told me afterward, the ribbon, reminded him of his little girl. That is, when she was actually little. I guess she's all grown up, now, and then some.

How old was he? Hughie asks.

He *looked* like middle forties, maybe fifty, but I calculated later on he was around sixty—

Sixty!

—but didn't act it at all, good-looking in this cowboy style you see out in Vegas, a suede hat with silver studs, and snakeskin boots, designer jeans, jeweled bracelet on one wrist and wristwatch on the other, even some rings—the rings all had special meanings. Like one was a birthstone, one used to belong to his great-grandfather, that sort of thing. Lynn says the serious gamblers are all superstitious, they don't do anything by chance. What Sonny reminded me of was one of these cigarette billboard ads, an older man I mean, with pale hair you can't tell is blond or silver, and longish sideburns, and a creased, kindly, slightly puzzled face as if he'd been looking too long into the sun. His voice was higher-pitched than you'd expect. Brady was younger, heavier, with a coarser skin. What the connection was between them I never did learn.

The two of them were taking a break from craps; I got the idea they'd done pretty well judging from the good mood they were in, especially Sonny, buying drinks for Lynn and me and some Japanese tourists we got to talking with at the bar in the Tropicana, then this expensive supper they bought us at the Barbary Coast where we saw some of the floor show, a kind of Ice Capades with singing and rainbow lights and acrobatics—it was beautiful to see, and Lynn and I loved it, but Sonny got restless so we had to leave. Brady was ragging him about not being able to stay away from the craps table for more than an hour or two like he needs his oxygen replenished, and Sonny laughs but you can tell he's annoyed. That kind of a man, you can get intimate with him to a degree and think you know him, but the least hint of familiarity he draws back and chills you out. I picked up on that right away.

Another thing Brady ragged him about was going to the john all the time and washing his hands. He's afraid of germs, Brady said, and Sonny said, You'd be too if you could see them with the naked eye, and we all laughed and Brady said, Can *you* see them with the naked eye? and Sonny laughed too but said in this serious voice, Sometimes. And I don't like it.

And I did notice, the short period of time I was in the man's company, he must have excused himself a dozen times to go to the lavatory. Only when he was shooting craps he didn't, of course—it was like he was another person then. When he was hot, I mean. Really rolling high and nothing could have stopped him.

So we went back to the Dunes and Sonny and Brady got into a game and Sonny was shooting and almost right away got hot. Won eighteen hundred dollars in less time than it takes me to say it! He had me stand on his left-hand side, told me not to move an inch if I could help it. At first he didn't want me to bet, thinking that might go against his own luck, but after a while, when he kept winning and so many other people were betting on the game, he said it might be all right so I started placing little bets on what they called the pass line—the easiest bet. And naturally I won too, though it didn't seem real or right, betting with chips he'd given me and following what he did.

Craps isn't my favorite game, it's so fast and nervous and wild, and so complicated, Christ—like some game that was invented to keep ordinary minds at a distance. All Lynn and I did was bet on the pass line and later on the come line—we wouldn't have wanted to bet no pass and go against Sonny—but these other gamblers got involved, and of course Brady was doing all kinds of things, special bets we couldn't follow. And the smart thing about Sonny was, he knew when to quit for awhile—with this big pile of chips he'd built up in half an hour—and let somebody else shoot, so he could bet or not bet, depending. He told me what to do and I did it and most of the time I won, but if I lost he told me to stop for a while till my luck returned; he said you can feel your luck in you like a pressure in the chest and head but not a cruel pressure, a feeling that's highwired and happy, and you can feel it drain away, sudden, he said, as water draining out of a sink. A gambler moves by instinct, he said, like a man dousing for water.

I had a granddaddy who could douse for water, I said.

We'll talk about it some other time, he said.

So after Brady shot for awhile and did OK, Sonny took over again and you could tell something would happen: this feeling all around the table, like the air's charged up. Of course we'd all been drinking this while, I don't know how long, Lynn and me excited and giggling like high school girls, arms around each other's waist, saying, This is something different, isn't it! This is something different from the old home routine! And Sonny started his roll and I placed bets on the pass line, which is the only bet I ever felt easy with, that I understood: before the shooter rolls the dice, you place your bet, and if he rolls seven or eleven you and him both win and he keeps the dice to roll again. If he hits two, three, or ten the bet is lost but he keeps his point and goes on rolling until either he makes his point and you both win or he shoots seven and the bet is lost. I *think* that's how the game goes.

That's how it goes, Hughie says. He's wider awake than I thought he would be, which is flattering. Except it's two, three, or twelve on that first roll.

And anyway I won my bets. But like I say it didn't seem real, or exactly right.

Around 4:30 A.M. Sonny quit for the night. He'd been playing in all about fifteen hours, he estimated, in the past twenty-four and needed some rest. As far as I could calculate—they didn't like to talk about these things, like it was in bad taste—he'd won about twenty-five thousand just the time I was with him.

Called me his good luck talisman, said he'd always want me by his side. All the time he was shooting he hadn't touched me, but now he put his arm around me so tight it was hard to walk and sort of leaned on me, calling me pretty girl, pretty Irene, Irene-y, I'll see you in my dreams. He was drunk I guess but not so you'd really notice. Had a way of talking that was a combination of a high-class gentleman and a country boy—a sort of twangy accent, warm and rich like Johnny Cash.

He *was* sweet. Next day down in the promenade—we were staying in the big Hilton, there's all these boutiques and special stores there—he bought me a Japanese kimono, the most beautiful thing, turquoise with a brocade design like a sunburst, gold, red, green: just so beautiful. And some black silk pants to go with the kimono, and some gold lamé sandals with spike heels. And some gold teardrop earrings, and a bottle of perfume. And—

Uh-huh, says Hughie, his leg muscles twitching the way they do when he's asleep but he isn't asleep now, I get the drift of it.

It wasn't *that*, I tell Hughie, I liked him for himself. He was a fine, sweet, generous, thoughtful man. And a gentleman.

Hughie keeps quiet, not wanting to pick a fight and get kicked out of here on his ass as he's in danger of being. My heart's beating hard just at that one thing he said, his sly innuendo that I don't have to swallow any more than I swallowed any of his shit and he knows it— he's the boy who knows it no matter what he goes around town telling his buddies.

He was a gentleman, I say. There aren't many of that kind around.

Hughie doesn't say a word but I know he's fully awake and listening.

I *will* say, though, when we first got to his room—a real nice room in the Hilton Tower, nothing like what Lynn and I were sharing at our motel—I started in feeling very strange and wanted to just say good night and leave. Before, you know, it was too late and Sonny got the wrong idea. I'm just standing there, afraid if I sit down I'll fall asleep— I was more exhausted all of a sudden than I've ever been in my life—

and my eyes weren't focusing right, everything sort of swimmy and blurry. I was drunk but that wasn't the only thing. There's this man I don't even know whistling to himself and taking off his shirt and his chest is covered in what looks like actual fur: gray-grizzled, silvery, matted. And his nipples dark as a woman's. And fat loose around his waist though his ribs were showing. And some sort of scar, or burn, on his back that looked just terrible. It's like him and me were married and had been married a long time, he's tossing his things around, whistling loud and happy, has me help him with his boots—these snakeskin boots like nothing you've ever seen, Lynn says something like that would go for five hundred dollars if not a thousand. You don't even see them in any store around here.

So I'm feeling very, very strange, this sickish feeling in my stomach, and Sonny's in the bathroom running the water loud and still whistling. He's happier now than down in the casino, like it was all held in, down there, and now it's coming out—just how happy he is, and how powerful it is, that kind of happiness!—like it would be too much for an ordinary person.

Sonny comes out of the bathroom drying his hands on a towel and when he sees me it's like he's almost forgotten I was there: this big smile comes over his face that looks as if it could stretch his face out of shape. Kisses me, and stands back staring at me, tells me how much I mean to him, how pretty I am, will I be his pretty pretty girl forever, and he takes the velvet bow out of my hair and kisses it solemn and serious and I'm thinking to myself, God, am *I* doing this? This is *me*? In a hotel room with some guy who, nice as he is, I don't know, just met? And I'm laughing too, giggling and scared, 'cause it's so easy, you could see doing this every night, I don't mean for the money or even for the man but just—the fact of how easy it is, once it starts.

Hughie stirs. Irene, he says, and it's the first time I have heard him call me Irene in a long time, this is a hard story to hear.

I told you, be quiet. Or don't you want to hear it?

I *want* to hear it, Hughie says, but I guess I want some parts of it to go by fast.

There's nothing to go by fast, I say, since all that happens is I sort of pass out on one of the beds and Sonny loosens my clothes and takes off my shoes and that's all—he sleeps in his own bed like a gentleman. And that's all.

Then the next morning I wake up pretty late, around eleven, and already he's in the shower, he orders us breakfast from room service which neither one of us can stomach, except for the Bloody Marys, and we go downstairs and pick out those nice things—which were a surprise to me, I swear, completely unexpected. Where Brady and Lynn are, I don't know, and I didn't like to make any inquiries.

Later on we drove over to Vegas World in this special car of Sonny's, Italian, hand-built, he said, like a custom-made suit, some sort of Ferrari with a long name, bright red like lipstick and capable Sonny said of doing 175 miles an hour under the right road conditions. How'd I like to go for a drive in the desert maybe the next day? Sonny asked. Out to Death Valley maybe. I told him I'd like that a lot, but I seemed to know we'd never get there, that something was due to happen; it was like a movie where things are going so well you know they can't last. Also, it was only a few blocks to Vegas World but the sunlight hurt our eyes, even with dark sunglasses. What the actual desert would be like I didn't want to think.

(It's kind of a startling thing, leaving the inside world and going to the outside, that you've sort of forgotten is still there. This ordinary sunshine and ordinary sidewalks and traffic lights and things, and people in it that didn't seem to have anything to do with all that was happening in the casinos. It made me feel sort of sickish, I told Sonny, and he said yes but you get used to it.)

At Vegas World it's sort of like a circus for adults but Sonny wasn't interested in any of it, just headed straight for the casino. And what a crowd packed in! Not just every slot machine taken, but people waiting for some to open up. Sonny staked me to some blackjack again, but I didn't do too well, then for a few turns at roulette, ditto; he didn't play because as he said you get to know which game is yours and which isn't.

Also, he said, the games were too simple. Didn't command his fullest concentration.

So it was back at craps, and he had me stand close beside him, on his left, wearing my new outfit, including the shoes, and the black velvet ribbon in my hair. And again Sonny got on a roll, couldn't seem to make a mistake; he doubled his bet, and won, and doubled, and won, and there was this feeling of—it's hard to explain—a kind of excitement at the table, happiness so strong it's scary. That it could go through you like electricity, and kill you, bend your skull out of shape. Some of it's because other people get caught up in the betting, strangers that a few minutes ago didn't know one another but suddenly they're all united, close as old friends or something deeper, sisters and brothers—the exact same blood.

So he did real well again but never allowed himself to show what he was feeling. I could never be like that, I guess; I could never be a real gambler! All my feelings show on my face.

So we went back to the Hilton, this is maybe 6 P.M. that day, and Sonny's in a state like I don't believe I have ever seen any person in, giving off heat like a radiator, I swear I could almost feel the waves of it, and I was pretty high too, and we're kissing a little, sort of fooling around, but more like kids, or puppies, than, you know—like he's too worked up for anything to actually happen. His skin is burning like fever, but without sweat. And his eyes, this tawny cat color, the eyeball and the iris or whatever it's called sort of run together, like a man with jaundice, and I notice he's breathing hard, and loud, but don't make much of it. Whatever we're doing he stops all of a sudden and goes into the bathroom to wash his hands—I mean, I guess that's what he was doing—then he comes back and looks at me and says, Get dressed, honey, let's go back to the casino. And I can't believe it.

So we go back out again, this time down to the Sands, and in the car he's talking a mile a minute, to me you'd naturally think but really to himself. I listened hard but I can't remember much of it now. He did want me to marry him, that's for sure—come back with him to Oklahoma City to this new house he planned to build. He didn't ask me anything about myself, such as did I have any children, let alone did I want any children, so I sat there nodding and agreeing but thinking he probably wasn't serious, really. What he said, he meant, but only while he was saying it.

Then at the Sands his luck turned on him after about an hour, I don't know why. I mean—I don't know why he didn't know it was going to turn, the way he'd said he always did. Right in the middle of one of these red-hot rolls—what you would think was a red-hot roll—when he'd made, I calculated, about twenty-two thousand in not much more time than it's taking me to say so, he rolled the wrong numbers and lost the bet; and that was the beginning of the end. The two or three guys that'd been betting don't come won really big, and Sonny just stood there like he couldn't believe he was seeing what he was seeing. And the terrible thing is, the girl just raked in the chips like nothing had gone wrong, or even changed. Not the slightest understanding in her face of what had happened.

Now, *I* seemed to know that poor man should quit right then but he didn't pay the least heed to me, and when I put my hand on his arm he pushed away like I was something nasty. Don't touch! he said.

And this feeling came over me like the floor was tilting, and I thought, I know the truth of why we're here on earth, human beings here on earth: it's to love one another if we can, but if we can't—if we try, but can't—we're here to show kindness and gentleness and mercy and respect to one another, and to protect one another. I don't know how I knew but I *knew*.

But would he pay any attention to me? He wouldn't. Saying he wanted to marry me one minute and telling me to go to hell, calling me cunt, the next. For all the good I meant to do him.

So his luck ran out, and I don't know how much he lost, but people made big money betting against him, and in the end nobody wanted to look at him. I should mention he was wearing the suede cowboy hat and the same black silk shirt with one of these little string neckties he'd been wearing the day before, and the fancy boots. And a leather belt with a big silver buckle. And hot as he was he wasn't sweating much. (*I* was the one that was sweating now!)

I recall one final sight: the girl in her costume with *Sands* stitched in gold on the back, black jumpsuit and tight belt and black spike heels, hair blonder and puffier than mine, she took this little Plexiglas rake of hers and just raked Sonny's chips away, and took a crumpled-up five-hundred-dollar bill from him the same way except that she pushed it down a little slot in the table like a mail slot. And it just disappeared.

So finally Sonny turned away, his face like paper that's been burnt though but hasn't burst into actual flames yet. Finish up your drink, Blondie, he says to me, smiling. I'm hurt to think the man has forgotten my name.

We went back to the Hilton and he made some calls, then went out, saying he'd be gone awhile. I watched some television and washed my hair and finished this champagne we'd got the night before, and it got late but I was too worked up to sleep. I had the drapes open looking over at Vegas World—that's the tallest building, all colored lights like fireworks. But everywhere on the Strip there's lights: the Sahara, the Oasis, the Golden Nugget, Caesar's Palace, all the rest. Off in the distance the mountains you can't see and I never did get to see except from the air and going to and from the airport in the cab.

Around 4 A.M. when I was actually asleep a little, with all the lights on, Sonny came back to the room. He had that look so drunk it might be said to be sober. He sat on the edge of the bed and kneaded his chest with both hands like it hurt him inside. In this calm voice he said, I have led the wrong life. I have done wrong things. At the very time of doing them I knew they were wrong, but I did them nonetheless. I did them *nonetheless*—this word drawn out slow, in a whisper.

He started to cry so it was painful to watch. Begging me not to leave him now his luck had run temporarily out.

I was crying too. I told him I'd stay with him as long as he wanted.

He said, I'm not from where I said. I'm from a different place. Not even Oklahoma. I've been a bad husband and father. There's people back home loved me and gave me their trust, and I let them down. I let them down a lot of times. Right now they don't even know where I am.

I was sort of cradling his head, stooping over him. I said, Don't think about that now, Sonny, and he shot back, Don't think about it *now*? When the fuck *am* I supposed to think about it, then?

But right away he changed his tone back. Said, Dolly, I'm a dead man.

What? I asked.

I'm dying, I'm a dying man, he said. I'm next thing to dead.

Are you serious? Should I call a—

You can't leave me just yet, he said, gripping my arm hard. You know I'm crazy about you; I'd love you if I could.

That didn't make any sense so I said, You can love me, why can't you love me? And he says right away, in this voice like we've been quarreling, Dolly, if I *could*, I *would*.

He grabs me around the hips so hard it hurts and pulls me down onto the bed. Then he's on me pawing and grunting and making this terrible hoarse sobbing noise, and I'm there not helping him much but just waiting for it to get over. I think, He can't do it, he's too drunk, or too sick, or too old, and that's more or less the way it was, I guess, but I wasn't paying close attention, shutting my eyes tight and seeing all kinds of things that had nothing to do with him or what was going on. I could see the wheat field out behind here, the way the wind makes it look like waves. And the Grand Canyon, when the pilot turned the plane for us, explained some things to us, those natural rock formations, what a canyon actually is.

And other things too. Lying there with my eyes shut like they are now, my mind taking me far away from where I was.

Afterward I couldn't wake him. It was almost noon and he was lying on his back with his mouth open and saliva on the pillow and I seemed to know he wasn't just sleeping or even blacked out but something more serious. I tried to wake him, slapped his face and got a washcloth soaked in cold water, and that didn't help; oh, Christ, I'm thinking, the man is in a coma, he's going to die. The loud wheezing breath in a rhythm not like a normal breath: he's going to die. No matter what I do, shaking him, shouting in his ear, *I can't wake him up.*

I remembered something I'd read about brain death, a coma caused by too much alcohol and pills—did I mention Sonny'd been taking some kind of pills, just popping them now and then, not too many, and I didn't know if they were for his health, or what, like my daddy has to take heart pills every day of his life and glycerine if he gets pains in his chest—but I didn't want to ask Sonny; I figured it was too personal a question.

I got so scared, I guess I panicked. Thinking if he's going to die I will be involved. I would be a witness, and maybe arrested. Called to testify. Or charged with murder like that woman, that actress, who gave John Belushi a shot of heroin and he died. And she was tried and found guilty of murder!

So I got dressed and left. I left the kimono behind, and the jewelry, and even the perfume, and the shoes—it was the only decent thing to do. I wasn't thinking too clearly but I thought he could sell them back, maybe, to the stores. Or pawn them. I found some hundred-dollar bills loose in my purse and left them too, on the bedside table where he couldn't miss them.

So I went downstairs to the lobby, and in the lobby I called the house physician and told him Sonny's room number and hung up quick before he could ask any questions. I went back to our motel and nobody was there, thank God, and I took a long bath and tried to keep myself from thinking. I fell asleep in the bath and sometime that afternoon Lynn helped me out and dried me and seeing my face she just said, Don't tell me, so I didn't tell her. I never did tell her much of it.

Before we left Vegas I called Sonny's room but the phone just rang and rang. I asked at the desk was Sonny Drexel still registered and the girl said there wasn't any Sonny Drexel listed and had not been, and I said, That can't be right, and the girl repeated what she'd said, and I asked who was registered in 2023 up in the tower and she said, in the snottiest voice possible, The Hilton does not give out such information.

And that was the end of that. Like that—it was the end of that.

Hughie? You listening?

But Hughie's asleep by now. Warm moist breath against my neck like a baby's. Pressing heavy against me, foot twitching between mine, like always. He's here, then he's gone.

Stuart Kaminsky's two series detectives are about as different as night and day. Toby Peters is a down-and-out private eye working the glamorous side of Hollywood and meeting such celebrities as Errol Flynn, Mae West, and the Marx Brothers. Porfiry Rostnikov is a Russian detective who is assigned "impossible cases" by his superiors to keep him in line. Both are incredibly well-done series, with the attention to detail in each varied and exact. He has also written biographies of prominent Hollywood personalities such as Clint Eastwood and John Huston. Luckily, in between all these books he finds the time to write and polish short story gems like the following

Blowout in Little Man Flats

Stuart M. Kaminsky

The last murder in Little Man Flats was back in, let me see, 1963, before Kennedy was shot by who knows how or why," Sheriff George Fingerhurt told his prime suspect. "Want some tea? Do you good in this heat."

"No . . . thanks."

"Suit yourself."

Fingerhurt sat back drinking his herbal peppermint tea from the Rhett Butler cup his daughter had brought him from Atlanta. George Fingerhurt liked Rhett Butler and herbal tea. Rhett was cool, never mind the temperature—like today, pushing a hundred in the shade.

"Got a theory about tea, got it from my grandfather Ocean Fingerhurt who was half Apache. Grandpa Ocean said hot tea cooled you off. Since Grandpa Ocean had got lost and wound up in Little Man Flats, New Mexico, back in 1930, when he thought he was in southern California, he was hardly a man to trust, at least not about directions. He was better about tea. Sure you don't want to change your mind?"

"Okay," said the suspect. "I'll have some tea."

"Gets dry out here," said the sheriff, pouring a cup of dark-green tea into a Scarlett O'Hara cup and handing it to the truckdriver, whose name, as he had told the sheriff, was Tector (Teck) Gorch. "Careful—hot."

"Obliged," said Teck.

They drank for about a minute, and Teck looked out the window.

"Quite a crowd," the sheriff said.

"Umm," Teck grunted.

There were eight people outside the one-story adobe town hall and sheriff's office. One of them was Ollie Twilly, from the feed store, wide-brimmed Stetson shading his eyes as he leaned back against the front fender of his '88 Ford pickup. Ollie had reason to be there. His brother Stan was one of the three people who had been killed, probably by the trucker sitting across from George drinking herbal tea.

The trucker was, George figured, maybe thirty-five, forty. One of those solid mailbox types. Curly hair cut a little long, could use a shave, but considering what had happened, made sense he hadn't considered the social graces. Teck the trucker was wearing slightly washed-out blood-specked jeans and a bloody T-shirt with the words I'M HAVING A BAD DAY written across the front in black. Amen to that sentiment, George thought.

"Last murder, back when I was a boy," George explained after a careful sip. "Indian named Double Eagle out of Gallup on a motorcycle went ravin' down 66 and plowed into Andrew Carpenter. Jury figured it was on purpose. Not much point to it. Andrew was near ninety. Am I getting too folksy for you? I haven't had much practice with murder cases. Haven't had any, really."

Teck shrugged and tried to think. The tea was making him feel a little cooler, but the sheriff was making him nervous. Fingerhurt was wearing matching khaki trousers and short-sleeved shirt. His black hair was freshly cut, combed straight back, and he looked a hell of a lot like the crying Indian in the TV commercials about polluting the rivers.

A sweat-stained khaki cowboy hat sat on the empty desk.

"Hey," said Fingerhurt, pointing out the window. "Crowd's growing. Those two are Mr. and Mrs. Barcheck, what passes for society in Little Man Flats. Own a lot of the town, including the Navajo Fill-up."

Teck looked out the window for the first time.

"Nice-lookin' woman," the sheriff said. "Not enough meat for me, but we're not in Santa Fe, so one's voyeuristic choices are limited. You wanna just tell your story? State police'll be here in a half hour, maybe less, to pick you up. Won't have a good report on what it looks like up there till Red comes in." Teck held his cup in two hands, feeling warm moisture seep into his palms.

"Red's my deputy, one you saw out at the Fill-up."

"His hair isn't red," said Teck.

"Never was. His father had red hair, was called Red. Deputy was Little Red. When his daddy died, deputy was just plain Red."

"Interesting," said Teck.

It was the sheriff's turn to shrug.

"Say, listen, information like that counts for lore in Little Man Flats."

He looked out the window and observed, "Crowd's getting bigger. I'd say twenty out there, coming to take a look at you. Four, five more people, and practically the whole town'll have turned out. State troopers are gonna be here soon, asking if I found anything. You want to tell your story? I'll take notes."

"I'm arrested? I need a lawyer?"

"You're here for questioning in the murder of Miss Rose Bryant Fernandez, Mr. Stanley Twilly, and a man who had a wallet in his back pocket strongly suggesting he was Lincoln Smart. You know the man?"

"Trucker, like me," said Teck. "Knew him to say hello. Where's my rig?"

"Safe, gathering dust out at the Fill-up, where you parked it. Wanna tell me what happened out there?"

"Someone cut your population almost in half," said Teck without a smile.

Sheriff Fingerhurt shook his head. He put down his Rhett Butler cup and folded his hands, looking unblinking at the trucker.

"Educated?"

"A little too much," said Teck. "Almost finished college. Almost a lot of things."

"Feeling a little sorry for yourself?"

"Considering, I think I've got a right."

"Maybe so. Story?"

Teck sat back, looked out the window at the gathered crowd, focused on a little boy about nine, who was looking directly back at him and covering his eyes to shade out the sun.

"Came thundering in a little before four in the morning," Teck began, nodding his agreement to the sheriff, who had pulled a tape recorder out of a desk drawer. Fingerhurt pushed the button and sat back.

"Came thundering in before four in the morning," Teck repeated. "Wanted to make Gallup, usually do. Never stopped at the Navajo Fill-up overnight before. One bad tire out of sixteen didn't stop me. I'd have even tried outlasting the knock in the diesel, even with nothing but desert for fifty more miles. Rain and backache did me in. Learned enough in eleven years in the high cab to know that when the back says stop, you stop, or you will have one hell of a tomorrow."

Sheriff Fingerhurt nodded and shook his head.

"Grit and sand on my neck, air conditioner gone lazy, shirt sticking to my chest, back, and deep down into my behind," Teck continued. "I was a sorry mess by one in the A.M. I never stopped in your town before last night except for diesel. I don't know the two locals who got killed, and I barely knew Linc."

"Lincoln Smart, the other driver?" asked the sheriff.

"There was only one rig in the opening beyond the pumps. Linc's big silver-and-blue, bigger than mine. I own my truck out there, and I've got a load of furniture from a factory just outside of Baines, Arkansas. Taking it to a pair of stores in Bakersfield."

"Where you from, Teck?"

"Tupelo. Tupelo, Mississippi."

"Elvis's town?"

"Yeah."

"You ever see the King himself?"

"He was long gone when I was growing up."

Sheriff Fingerhurt sat back, shaking his head.

"Well," Teck went on, "I—"

"Married?" asked the sheriff.

"Divorced. One kid. A boy, about seven or eight."

"You don't know?"

"Seven. His birthday's February 11. I just forget the year. Haven't seen him for three years. My ex-wife won't let me."

"Sorry," said Fingerhurt.

"I got bigger things to worry about today," Teck said, putting down his now empty cup.

"Yeah," said the sheriff.

"Got out of my rig, with my rain poncho over my head, duffel in my hand, locked up, and went inside the café. Woman behind the counter was reading a paperback."

"Remember what it was?"

"Make a difference?"

"Who knows?" said Fingerhurt.

"Woman behind the counter looked up at me like I was a surprise she could have done without," Teck went on. "People tend not to be overjoyed when I walk in, but this woman—"

"Rosie Fernandez," Fingerhurt supplied.

"I guess," Teck said with a shrug, looking out the window.

The small crowd had grown. There were more men now, and they were talking, arguing.

"You ever have a lynching in this town?" Teck said, his eyes meeting those of Ollie Twilly, whose Stetson was now tilted back on his head. Ollie either had a very high forehead or he was bald. Bald or balding, he was clearly in one hell of a bad mood.

"Not a white man," said the sheriff. "Last Indian was shot in 1928 by a mob for drunk talk to a white woman."

"Your grandfather picked one hell of a town to settle in," Teck said.

"He was lost."

"We keep this up, I won't get my story told before the troopers get here," Teck said.

"Go on. Rose Fernandez was behind the counter, reading a paperback."

"Dean Koontz. It was Dean Koontz."

"Read one by him," said Fingerhurt. "People turned into machines in a small town. Scared shit out of me."

"I asked her for a room and something to eat," Teck went on. "I wasn't particular as long as it wasn't trout. I'm allergic."

"We don't have much call for trout in New Mexico," the sheriff said.

Outside the window, the crowd was getting louder, and there was, the sheriff noted, a very bad sign even a white man could read. The children were being sent off, as if there might be something the adults didn't want them to see.

"I think they're working themselves up to come here and lynch me," said Teck, following the sheriff's line of vision.

"Closest yucca that'll hold your weight is two miles out of town," said the sheriff, reaching for his hat. "Shoot you is what I'm thinking."

"Like the Indian in 1928?"

"Something like that," George Fingerhurt agreed. "But we'll stop 'em."

"We?"

"Me and Red. He's pulling up."

About twenty-five yards beyond the window where the crowd had gathered, a dust-covered pickup pulled in and a man in jeans, a khaki shirt, and a hat climbed out.

People flocked around him as he strode forward, shaking his head.

"He found something," the sheriff said.

"How can you tell? Your Indian blood?"

"Got the look. Known Red for almost forty years. You know things like that about people you know."

The door behind Teck flew open, and voices from outside came in, full of fear and anger. Red closed the door and stepped in. He was thinner and, considering the mood of the mob, less formidable than Teck would have liked. Red looked at the sheriff and then at Teck.

"Wanna talk in the other room, George?"

"What'd you find?" asked the sheriff.

"You sure you—"

"You found what, Red?"

"Troopers came with a truck. All over the place. Told me I could go. They'd be here quick. Said we shoulda held Gorch at the murder site. Found this under Rosie's body. Said you should have a look at it."

Red stepped to the sheriff's desk, avoiding Teck's eyes, pulled a crumpled paper bag out of his jeans pocket, and handed it to George Fingerhurt. The sheriff held the bag open behind the desk, looked into it and then out the window and then at Red.

"Damn," said Fingerhurt.

"Damn right, damn," said Red.

"Sheriff. . . ." Teck tried, but the door behind him opened with a jolt. He turned and found himself facing Ollie Twilly, both Barchecks, and a variety of others, mostly with the look and matching intellect of bewildered cattle. Twilly was carrying a shotgun.

"We want him," said Ollie, pointing his shotgun barrel at Teck, who jumped up and stood with his back to the wall behind the still seated sheriff.

"You all want him? You too, Mrs. Barcheck?" Fingerhurt asked.

"Yes," she said.

She was, indeed, a fine-looking woman, freckled brown with yellow hair tied back, could have been any age from thirty to fifty, Teck thought, and wondered how he could do such thinking with a shotgun cocked and aimed in the general area of his gut.

"And what'll you do with him?" asked the sheriff.

"Take him out. Shoot him," said Twilly. "Shoot him through the brains like the dog he is."

The shotgun came up toward Teck Gorch's face, and Ollie Twilly continued with:

"You shot my brother like a dog, and I'm—"

"How'd you know Stan was shot, Mr. Twilly?" the sheriff asked, as two of the more oxlike men stepped toward Teck.

"Red told us," said Andrew Barcheck, who was decidedly a slouching Saint Bernard to his wife's well-groomed poodle.

The sheriff closed his eyes and shook his head before he looked up at Red, whose left cheek twitched.

"George, you and Red go out for a shake at Veronica's," said Ollie Twilly. "When you come back—"

"No, Mr. Twilly," said the sheriff.

"We'll have your goddamn job, George," Twilly said through gritted teeth.

"You couldn't live on my salary, Mr. Twilly. You take him. You shoot him. Red and I arrest you for murder," said the sheriff. "Is it worth going to jail for, Mr. Twilly?"

"Yes."

The two bovine men were now about three feet in front of Teck, who had sucked in his stomach, feeling more than a little sick.

"Rest of you feel the same way?" the sheriff asked. "You got murder looking at you, conspiracy, impeding a lawman in the dispatching of his duty. Hell, folks, you're looking at a lot of bleak years in the state house."

"No jury will convict us. Not after what he did."

"Act your age, Ollie," Mrs. Barcheck said. "There isn't a jury that wouldn't convict us."

"Then by shit and a wild pig," shouted Twilly, "I don't give a crap. I'll shoot him right here."

The two bulls in front of Teck jumped out of the line of fire.

"Man was telling his side when you came in," said the sheriff. "Think you can hold off till he finishes? Give him that?"

"Let him speak, Ollie," Mr. Barcheck said.

Someone behind the front line let out a groan and an "Oh, shit."

"Miguel, that you?" the sheriff called.

A heavy, hard-breathing dark man with bad skin worked his way forward through the crowd.

"Let him say," Miguel said.

"No," said Twilly, the gun now firmly against the chest of Miguel.

"My sister got killed last night too," Miguel Fernandez said. "We can listen. Who knows what Leon Harvey Oswald would have said if the Jew guy hadn't shot him?"

"Lee. Oswald's name was Lee," Mrs. Barcheck corrected.

"And the man who shot him was Jack Ruby."

"This isn't goddamn Trivial Pursuit," screamed Twilly. "Can't you see Fingerhurt's stalling till the state police get here?"

"I'll look out the window," said Miguel. "We see them coming, and you can shoot."

Defeated for the moment, Ollie Twilly let the shotgun point toward the floor.

"Finish your story, Tector," the sheriff said.

Teck, back to the wall, looked at the faces of anger, hate, and confusion around the room.

"I don't think I. . . ." Teck began, and then said, "I walked in, soaking wet, told the woman I needed a room for the night and a mechanic in the morning. She said . . ."

Teck's eyes met Miguel's and then went to the sheriff.

"I don't . . ."

"Tector," said the sheriff, "I don't see a hell of a lot of choice here, do you?"

"She said all she had was eggs any way I wanted 'em, and if I wanted company in bed for a couple of hours, she could handle that too, for a reasonable fee."

Teck's eyes were watching Miguel Fernandez. Fernandez betrayed nothing but heavy breathing.

"I said I'd think on it," Teck went on.

"A fine-looking woman, Rosie," said the sheriff. "Some meat on her bones. Nothing to hold back here, Teck. Rosie was the town—begging your pardon, Mrs. Barcheck—lady of the afternoon and evening."

"She was a whore, yes," said Miguel, "but she was a good person. Anybody in this room say anything else?"

No one in the room had anything else to say relating to Rosie Fernandez's behavior, so the sheriff nodded at Teck, who went on.

"She said she'd make me two over-easy sandwiches with mayo and onions and figured from the onion order that I wasn't interested in company. I said I wanted to change into something dry, and she told me to go up the stairs off in the corner and go into room three, where I could shower and get decent and dry."

"What else?" the sheriff said.

"Jukebox in the corner near the window was playing Patsy Cline," Teck said hopefully.

"She was reading Dean Koontz and listening to Patsy Cline," the sheriff said.

"Stairs were dark. I started up. This guy passed me coming down."

"Guy?" asked Fingerhurt. "What'd he look like?"

"Don't know. Wasn't really looking. About my height, weight. Maybe."

"Met himself coming and going," said Twilly. "We heard enough here yet?"

"Wait," Teck said. "He had a big silver belt buckle."

"Every man in this room and a few of the women are wearing big silver belt buckles," the sheriff said. "Even me and Red."

"I'm telling you what I remember," Teck pleaded. "I'm telling the truth."

"Okay. Sha-hair-a-zadie," said Ollie Twilly. "Keep going."

"Not much more to tell. I went to room three, got my clean jeans, socks, and the shirt I'm wearing out of my bag, took a quick shower, got dressed, and headed back down. Patsy Cline was still singing, eggs were burning bad, and Miss Fernandez was laying there in the middle of the room, dead and bloody. I tried to help her, but she was—"

"And you were covered in her blood," the sheriff said.

"Yes."

"And then?"

"I called for help. No one answered. The rain was harder. It was pushing dawn. I ran back up the stairs and knocked at doors and yelled. No answer. One of the doors was open. Linc Smart was naked, bloody, and dead. I kept opening doors. One was an office. Bald man was laying across the desk, dead."

"That was my brother. That was Stan," cried Ollie. "You lying son of a bitch and a half."

"No," said Teck, holding up his hands to ward off the anticipated shotgun blast. "No lie. I found the phone, called the operator, told her that someone had murdered who knows how many people at the Navajo Fill-up. And that was it."

The sheriff's eyes met Teck's and then moved for an instant to the running tape recorder before returning to Teck's face.

"Question, Mr. Gorch," the sheriff said. "You didn't hear gunshots when you drove up to the Fill-up and walked in?"

"No. It was raining hard. Whoever it was must have shot Linc and the other guy before I got to the door."

"How many times were they shot, Red?" the sheriff asked.

"The trucker three times, Mr. Stanley Twilly twice. Then Miss Rosie twice."

"Why," the sheriff asked, "did Miss Rosie sit there reading a Dean Koontz and offer you eggs and companionship if she just heard five shots?"

"Yes," said Miguel, turning angrily toward Teck.

"I don't know," said Teck.

"And why didn't you hear Rosie getting shot?" the sheriff went on.

"I was in the shower. It was raining hard. I don't know."

"This is the stupidest damn story," Ollie said. "Everybody step back. Fairy tale's over."

The shotgun came up toward Teck again.

"Why would I kill those people?" Teck said.

"You thought Rose was alone," said Ollie. "You went for her behind the counter. She fought you, threatened to call the sheriff. You shot her. Then you panicked and went to look for any witnesses who might have seen you. You shot that truckdriver and my brother."

"And then I called the police?" Teck cried.

"Maybe you were trying to be tricky," Miguel Fernandez said. "Maybe you just got damned confused, decided you couldn't get away, tire tracks, whatever. So you made up your story."

"No," cried Teck. "Sheriff."

"What'd he do with the gun?" Sheriff Fingerhurt asked.

"Threw it away, maybe buried it couple hundred yards off in the desert," said Barcheck. "What's the difference?"

"Troopers are coming down the street," said Miguel softly, turning his eyes to Teck's frightened face.

"That does it," said Ollie. "Everybody stand back. We in this together?"

The two bulls who had approached Teck grunted something. The rest of the crowd was shuffling, silent now that the troopers were a minute or two away.

"I've got one thing I can't figure," said the sheriff. "If his story is true, why didn't Rose call me and Red, or go upstairs to see what was happening? Why did she sit there reading a book?"

"He made up a dumb story," said Miguel.

"Miguel," said the sheriff, "how long I know you?"

"Your whole life."

"What if Rose did hear the shots? What if Rose knew Stan and the trucker were dead when Gorch came in looking for a warm room and meal? What if he surprised her, she picked up a book, looked as if she didn't want company, and then, to keep him from getting suspicious, offered to bed down with him for the night, not forgetting to say it wasn't free. Gorch goes upstairs. Killer comes down. Rose tells him about Gorch. Killer gets the idea of blaming everything on the dumb trucker. Sorry, Tector."

"No offense," said Teck.

"Why would anyone want to kill my brother?" Ollie said.

"Property, money's my guess," said Sheriff Fingerhurt. "Killer probably considered burying Stan and the dead trucker and having Rose say Stan just got fed up, grabbed some cash, and took off for northern California."

The troopers' car door opened and then slammed shut a beat later. All eyes turned to the window. Two troopers were walking toward the Little Man Flats municipal building, where most of the adult population was gathered in the sheriff's office.

"That's crazy," shouted Ollie.

The sheriff lifted his right hand and displayed a crinkled brown paper bag.

"Red found this on the floor under Rose's body," he said, pulling a bright silver buckle out of the bag and holding it up for the congregation to see. The silver was hammered into the shape of a buffalo, with huge horns in relief.

"So," said Miguel, "everybody around here has a belt buckle like that, something like that. It could be this guy's, this truckdriver's."

"Right," said the sheriff, "but he's got a buckle on his belt, and he had time to look for it if Rose pulled it off in a struggle with him. But the killer, the killer heard the shower go off, made a decision not to kill the trucker, and ran without finding the buckle. Hell, maybe he didn't even notice till he got home or too far to turn back."

The door behind the crowd opened, and a deep voice said:

"What the hell is going on in here?"

"I'm not interested in who has a buffalo-head silver buckle," said Fingerhurt, ignoring the troopers who were muscling their way forward through the gathering. "I'm interested in who *doesn't* have one anymore. With the cooperation of the troopers who have just arrived, I'm going to ask a few of you who I know have buffalo buckles to go back to their houses with me and show me the buckle. Miguel, Dan Sullivan, Mr. Barcheck, and you, Ollie."

The troopers were in front now, near twins, well built, unwrinkled uniforms, hats flat on their heads and brims perfectly parallel to the ground.

"What's going on, George?" the older of the two said.

The sheriff held up a finger to show that he needed only a minute more.

"All right with me," said Barcheck.

"Me too," said Miguel.

"I'm wearing mine," said Danny Sullivan, stepping forward to show the buckle in question.

"Mr. Twilly?" Sheriff Fingerhurt asked.

"Lost," he said defiantly. "I looked for it a few days ago. Someone stole it."

"You wore it yesterday, Oliver," Mrs. Barcheck said.

"Hey, that's right," said Danny Sullivan. "You sat next to me at Veronica's for lunch. You were wearing the buckle. You had the meat loaf with chilies, and I had . . . who the hell cares what I had?"

"Is there a punch line here, George?" the older trooper said, doing a magnificent job of hiding his complete confusion.

"I think Mr. Twilly here has some questions to answer," the sheriff said.

The shotgun was coming up again, but before Twilly could level it at anyone, Teck Gorch pushed himself from the wall with a rebel yell and threw himself at the armed man. The shotgun barrel was still coming up toward Teck's face when Miguel Fernandez punched Twilly in the gut. Twilly went down with Teck on top of him, and the shotgun spun around in the air like the bone at the beginning of *2001*.

Three people made it out the door. Some went for the floor. Barcheck pushed his wife against the wall. The troopers and Red dived behind the desk, where Sheriff George Fingerhurt sat shaking his head.

The gun hit the ceiling, dropped quickly to the floor with a clatter-clack, and didn't discharge.

It took Red about twenty seconds to clear everyone but the troopers, the sheriff, Teck, and Ollie out of the room.

It took Ollie Twilly two minutes and some resuscitation from the younger trooper to revive enough to deny everything, from his affair with Rose to the murder of his brother. He even managed to deny a variety of crimes, including felonies of which no one had yet accused him.

Within four minutes, the troopers were being led by Red, with Ollie in tow, for a tour of Ollie's home and office.

"Can I go now?" Teck asked when he was alone with the sheriff again.

"Nope," said Fingerhurt. "You're our key witness."

"But . . ."

"Up to the troopers now," the sheriff said. "They can let you go when they take you off my hands, but who knows. Maybe they'll get a statement and let you deliver your furniture to Bakersfield."

"Okay if I go back to my rig and pick up some clean clothes?"

"Sure," said the sheriff. "I'll give you a lift."

George Fingerhurt backed his wheelchair from behind the desk and carefully maneuvered it through the space between it and the window. From that point, it was out the door, down the ramp, and another day starting.

Bill Pronzini is a fixture in the mystery world, and that world is all the better for his presence. His Nameless Detective series is synonymous with classic mystery fiction that gets better with each book. He also writes powerful western stories and has collaborated with such authors as Barry Malzberg, John Lutz, Colin Wilcox, and Marcia Muller. The dozens of mystery anthologies he's edited bring together some of the finest writers of the twentieth century. Here he joins forces with another fine writer, Jeffrey Wallmann, to uncover a tale of cover-ups and murder in the Oregon countryside.

Jeffrey Wallmann has written several excellent short stories, appearing in Ellery Queen's Mystery Magazine *and* Alfred Hitchcock's Mystery Magazine. *In this collaboration with Bill Pronzini, the two authors combine their formidable talents on a tale of a lost dog and found crime.*

Coyote and Quarter-Moon

Bill Pronzini and Jeffrey Wallmann

With the Laurel County Deputy Sheriff beside her, Jill Quarter-Moon waited for the locksmith to finish unlatching the garage door. Inside, the dog—a good-sized Doberman; she had identified it through the window—continued its frantic barking.

The house to which the garage belonged was only a few years old, a big ranch-style set at the end of a cul-de-sac and somewhat removed from its neighbors in the expensive Oregon Estates development. Since it was a fair Friday morning in June, several of the neighbors were out and mingling in a wide crescent around the property; some of them Jill recognized from her previous visit here. Two little boys were chasing each other around her Animal Regulation Agency truck, stirring up a pair of other barking dogs nearby. It only added to the din being raised by the Doberman.

At length the locksmith finished and stepped back. "It's all yours," he said.

"You'd better let me go in with you," the deputy said to Jill.

There was a taint of chauvinism in his offer, but she didn't let it upset her. She was a mature twenty-six, and a full-blooded Umatilla Indian, and she was comfortable with both her womanhood and her role in society. She was also strikingly attractive, in the light-skinned way of Pacific Northwest Indians, with hip-length brown hair and a long willowy body. Some men, the deputy being one of them, seemed to feel protective, if not downright chivalric, toward her. Nothing made her like a man less than being considered a pretty-and-helpless female.

She shook her head at him and said, "No thanks. I've got my tranquilizer dart gun."

"Suit yourself, then." The deputy gave her a disapproving frown and stepped back out of her way. "It's your throat."

Jill drew a heavy padded glove over her left hand, gripped the dart gun with her right. Then she caught hold of the door latch and depressed it. The Doberman stopped barking; all she could hear from inside were low growls. The dog sensed that someone was coming in, and when she opened the door it would do one of two things: back off and watch her, or attack. She had no way of telling beforehand which it would be.

The Doberman had been locked up inside the garage for at least thirty-six hours. That was how long ago it had first started howling and barking and upsetting the neighbors enough so that one of them had complained to the Agency. The owner of the house, Jill had learned in her capacity as field agent, was named Edward Benham; none of the neighbors knew him—he'd kept to himself during the six months he had lived here—and none of them knew anything at all about his dog. Benham hadn't answered his door, nor had she been able to reach him by telephone or track down any local relatives. Finally she had requested, through the Agency offices, a court order to enter the premises. A judge had granted it, and along with the deputy and the locksmith, here she was to release the animal.

She hesitated a moment longer with her hand on the door latch. If the Doberman backed off, she stood a good chance of gentling it enough to lead it out to the truck; she had a way with animals, dogs in particular—something else she could attribute to her Indian heritage. But if it attacked she would have no choice except to shoot it with the tranquilizer gun. An attack-trained, or even an untrained but high-strung, Doberman could tear your throat out in a matter of seconds.

Taking a breath, she opened the door and stepped just inside the entrance. She was careful to act natural, confident; too much caution could be as provoking to a nervous animal as movements too bold or too sudden. Black and short-haired, the Doberman was over near one of the walls—yellowish eyes staring at her, fangs bared and gleaming in the light from the open doorway and the single dusty window. But it stood its ground, forelegs spread, rear end flattened into a crouch.

"Easy," Jill said soothingly. "I'm not going to hurt you."

She started forward, extending her hand, murmuring the words of a lullabye in Shahaptian dialect. The dog cocked its head, ears perked, still growling, still tensed—but it continued to stay where it was and its stub of a tail began to quiver. That was a good sign, Jill knew. No dog wagged its tail before it attacked.

As her eyes became more accustomed to the half light, she could see that there were three small plastic bowls near the Doberman; each of them had been gnawed and deeply scratched. The condition of the bowls told her that the dog had not been fed or watered during the past thirty-six hours. She could also see that in one corner was a wicker sleeping basket about a foot and a half in diameter, and that on a nearby shelf lay a curry comb. These things told her something else, but just what it meant she had no way of knowing yet.

"Easy, boy . . . calm," she said in English. She was within a few paces of the dog now and it still showed no inclination to jump at her. Carefully she removed the thick glove, stretched her hand out so that the Doberman could better take her scent. "That's it, just stay easy, stay easy . . ."

The dog stopped growling. The tail stub began to quiver faster, the massive head came forward and she felt the dryness of its nose as it investigated her hand. The yellow eyes looked up at her with what she sensed was a wary acceptance.

Slowly she put away the tranquilizer gun and knelt beside the animal, murmuring the lullabye again, stroking her hand around its neck and ears. When she felt it was ready to trust her she straightened and patted the dog, took a step toward the entrance. The Doberman followed. And kept on following as she retraced her path toward the door.

They were halfway there when the deputy appeared in the doorway. "You all right in there, lady?" he called.

The Doberman bristled, snarled again low in its throat. Jill stopped and stood still. "Get away, will you?" she said to the deputy, using her normal voice, masking her annoyance so the dog wouldn't sense it. "Get out of sight. And find a hose or a faucet, get some water puddled close by. This animal is dehydrated."

The deputy retreated. Jill reached down to stroke the Doberman another time, then led it slowly out into the sunlight. When they emerged she saw that the deputy had turned on a faucet built into the garage wall; he was backed off to one side now, one hand on the weapon holstered at his side, like an actor in a B movie. The dog paid no attention to him or to anyone else. It went straight for the water and began to lap at it greedily. Jill went with it, again bent down to soothe it with her hands and voice.

While she was doing that she also checked the license and rabies tags attached to its collar, making a mental note of the numbers stamped into the thin aluminum. Now that the tenseness of the situation had eased, anger was building within her again at the way the dog had been abused. Edward Benham, whoever he was, would pay for that, she thought. She'd make certain of it.

The moment the Doberman finished drinking, Jill stood and faced the bystanders. "All of you move away from the truck," she told them. "And keep those other dogs quiet."

"You want me to get the back open for you?" the deputy asked.

"No. He goes up front with me."

"Up front? Are you crazy, lady?"

"This dog has been cooped up for a long time," Jill said. "If I put him back, in the cage, he's liable to have a fit. And he might never trust me again. Up front I can open the window, talk to him, keep him calmed down."

The deputy pursed his lips reprovingly. But as he had earlier, he said, "It's your throat," and backed off with the others.

When the other dogs were still Jill caught hold of the Doberman's collar and led it down the driveway to the truck. She opened the passenger door, patted the seat. The Doberman didn't want to go in at first, but she talked to it, coaxing, and finally it obeyed. She shut the door and went around and slid in under the wheel.

"Good boy," she told the dog, smiling. "We showed them, eh?"

Jill put the truck in gear, turned it around, and waved at the scowling deputy as she passed him by.

★   ★   ★

At the agency—a massive old brick building not far from the university—she turned the Doberman over to Sam Wyatt, the resident veterinarian, for examination and treatment. Then she went to her desk in the office area reserved for field agents and sat down with the Benham case file.

The initial report form had been filled out by the dispatcher who had logged the complaint from one of Benham's neighbors. That report listed the breed of Benham's dog as an Alaskan husky, female—not a Doberman, male. Jill had been mildly surprised when she went out to the house and discovered that the trapped dog was a Doberman. But then, the Agency was a bureaucratic organization, and like all bureaucratic organizations it made mistakes in paperwork more often than it ought to. It was likely that the dispatcher, in checking the registry files for the Benham name, had either pulled the wrong card or miscopied the information from the right one.

But Jill kept thinking about the sleeping basket and the curry comb inside the garage. The basket had been too small for the Doberman but about the right size for a female husky. And curry combs were made for long-haired, not short-haired dogs.

The situation puzzled as well as angered her. And made her more than a little curious. One of the primary character traits of the Umatilla was inquisitiveness, and Jill had inherited it along with her self-reliance and her way with animals. She had her grandmother to thank for honing her curiosity, though, for teaching her never to accept any half-truth or partial answer. She could also thank her grandmother who had been born in the days when the tribe lived not on the reservation in northeastern Oregon but along the Umatilla River—the name itself meant "many rocks" or "water rippling over sand"—for nurturing her love for animals and leading her into her present job with the Agency. As far back as Jill could remember, the old woman had told and retold the ancient legends about "the people"—the giant creatures, Salmon and Eagle and Fox and the greatest of all, Coyote, the battler of monsters, who ruled the earth before the human beings were created, before all animals shrank to their present size.

But she was not just curious about Benham for her own satisfaction: she had to have the proper data for her report. If the Agency pressed charges for animal abuse, which was what she wanted to see happen, and a heavy fine was to be levied against Benham, all pertinent information had to be correct.

*   *   *

She went to the registry files and pulled the card on Edward Benham. The dispatcher, it turned out, *hadn't* made a mistake after all: the breed of dog listed as being owned by Benham was an Alaskan husky, female. Also, the license and rabies tag numbers on the card were different from those she had copied down from the Doberman's collar.

One good thing about bureaucratic organizations, she thought, was that they had their filing systems cross-referenced. So she went to the files arranged according to tag numbers and looked up the listed owner of the Doberman.

The card said: *Fox Hollow Kennels, 1423 Canyon Road, Laurel County, Oregon.*

Jill had heard of Fox Hollow Kennels; it was a fairly large place some distance outside the city, operated by a man named Largo or Fargo, which specialized in raising a variety of purebred dogs. She had been there once on a field investigation that had only peripherally concerned the kennel. She was going to make her second visit, she decided, within the next hour.

The only problem with that decision was that her supervisor, Lloyd Mortisse, vetoed it when she went in to tell him where she was going. Mortisse was a lean, mournful-looking man in his late forties, with wild gray hair that reminded Jill of the beads her grandmother had strung into ornamental baskets. He was also a confirmed bureaucrat, which meant that he loved paperwork, hated anything that upset the routine, and was suspicious of the agents' motives every time they went out into the field.

"Call up Fox Hollow," he told her. "You don't need to go out there; the matter doesn't warrant it."

"I think it does."

"You have other work to do, Ms. Quarter-Moon."

"Not as important as this, Mr. Mortisse."

She and Mortisse were constantly at odds. There was a mutual animosity, albeit low-key, based on his part by a certain condescension—either because she was a woman or an Indian, or maybe both—and on her part by a lack of respect. It made for less than ideal working conditions.

He said, "And I say it's not important enough for you to neglect your other duties."

"Ask that poor Doberman how important it is."

"I repeat, you're not to pursue the matter beyond a routine telephone call," Mortisse told her sententiously. "Now is that understood?"

"Yes. It's understood."

Jill pivoted, stalked out of the office, and kept right on stalking through the rear entrance and out to her truck. Twenty minutes later she was turning onto the long gravel drive, bordered by pine and Douglas fir, that led to the Fox Hollow Kennels.

She was still so annoyed at Mortisse, and preoccupied with Edward Benham, that she almost didn't see the large truck that came barreling toward her along the drive until it was too late. As it was, she managed to swerve off onto the soft shoulder just in time, and to answer the truck's horn blast with one of her own. It was an old Ford stakebed, she saw as it passed her and braked for the turn onto Canyon Road, with the words *Fox Hollow Kennels* on the driver's door. Three slat-and-wire crates were tied together on the bed, each of which contained what appeared to be a mongrel dog. The dogs had begun barking at the sound of the horns and she could see two of them pawing at the wire mesh.

Again she felt both her curiosity and her anger aroused. Transporting dogs in bunches via truck wasn't exactly inhuman treatment, but it was still a damned poor way to handle animals. And what was an American Kennel Club-registered outfit which specialized in purebreds doing with mongrels?

Jill drove up the access drive and emerged into a wide gravel parking area. The long whitewashed building that housed Fox Hollow's office was on her right, with a horseshoe arrangement of some thirty kennels and an exercise yard behind it. Pine woods surrounded the complex, giving it a rustic atmosphere.

When she parked and got out, the sound of more barking came to her from the vicinity of the exercise yard. She glanced inside the office, saw that it was empty, and went through a swing-gate that led to the back. There, beside a low fence, a man stood tossing dog biscuits into the concrete run on the other side, where half a dozen dogs—all of these purebred setters—crowded and barked together. He was in his late thirties, average-sized, with bald head and nondescript features, wearing Levi's and a University of Oregon sweatshirt. Jill recognized him as the owner, Largo or Fargo.

"Mr. Largo?" she said.

He turned, saying, "The name is Fargo." Then he set the food sack down and wiped his hands on his Levi's. His eyes were speculative as he studied both her and her tan Agency uniform. "Something I can do for you, miss?"

Jill identified herself. "I'm here about a dog," she said, "a male Doberman, about three years old. It was abandoned inside a house in Oregon Estates at least two days ago; we went in and released it this morning. The house belongs to a man named Benham, Edward Benham, but the Doberman is registered to Fox Hollow."

Fargo's brows pulled down. "Benham, did you say?"

"That's right. Edward Benham. Do you know him?"

"Well, I don't recognize the name."

"Is it possible you sold him the Doberman?"

"I suppose it is," Fargo said. "Some people don't bother to change the registration. Makes a lot of trouble for all of us when they don't."

"Yes, it does. Would you mind checking your records?"

"Not at all."

He led her around and inside the kennel office. It was a cluttered room that smelled peculiarly of dog, dust, and cheap men's cologne. An open door on the far side led to an attached workroom; Jill could see a bench littered with tools, stacks of lumber, and several slat-and-wire crates of the type she had noticed on the truck, some finished and some under construction.

Along one wall was a filing cabinet and Fargo crossed to it, began to rummage inside. After a time he came out with a folder, opened it, consulted the papers it held, and put it away again. He turned to face Jill.

"Yep," he said, "Edward Benham. He bought the Doberman about three weeks ago. I didn't handle the sale myself, one of my assistants took care of it. That's why I didn't recognize the name."

"Is your assistant here now?"

"No, I gave him a three-day weekend to go fishing."

"Is the Doberman the only animal Benham has bought from you?"

"As far as the records show, it is."

"Benham is the registered owner of a female Alaskan husky," Jill said. "Do you know anyone who specializes in that breed?"

"Not offhand. Check with the American Kennel Club; they might be able to help you."

"I'll do that." Jill paused. "I passed your truck on the way in, Mr. Fargo. Do you do a lot of shipping of dogs?"

"Some, yes. Why?"

"Just curious. Where are those three today bound?"

"Portland." Fargo made a deliberate point of looking at his watch. "If you'll excuse me, I've got work to do . . ."

"Just one more thing. I'd like to see your American Kennel Club registration on the Doberman you sold Benham."

"Can't help you there, I'm afraid," Fargo said. "There wasn't any AKC registration on that Doberman."

"No? Why not? He's certainly a purebred."

"Maybe so, but the animal wasn't bred here. We bought it from a private party who didn't even know the AKC existed."

"What was this private party's name?"

"Adams. Charles Adams. From out of state—California. That's why Fox Hollow was the first to register the dog with you people."

Jill decided not to press the matter, at least not with Fargo personally. She had other ways of finding out information about him, about Fox Hollow, and about Edward Benham. She thanked Fargo for his time, left the office, and headed her truck back to the Agency.

When she got there she went first to see Sam Wyatt, to check on the Doberman's health. There was nothing wrong with the animal, Wyatt told her, except for minor malnutrition and dehydration. It had been fed, exercised, and put into one of the larger cages.

She looked in on it. The dog seemed glad to see her; the stub of a tail began to wag when she approached the cage. She played her fingers through the mesh grille, let the Doberman nuzzle them.

While she was doing that the kennel attendant, a young redhead named Lena Stark, came out of the dispensary. "Hi, Jill," she said. "The patient looks pretty good, doesn't he?"

"He'll look a lot better when we find him a decent owner."

"That's for sure."

"Funny thing—he's registered to the Fox Hollow Kennels, but they say he was sold to one Edward Benham. It was Benham's garage he was locked up in."

"Why is that funny?"

"Well, purebred Dobermans don't come cheap. Why would anybody who'd pay for one suddenly go off and desert him?"

"I guess that is kind of odd," Lena admitted. "Unless Benham was called out of town on an urgent matter or something. That would explain it."

"Maybe," Jill said.

"Some people should never own pets, you know? Benham should have left the dog at Fox Hollow; at least they care about the welfare of animals."

"Why do you say that?"

"Because every now and then one of their guys comes in and takes most of our strays."

"Oh? For what reason?"

"They train them and then find homes for them in other parts of the state. A pretty nice gesture, don't you think?"

"Yes," Jill said thoughtfully. "A pretty nice gesture."

She went inside and straight to the filing room, where she pulled the Fox Hollow folder. At her desk she spread out the kennel's animal licensing applications and studied them. It stood to reason that there would be a large number and there were; but as she sifted through them Jill was struck by a peculiarity. Not counting the strays Fox Hollow had "adopted" from the Agency, which by law had to be vaccinated and licensed before being released, there were less than a dozen dogs brought in and registered over the past twelve months. For a kennel which claimed to specialize in purebreds, this was suspiciously odd. Yet no one else had noticed it in the normal bureaucratic shuffle, just as no one had paid much attention to Fox Hollow's gathering of Agency strays.

And why *was* Fox Hollow in the market for so many stray dogs? Having met Fargo, she doubted that he was the humanitarian type motivated by a desire to save mongrels from euthanasia, a dog's fate if kept unclaimed at the Agency for more than four days. No, it sounded as if he were in some sort of strange wholesale pet business—as if the rest of the state, not to mention the rest of the country, didn't have their own animal overpopulation problems.

But where did Edward Benham, and the Doberman, fit in? Jill reviewed the Benham file again, but it had nothing new to tell her. She wished she knew where he'd gone, or of some way to get in touch with him. The obvious way, of course, was through his place of employment; unfortunately, however, pet license applications did not list employment of owners, only home address and telephone number. Nor had any of his neighbors known where he worked.

Briefly she considered trying to bluff information out of one of the credit-reporting companies in the city. Benham had bought rather than rented or leased his house, which meant that he probably carried a mortgage, which meant credit, which meant an application listing his employment. The problem was that legitimate members of such credit companies used special secret numbers to identify themselves when requesting information, so any ruse she might attempt would no doubt fail, and might even backfire and land her in trouble with Mortisse.

Then she thought of Pete Olafson, the office manager for Mid-Valley Adjustment Bureau, a local bad-debt collection service. Mid-Valley could certainly belong to a credit-reporting company. And she knew Pete pretty well, had dated him a few times in recent months. There wasn't any torrid romance brewing between her and the sandy-haired bachelor, but she knew he liked her a good deal—maybe enough to bend the rules a little and check Benham's credit as a favor.

She looked up Mid-Valley's number, dialed it, and was talking to Pete fifteen seconds later. "You must be a mindreader, Jill," he said after she identified herself. "I was going to call you later. The University Theater is putting on *Our Town* tomorrow night and I've wangled a couple of free passes. Would you like to go?"

"Sure. If you'll do me a favor in return."

Pete sighed dramatically. "Nothing is free these days, it seems. Okay, what is it?"

"I want to know where a man named Edward Benham is employed. Could you track down his credit applications and find out from them?"

"I can if he's got credit somewhere."

"Well, he owns his home, out in Oregon Estates. The name is Benham, B-e-n-h-a-m, Edward. How fast can you find out for me?"

"It shouldn't take long. Sit tight; I'll get back to you."

Jill replaced the handset and sat with her chin propped in one palm brooding. If the lead to Edward Benham through Pete didn't pan out, then what? Talk to his neighbors again? Through them she could find out the name of the real estate agent who had sold Benham his home . . . but it was unlikely that they would divulge personal information about him, since she had no official capacity. Talk to Fargo again? That probably wouldn't do her any good either. . . .

The door to Lloyd Mortisse's private office opened; Jill saw him thrust his wild-maned head out and look in her direction. It was not a look of pleasure. "Ms. Quarter-Moon," he said. "Come into my office, please."

Jill complied. Mortisse shut the door behind her, sat down at his desk, and glared at her. "I thought," he said stiffly, "that I told you not to go out to Fox Hollow Kennels."

Surprised, Jill asked, "How did you know about that?"

"Mr. Fargo called me. He wanted to know why you were out there asking all sorts of questions. He wasn't particularly pleased by your visit; neither am I. Why did you disobey me?"

"I felt the trip was necessary."

"Oh, you felt it was necessary. I see. That makes it all right, I suppose."

"Look, Mr. Mortisse—"

"I do not like disobedience," Mortisse said. "I won't stand for it again, is that clear? Nor will I stand for you harassing private facilities like Fox Hollow. This Agency's sole concern in the Benham matter is to house the Doberman for ninety-six hours or until it is claimed. And I'll be the one, not you, to decide if any misdemeanor animal-abuse charges are to be filed against Mr. Benham."

Jill thought that it was too bad these weren't the old days, when one of the Umatilla customs in tribal disputes was to hold a potlatch— a fierce social competition at which rival chiefs gave away or destroyed large numbers of blankets, coppers, and slaves in an effort to outdo and therefore vanquish each other. She would have liked nothing better than to challenge Mortisse in this sort of duel, using bureaucratic attitudes and red tape as the throwaway material. She also decided there was no point in trying to explain her suspicions to him; he would only have said in his supercilious way that none of it was Agency business. If she was going to get to the bottom of what was going on at Fox Hollow, she would have to do it on her own.

"Do you understand?" Mortisse was saying. "You're to drop this matter and attend to your assigned duties. And you're not to disobey a direct order again, under any circumstances."

"I understand," Jill said thinly. "Is that all?"

"That's all."

She stood and left the office, resisting an impulse to slam the door. The wall clock said that it was 4:10—less than an hour until quitting time for the weekend. All right, she thought as she crossed to her desk. I'll drop the matter while I'm on Agency time. But what I do and where I go on my own time is *my* business, Mortisse or no Mortisse.

★   ★   ★

It was another ten minutes, during which time she typed up a pair of two-day-old reports, before Pete Olafson called her back. "Got what you asked for, Jill," he said. "Edward Benham has a pretty fair credit rating, considering he's modestly employed."

"What does he do?"

"He's a deliveryman, it says here. For a kennel."

Jill sat up straight. "Kennel?"

"That's right," Pete said. "Place called Fox Hollow outside the city. Is that what you're after?"

"It's a lot more than I expected," Jill told him. Quickly she arranged tomorrow night's date with him, then replaced the receiver and sat mulling over this latest bit of news.

If she had needed anything more to convince her that something was amiss at Fox Hollow, this was it. Fargo had claimed he didn't know Edward Benham; now it turned out that Benham worked for Fargo. Why had he lied? What was he trying to cover up? And where was Benham? And where did the Doberman fit in?

She spent another half hour at her desk, keeping one eye on the clock and pretending to work while she sorted through questions, facts, and options in her mind. At ten minutes of five, when she couldn't take any more of the inactivity, she went out into the kennel area to see Lena Stark.

"Release the Doberman to me, will you, Lena?" she asked. "I'll bring him back later tonight and check him in with the night attendant."

"Why do you want him?"

"I like his looks and I want to get better acquainted. If it turns out neither Fox Hollow nor Benham decides to claim him, I may just adopt him myself."

"I don't know, Jill . . ."

"He's all right, isn't he? Sam Wyatt said he was."

"Sure, he's fine. But the rules—"

"Oh, hang the rules. Nobody has to know except you and me and the night attendant. I'll take full responsibility."

"Well . . . okay, I guess you know what you're doing."

Lena opened the cage and the Doberman came out, stubby tail quivering, and nuzzled Jill's hand. She led it out through the rear door, into the parking lot to where her compact was parked. Obediently, as if delighted to be free and in her company, the dog jumped onto the front seat and sat down with an expectant look.

Jill stroked its ears as she drove out of the lot. "I don't want to keep calling you 'boy'," she said. "I think I'll give you a name, even it it's only temporary. How about Tyee?" In the old Chinook jargon, the mixed trade language of Indians and whites in frontier days, *tyee* was the word for chief. "You like that? Tyee?"

The dog cocked its head and made a rumbly sound in its throat.

"Good," Jill said. "Tyee it is."

She drove across the city and into Oregon Estates. Edward Benham's house, she saw when she braked at the end of the cul-de-sac, looked as deserted as it had this morning. This was confirmed when she went up and rang the doorbell several times without getting a response.

She took Tyee with her and let him sniff around both front and back. The Doberman showed none of the easy familiarity of a dog on its own turf; rather, she sensed a wary tenseness in the way he moved and keened the air. And when she led him near the garage he bristled, Jill thought. But then why had he been locked in Benham's garage?

She would have liked to go inside for a better look around, but the locksmith had relocked the doors, as dictated by law, before leaving the premises that morning. The house was securely locked too, as were each of the windows. And drawn drapes and blinds made it impossible to see into any of the rooms from outside.

Jill took Tyee back to her compact. She sat for a time, considering. Then she started the engine and pointed the car in an easterly direction.

It was just seven o'clock when she came up the access drive to Fox Hollow Kennels and coasted to a stop on the gravel parking area near the main building. There were no other vehicles around, a *Closed* sign was propped in one dusty pane of the front door, and the complex had a deserted aura; even the dogs in the near kennels were quiet.

She got out, motioning for Tyee to stay where he was on the front seat. The setting sun hung above the tops of the pines straight ahead, bathing everything in a dark-orange radiance. Jill judged that there was about an hour of daylight left, which meant that an hour was all she would have to look around. Prowling in daylight was risky enough, though if she were seen she might be able to bluff her way out of trouble by claiming she had brought Tyee back to his registered owner. If she were caught here after dark, no kind of bluff would be worth much.

The office door was locked, but when she shook it, it rattled loosely in its frame. Jill bent for a closer look at the latch. It was a spring-type lock, rather than a deadbolt. She straightened again, gnawing at her lower lip. Detectives in movies and on TV were forever opening spring locks with credit cards or pieces of celluloid; there was no reason why she couldn't do the same thing. No reason, that was, except that it was illegal and would cost her her job, if not a prison term, were she to be caught. She could imagine Lloyd Mortisse smiling like a Cheshire Cat at news of her arrest.

But she was already here, and the need to sate her curiosity was overpowering. The debate with her better judgment lasted all of ten seconds. Then she thought: Well, fools rush in—and she went back to the car to get a credit card from her purse.

Less than a minute of maneuvering with the card rewarded her with a sharp click as the lock snapped free. The door opened under her hand. Enough of the waning orange sunlight penetrated through the windows, she saw when she stepped inside, so that she didn't need any other kind of light. She went straight to the filing cabinets, began to shuffle through the folders inside.

The kennel records were in something of a shambles; Jill realized quickly that it would take hours, maybe even days, to sort through all the receipts, partial entries, and scraps of paper. But one file was complete enough to hold her attention and to prove interesting. It consisted of truck expenses—repair bills, oil company credit card receipts, and the like—and what intrigued her was that, taken together, they showed that the Fox Hollow delivery truck consistently traveled to certain towns in Oregon, northern California, and southern Washington. Forest Grove, Corvallis, Portland, McMinnville, Ashland, La Grande, Arcata, Kirkland. . . . These, and a few others, comprised a regular route.

Which might explain why Edward Benham was nowhere to be found at the moment; some of the towns were at least an overnight's drive away, and it was Benham's signature that was on most of the receipts. But the evident truck route also raised more questions. Why such long hauls for a small kennel? Why to some points out of state? And why to these particular towns, when there were numerous others of similar size along the way?

"Curiouser and curiouser," Jill murmured to herself.

She shut the file drawers and turned to the desk. Two of the drawers were locked; she decided it would be best not to try forcing them.

None of the other drawers, nor any of the clutter spread across the top, told her anything incriminating or enlightening.

The door to the adjacent workroom was closed, but when she tried the knob it opened right up. That room was dimmer but there was still enough daylight filtering in to let her see the tools, workbench, stacks of lumber, finished and unfinished crates. She picked through the farrago of items on the bench; caught up slats and corner posts of an unassembled cage, started to put them down again. Then, frowning, she studied one of the wooden posts more carefully.

The post was hollow. So were the others; the inner lengths of all four had been bored out by a large drill bit. When fitted into the frame of a fully constructed cage the posts would appear solid, their holes concealed by the top and bottom sections. Only when the cage was apart, like now, would the secret compartments be exposed, to be filled or emptied.

Of what?

Jill renewed her search. In a back corner were three rolls of cage wire—and caught on a snag of mesh on one roll was a small cellophane bag. The bag was out of easy sight and difficult to reach, but she managed to retrieve it. It looked new, unopened, and it was maybe 3x5 inches in size. The kind of bag—

And then she knew. All at once, with a kind of wrenching insight, she understood what the bag was for, why the corner posts were hollowed out, what Fox Hollow was involved in. And it was ugly enough and frightening enough to make her feel a chill of apprehension, make her want to get away from there in a hurry. It was more than she had bargained for—considerably more.

She ran out of the workroom, still clutching the cellophane bag in her left hand. At the office door she peered through the glass before letting herself out, to make sure the parking area remained deserted. Then she set the button-lock on the knob, stepped outside, pulled the door shut, and started across to her compact.

Tyee was gone.

She stopped, staring in at the empty front seat. She had left the driver's window all the way down and he must have jumped out. Turning, she peered through gathering shadows toward the kennels. But the dogs were still quiet back there, and they wouldn't be if the Doberman had gone prowling in that direction. Where, then? Back down the drive? The pine woods somewhere?

Jill hesitated. The sense of urgency and apprehension demanded that she climb into the car, Tyee or no Tyee, and drive away pronto. But she couldn't just leave him here while she went to tell her suspicions to the county sheriff. The law would not come out here tonight no matter what she told them; they'd wait until tomorrow, when the kennel was open for business and when they could obtain a search warrant. And once she left here herself she had no intention of coming back again after dark.

She moved away from the car, toward the dark line of evergreens beyond. It was quiet here, with dust settling, and sounds carried some distance; the scratching noises reached her ears when she was still twenty paces from the woods. She'd heard enough dogs digging into soft earth to recognize the sound and she quickened her pace. Off to one side was a beaten-down area, not quite a path, and she went into the trees at that point. The digging sounds grew louder. Then she saw Tyee, over behind a decayed moss-festooned log, making earth and dry needles fly out behind him with his forepaws.

"What are you doing?" she called to him. "Come here, Tyee."

The Doberman kept on digging, paying no attention to her. She hurried over to him, around the bulky shape of the log. And then she stopped abruptly, made a startled gasping sound.

A man's arm and clenched hand lay partially uncovered in the soft ground.

Tyee was still digging, still scattering dirt and pine needles. Jill stood frozen, watching part of a broad back encased in a khaki shirt appear.

Now she knew what had happened to Edward Benham.

She made herself move, step forward and catch hold of the Dober-man's collar. He resisted at first when she tried to tug him away from the shallow grave and what was in it; but she got a firmer grip and pulled harder, and finally he quit struggling. She dragged him around the log, back out of the trees.

Most of the daylight was gone now; the sky was grayish, streaked with red, like bloody fingermarks on faded cloth. A light wind had come up and she felt herself shiver as she took the Doberman toward her compact. She was anything but a shrinking violet, but what she had found at Fox Hollow tonight was enough to frighten Old Chief Joseph or any of the other venerable Shahaptian warriors. The sooner she was sitting in the safety of the Laurel County Sheriff's office, the better she—

And the sudden figure of a man came out from behind her car.

★　　★　　★

She was ten feet from the driver's door, her right hand on Tyee's collar, and the man just rose up into view like Nashlah, the legendary monster of the Columbia River. Jill made an involuntary cry, stiffened into a standstill. The Doberman seemed to go as tense as she did; a low rumble sounded in his throat as the man came toward them.

Fargo. With a gun in his hand.

"You just keep on holding that dog," he said. He stopped fifteen feet away, holding the gun out at arm's length. "You're both dead if you let go his collar."

She was incapable of speech for five or six seconds. Then she made herself say, "There's no need for that gun, Mr. Fargo. I'm only here to return the Doberman. . . ."

"Sure you are. Let's not play games. You're here because you're a damned snoop. And I'm here because you tripped a silent alarm connected to my house when you broke into the office."

It was not in Jill's nature to panic in a crisis; she got a grip on her fear and held it down, smothered it. "The office door was unlocked," she said. "Maybe you think you locked it when you left but you didn't. I just glanced inside."

"I don't buy that either," Fargo said. "I saw you come out of the office; I left my car down the road and walked up here through the trees. I saw you go into the woods over there, too."

"I went to find the dog, that's all."

"But that's not what you found, right? He's got dirt all over his forepaws—he's been doing some digging. You found Benham. And now you know too much about everything."

"I don't know what you're talking about."

"I say you do. So does that cellophane bag you're carrying."

Jill looked down at her left hand; she had forgotten all about the bag. And she had never even considered the possibility of a silent alarm system. She had a lot to learn about being a detective—if she survived to profit from her mistakes.

"All right," she said. "It's drugs, isn't it? That's the filthy business you're in."

"You got it."

"Selling drugs to college kids all over the Pacific Northwest," she said. That was the significance of the towns on the Fox Hollow shipping route: they were all college or university towns. Humboldt State in Arcata, Lewis & Clark in Portland, Linfield College in McMinnville,

Eastern Oregon College in La Grande. And the state university right here in this city. That was also why Fox Hollow had taken so many stray dogs from the Agency; they needed a constant supply to cover their shipment of drugs—cocaine and heroin, probably, the kind usually packaged and shipped in small cellophane bags—to the various suppliers along their network. "Where does it come from? Canada?"

"Mexico," Fargo said. "They bring it up by ship, we cut and package and distribute it."

"To kennels in those other cities, I suppose."

"That's right. They make a nice cover."

"What happens to the dogs you ship?"

"What do you think happens to them? Dogs don't matter when you're running a multi-million-dollar operation. Neither do snoops like you. Nobody fouls up this kind of operation and gets away with it."

Tyee growled again, shifted his weight; Jill tightened her grip on his collar. "Did Benham foul it up? Is that why he's dead?"

"He tried to. His percentage wasn't enough for him and he got greedy; he decided to hijack a shipment for himself—substitute milk sugar and then make off with the real stuff. When he left here on Wednesday for Corvallis he detoured over to his house and made the switch. Only one of the crates had the drugs in it, like always; he had to let the dog out of that one to get at the shipment and it turned on him, tried to bite him."

"This dog, the Doberman."

"Yeah. He managed to lock it up inside his garage, but that left him with an empty crate and he couldn't deliver an empty, not without making the Corvallis contact suspicious. So he loaded his own dog, the Husky, inside the crate and delivered it instead. But our man checked the dope anyway, discovered the switch, and called me. I was waiting for Benham when he got back here."

"And you killed him."

Fargo shrugged. "I had no choice."

"Like you've got no choice with me?"

He shrugged again. "I forgot all about the Doberman, that was my mistake. If I hadn't, I wouldn't have you on my hands. But it just didn't occur to me the dog would raise a ruckus and a nosy Agency worker would decide to investigate."

"Why did you lie to me before about knowing Benham?"

"I didn't want you doing any more snooping. I figured if I gave you that story about selling him the Doberman, you'd come up against a dead-end and drop the whole thing. Same reason I called your supervisor: I thought he'd make you drop it. Besides, you had no official capacity. It was your word against mine."

"Lying to me was your second mistake," Jill said. "If you kill me, it'll be your third."

"How do you figure that?"

"I told somebody I came out here tonight. He'll go to the county sheriff if I disappear, and they'll come straight to you."

"That's a bluff," Fargo said. "And I don't bluff. You didn't tell anybody about coming here; nobody knows but you and me. And pretty soon it'll just be me." He made a gesture with the gun. "Look at it this way. You're only one person, but I got a lot of people depending on me: others in the operation, all those kids we supply."

All those kids, Jill thought, and there was a good hot rage inside her now. College kids, some of them still in their teens. White kids, black kids—Indian kids. She had seen too many Indian youths with drug habits; she had talked to the parents of a sixteen-year-old boy who had died from an overdose of heroin on the Umatilla reservation, of a seventeen-year-old girl, an honor student, killed in a drug raid at Trout Lake near the Warm Springs development. Any minority, especially its restless and sometimes disenchanted youth, was susceptible to drug exploitation; and Indians were a minority long oppressed in their own country. That was why she hated drugs, and hated these new oppressors, the drug dealers like Fargo, even more.

Fargo said, "Okay, we've done enough talking—no use in prolonging things. Turn around, walk into the woods."

"So you can bury me next to Benham?"

"Never mind that. Just move."

"No," she said, and she let her body go limp, sank onto her knees. She dropped the cellophane bag as she did so and then put that hand flat on the gravel beside her, keeping her other hand on Tyee's collar. The Doberman, sensing the increase of tension between her and Fargo, had his fangs bared now, growling steadily.

"What the hell?" Fargo said. "Get up."

Jill lowered her chin to her chest and began to chant in a soft voice—a Shahaptian prayer.

"I said get up!"

She kept on chanting.

Fargo took two steps toward her, a third, a fourth. That put less than five feet of ground between them. "I'll shoot you right where you are, I mean it—"

She swept up a handful of gravel, hurled it at his face, let go of Tyee's collar, and flung herself to one side.

The gun went off and she heard the bullet strike the ground near her head, felt the sting of a pebble kicked up against her cheek. Then Fargo screamed, and when Jill rolled over she saw that Tyee had done what she'd prayed he would—attacked Fargo the instant he was released. He had driven the man backward and knocked him down and was shaking his captured wrist as if it were a stick; the gun had popped loose and sailed off to one side. Fargo cried out again, tried to club the Doberman with his free hand. Blood from where Tyee's teeth had bitten into his wrist flowed down along his right arm.

Jill scrambled to her feet, ran to where the gun lay and scooped it up. But before she could level it at Fargo, he jackknifed his body backwards, trying to escape from the Doberman, and cracked his head against the front bumper of her compact; she heard the thunking sound it made in the stillness, saw him go limp. Tyee still straddled the inert form, growling, shaking the bloody wrist.

She went over there, caught the dog's collar again, talked to him until he let go of Fargo and back off with her. But he stood close, alert, alternately looking at the unconscious man and up at her. She knelt and hugged him, and there were tears in her eyes. She disliked women who cried, particularly self-sufficient Indian women, but sometimes . . . sometimes it was a necessary release.

"You know who you are?" she said to him. "You're not Tyee, you're Coyote. You do battle with monsters and evil beings and you save Indians from harm."

The Doberman licked her hand.

"The Great One isn't supposed to return until the year 2000, when the world changes again and all darkness is gone; but you're here already and I won't let you go away. You're mine and I'm yours from now on—Coyote and Quarter-Moon."

Then she stood, shaking but smiling, and went to re-pick the lock on the office door so she could call the Laurel County sheriff.

*Richard Matheson has written extensively for film and television as well as
fiction. His novelette "Duel" was made into a film and launched the career of
Steven Spielberg. Other novels* I Am Legend *and* The Shrinking Man *also
found their way onto the silver screen His work concerns itself with one
overarching theme: that of man against his universe. In "The Conqueror" this is
apparent only by the end of the story.*

The Conqueror

Richard Matheson

That afternoon in 1871, the stage to Grantville had only the two of us
as passengers, rocking and swaying in its dusty, hot confines under the
fiery Texas sun. The young man sat across from me, one palm braced
against the hard, dry leather of the seat, the other holding on his lap a
small black bag.

He was somewhere near 19 or 20. His build was almost delicate.
He was dressed in checkered flannel and wore a dark tie with a stickpin
in its center. You could tell he was a city boy.

From the time we'd left Austin two hours before, I had been wondering about the bag he carried so carefully in his lap. I noticed that his
light-blue eyes kept gazing down at it. Every time they did, his thin-
lipped mouth would twitch—whether toward a smile or a grimace I
couldn't tell. Another black bag, slightly larger, was on the seat beside
him, but to this he paid little attention.

I'm an old man, and while not usually garrulous, I guess I do like
to seek out conversation. Just the same, I hadn't offered to speak in the
time we'd been fellow passengers, and neither had he. For about an hour
and a half I'd been trying to read the Austin paper, but now I laid it
down beside me on the dusty seat. I glanced down again at the small
bag and noted how tightly his slender fingers were clenched around the
bone handle.

Frankly, I was curious. And maybe there was something in the
young man's face that reminded me of Lew or Tylan—my sons.
Anyhow, I picked up the newspaper and held it out to him.

"Care to read it?" I asked him above the din of the 24 pounding hoofs and the rattle and creak of the stage.

There was no smile on his face as he shook his head once. If anything, his mouth grew tighter until it was a line of almost bitter resolve. It is not often you see such an expression in the face of so young a man. It is too hard at that age to hold on to either bitterness or resolution, too easy to smile and laugh and soon forget the worst of evils. Maybe that was why the young man seemed so unusual to me.

"I'm through with it if you'd like," I said.

"No, thank you," he answered curtly.

"Interesting story here," I went on, unable to rein in a runaway tongue. "Some Mexican claims to have shot young Wesley Hardin."

The young man's eyes raised up a moment from his bag and looked at me intently. Then they lowered to the bag again.

"'Course I don't believe a word of it," I said. "The man's not born yet who'll put John Wesley away."

The young man did not choose to talk, I saw. I leaned back against the jolting seat and watched him as he studiously avoided my eyes.

Still I would not stop. What is this strange compulsion of old men to share themselves? Perhaps they fear to lose their last years in emptiness. "You must have gold in that bag," I said to him, "to guard it so zealously."

It was a smile he gave me now, though a mirthless one.

"No, not gold," the young man said, and as he finished saying so, I saw his lean throat move once nervously.

I smiled and struck in deeper the wedge of conversation.

"Going to Grantville?" I asked.

"Yes, I am," he said—and I suddenly knew from his voice that he was no Southern man.

I did not speak then. I turned my head away and looked out stiffly across the endless flat, watching through the choking haze of alkali dust, the bleached scrub which dotted the barren stretches. For a moment, I felt myself tightened with that rigidity we Southerners contracted in the presence of our conquerors.

But there is something stronger than pride, and that is loneliness. It was what made me look back to the young man and once more see in him something of my own two boys who gave their lives at Shiloh. I could not, deep in myself, hate the young man for being from a different part of our nation. Even then, imbued as I was with the stiff pride of the Confederate, I was not good at hating.

"Planning to live in Grantville?" I asked.

The young man's eyes glittered. "Just for a while," he said. His fingers grew yet tighter on the bag he held so firmly in his lap. Then he suddenly blurted, "You want to see what I have in—"

He stopped, his mouth tightening as if he were angry to have spoken.

I didn't know what to say to his impulsive, half-finished offer.

The young man very obviously clutched at my indecision and said, "Well, never mind—you wouldn't be interested."

And though I suppose I could have protested that I would, somehow I felt it would do no good.

The young man leaned back and braced himself again as the coach yawed up a rock-strewn incline. Hot, blunt waves of dust-laden wind poured through the open windows at my side. The young man had rolled down the curtains on his side shortly after we'd left Austin.

"Got business in our town?" I asked, after blowing dust from my nose and wiping it from around my eyes and mouth.

He leaned forward slightly. "You live in Grantville?" he asked loudly as overhead the driver, Jeb Knowles, shouted commands to his three teams and snapped the leather popper of his whip over their straining bodies.

I nodded. "Run a grocery there," I said, smiling at him. "Been visiting up North with my oldest—with my son."

He didn't seem to hear what I had said. Across his face a look as intent as any I have ever seen moved suddenly.

"Can you tell me something?" he began. "Who's the quickest pistolman in your town?"

The question startled me, because it seemed born of no idle curiosity. I could see that the young man was far more than ordinarily interested in my reply. His hands were clutching, bloodless, the handle of his small black bag.

"Pistolman?" I asked him.

"Yes. Who's the quickest in Grantville? Is it Hardin? Does he come there often? Or Longley? Do they come there?"

That was the moment I knew something was not quite right in that young man. For, when he spoke those words, his face was strained and eager beyond a natural eagerness.

"I'm afraid I don't know much about such things," I told him. "The town is rough enough; I'll be the first man to admit to that. But I go my own way and folks like me go theirs and we stay out of trouble."

"But what about Hardin?"

"I'm afraid I don't know about that either, young man," I said. "Though I do believe someone said he was in Kansas now."

The young man's face showed a keen and heartfelt disappointment. "Oh," he said and sank back a little.

He looked up suddenly. "But there are pistolmen there," he said, "*dangerous* men?"

I looked at him for a moment, wishing, somehow, that I had kept to my paper and not let the garrulity of age get the better of me. "There are such men," I said stiffly, "wherever you look in our ravaged South."

"Is there a sheriff in Grantville?" the young man asked me then.

"There is," I said—but for some reason did not add that Sheriff Cleat was hardly more than a figurehead, a man who feared his own shadow and kept his appointment only because the county fathers were too far away to come and see for themselves what a futile job their appointee was doing.

I didn't tell the young man that. Vaguely uneasy, I told him nothing more at all and we were separated by silence again, me to my thoughts, he to his—whatever strange, twisted thoughts they were. He looked at his bag and fingered at the handle, and his narrow chest rose and fell with sudden lurches.

A creaking, a rattling, a blurred spinning of thick spokes. A shouting, a deafening clatter of hoofs in the dust. Over the far rise, the buildings of Grantville were clustered and waiting.

A young man was coming to town.

Grantville in the postwar period was typical of those Texas towns that struggled in the limbo between lawlessness and settlement. Into its dusty streets rode men tense with the anger of defeat. The very air seemed charged with their bitter resentments—resentments toward the occupying forces, toward the rabble-rousing carpetbaggers and, with that warped evaluation of the angry man, toward themselves and their own kind. Threatening death was everywhere, and the dust was often red with blood. In such a town I sold food to men who often died before their stomachs could digest it.

I did not see the young man for hours after Jeb braked up the stage before the Blue Buck Hotel. I saw him move across the ground and up the hotel porch steps, holding tightly to his two bags.

Then some old friends greeted me and I forgot him.

I chatted for a while and then I walked by the store. Things there were in good order. I commended Merton Winthrop, the young man I had entrusted the store to in my three weeks' absence, and then I went home, cleaned up, and put on fresh clothes.

I judge it was near four that afternoon when I pushed through the batwings of the Nellie Gold Saloon. I am not nor ever was a heavy drinking man, but I'd had for several years the pleasurable habit of sitting in the cool shadows of a corner table with a whiskey drink to sip. It was a way that I'd found for lingering over minutes.

That particular afternoon I had chatted for a while with George P. Shaughnessy, the afternoon bartender, then retired to my usual table to dream a few presupper dreams and listen to the idle buzz of conversations and the click of chips in the back-room poker game.

That was where I was when the young man entered.

In truth, when he first came in, I didn't recognize him. For what a strange, incredible altering in his dress and carriage! The city clothes were gone; instead of a flannel coat he wore a broadcloth shirt, pearl-buttoned; in place of flannel trousers there were dark, tight-fitting trousers whose calves plunged into glossy, high-heeled boots. On his head a broad-brimmed hat cast a shadow across his grimly set features.

His boot heels had clumped him almost to the bar before I recognized him, before I grew suddenly aware of what he had been keeping so guardedly in that small black bag.

Crossed on his narrow waist, riding low, a brace of gunbelts hung, sagging with the weight of two Colt .44s in their holsters.

I confess to staring at the transformation. Few men in Grantville wore two pistols, much less slender young city men just arrived in town.

In my mind, I heard again the question he had put to me. I had to set my glass down for the sudden, unaccountable shaking of my hand.

The other customers of the Nellie Gold looked only briefly at the young man, then returned to their several attentions. George P. Shaughnessy looked up, smiling, gave the customary unnecessary wipe across the immaculate mahogany of the bar top, and asked the young man's pleasure.

"Whiskey," the young man said.

"Any special kind, now?" George asked.

"Any kind," the young man said, thumbing back his hat with studied carelessness.

It was when the amber fluid was almost to the glass top that the young man asked the question I had somehow known he would ask from the moment I had recognized him.

"Tell me, who's the quickest pistolman in town?"

George looked up. "I beg your pardon, mister?"

The young man repeated the question, his face emotionless.

"Now, what does a fine young fellow like you want to know that for?" George asked him in a fatherly way.

It was like the tightening of hide across a drum top the way the skin grew taut across the young man's cheeks.

"I asked you a question," he said with unpleasant flatness. "Answer it."

The two closest customers cut off their talking to observe. I felt my hands grow cold upon the table top. There was ruthlessness in the young man's voice.

But George's face still retained the bantering cast it almost always had.

"Are you going to answer my question?" the young man said, drawing back his hands and tensing them with light suggestiveness along the bar edge.

"What's your name, son?" George asked.

The young man's mouth grew hard and his eyes went cold beneath the shadowing brim of his hat. Then a calculating smile played thinly on his lips. "My name is Riker," he said as if somehow he expected this unknown name to strike terror into all our hearts.

"Well, young Mr. Riker, may I ask you why you want to know about the quickest pistolman in town?"

"Who *is* it?" There was no smile on Riker's lips now; it had faded quickly into that grim, unyielding line again. In back I noticed one of the three poker players peering across the top of half-doors into the main saloon.

"Well, now," George said, smiling, "there's Sheriff Cleat. I'd say that he's about—"

His face went slack. A pistol was pointing at his chest.

"Don't tell me lies," young Riker said in tightly restrained anger. "I know your sheriff is a yellow dog; a man at the hotel told me so. I want the *truth*."

He emphasized the word again with a sudden thumbing back of hammer. George's face went white.

"Mr. Riker, you're making a very bad mistake," he said, then twitched back as the long pistol barrel jabbed into his chest.

Riker's mouth was twisted with fury. "Are you going to *tell* me?" he raged. His young voice cracked in the middle of the sentence like an adolescent's.

"Selkirk," George said quickly.

The young man drew back his pistol, another smile trembling for a moment on his lips. He threw across a nervous glance at where I sat but did not recognize me. Then his cold blue eyes were on George again.

"Selkirk," he repeated. "What's the first name?"

"Barth," George told him, his voice having neither anger nor fear.

"Barth Selkirk." The young man spoke the name as though to fix it in his mind. Then he leaned forward quickly, his nostrils flaring, the thin line of his mouth once more grown rigid.

"You tell him I want to kill him," he said. "Tell him I—" He swallowed hastily and jammed his lips together. "Tonight," he said then. "Right here. At eight o'clock." He shoved out the pistol barrel again. "You *tell* him," he commanded.

George said nothing and Riker backed away from the bar, glancing over his shoulder once to see where the doors were. As he retreated, the high heel of his right boot gave a little inward and he almost fell. As he staggered for balance, his pistol barrel pointed restlessly around the room, and in the rising color of his face, his eyes looked with nervous apprehension into every dark corner.

Then he was at the doors again, his chest rising and falling rapidly. Before our blinking eyes, the pistol seemed to leap back into its holster. Young Riker smiled uncertainly, obviously desperate to convey the impression that he was in full command of the moment.

"Tell him I don't like him," he said as if he were tossing out a casual reason for his intention to kill Selkirk. He swallowed again, lowering his chin a trifle to hide the movement of his throat.

"Tell him he's a dirty rebel," he said in a breathless sounding voice. "Tell him—tell him I'm a Yankee and I *hate* all rebels!"

For another moment he stood before us in wavering defiance. Then suddenly he was gone.

George broke the spell. We heard the clink of glass on glass as he poured himself a drink. We watched him swallow it in a single gulp. "Young fool," he muttered.

I got up and went over to him.

"How do you like *that*?" he asked me, gesturing one big hand in the general direction of the doors.

"What are you going to do?" I asked him, conscious of the two men now sauntering with affected carelessness for the doors.

"What am I *supposed* to do?" George asked me. "Tell Selkirk, I guess."

I told George about my talk with young Riker and of his strange transformation from city boy to, apparently, self-appointed pistol killer.

"Well," George said when I was finished talking, "where does that leave me? I can't have a young idiot like that angry with me. Do you know his triggers were filed to a hair? Did you see the way he slung that Colt?" He shook his head. "He's a fool," he said. "But a dangerous fool—one that a man can't let himself take chances with."

"Don't tell Selkirk," I said. "I'll go to the sheriff and—"

George waved an open palm at me. "Don't joke now, John," he said. "You know Cleat hides his head under the pillow when there's a shooting in the air."

"But this would be a slaughter, George," I said. "Selkirk is a hardened killer, you know that for a fact."

George eyed me curiously. "Why are you concerned about it?" he asked me.

"Because he's a boy," I said. "Because he doesn't know what he's doing."

George shrugged. "The boy came in and asked for it himself, didn't he?" he said. "Besides, even if I say nothing, Selkirk will hear about it, you can be sure of that. Those two who just went out—don't you think *they'll* spread the word?"

A grim smile raised Shaughnessy's lips. "The boy will get his fight," he said "And may the Lord have mercy on his soul."

George was right. Word of the young stranger's challenge flew about the town as if the wind had blown it. And with the word, the threadbare symbol of our justice, Sheriff Cleat, sought the sanctuary of his house, having either scoffed at all storm warnings or ignored them in his practiced way.

But the storm *was* coming; everyone knew it. The people who had found some reason to bring them to the square—they knew it. The men thronging the Nellie Gold who seemed to have developed a thirst quite out of keeping with their normal desires—they knew it. Death is a fascinating lure to men who can stand aside and watch it operate on someone else.

I stationed myself near the entrance of the Nellie Gold, hoping that I might speak to young Riker, who had been in his hotel room all afternoon, alone.

At seven-thirty, Selkirk and his ruffian friends galloped to the hitching rack, tied up their snorting mounts, and went into the saloon. I heard the greetings offered them and their returning laughs and shouts. They were elated, all of them; that was not hard to see. Things had been dull for them in the past few months. Cleat had offered no resistance, only smiling fatuously to their bullying insults. And, in the absence of any other man willing to draw his pistol on Barth Selkirk, the days had dragged for him and for his gang, who thrived on violence. Gambling and drinking and the company of Grantville's lost women was not enough for these men. It was why they were all bubbling with excited anticipation that night.

While I stood waiting on the wooden sidewalk, endlessly drawing out my pocket watch, I heard the men shouting back and forth among themselves inside the saloon. But the deep, measured voice of Barth Selkirk I did not hear. He did not shout or laugh then or ever. It was why he hovered like a menacing wraith across our town. For he spoke his frightening logic with the thunder of his pistols and all men knew it.

Time was passing. It was the first time in my life that impending death had taken on such immediacy to me. My boys had died a thousand miles from me, falling while, oblivious, I sold flour to the blacksmith's wife. My wife had died slowly, passing in the peace of slumber, without a cry or a sob.

Yet now I was deeply in this fearful moment. Because I had spoken to young Riker, because—yes, I knew it now—he had reminded me of Lew, I now stood shivering in the darkness, my hands clammy in my coat pockets, in my stomach a hardening knot of dread.

And then my watch read eight. I looked up—and I heard his boots clumping on the wood in even, unhurried strides.

I stepped out from the shadows and moved toward him. The people in the square had grown suddenly quiet. I sensed men's eyes on me as I walked toward Riker's approaching form. It was, I knew, the distortion of nerves and darkness, but he seemed taller than before as he walked along with measured steps, his small hands swinging tensely at his sides.

I stopped before him. For a moment, he looked irritably confused. Then that smile that showed no humor flickered on his tightly drawn face.

"It's the grocery man," he said, his voice dry and brittle.

I swallowed the cold tightness in my throat. "Son, you're making a mistake," I said, "a very bad mistake."

"Get out of my way," he told me curtly, his eyes glancing over my shoulder at the saloon.

"Son, *believe* me. Barth Selkirk is too much for you to—"

In the dull glowing of saloon light, the eyes he turned on me were the blue of frozen, lifeless things. My voice broke off, and without another word, I stepped aside to let him pass. When a man sees in another man's eyes the insensible determination that I saw in Riker's, it is best to step aside. There are no words that will affect such men.

A moment more he looked at me and then, squaring his shoulders, he started walking again. He did not stop until he stood before the batwings of the Nellie Gold.

I moved closer, staring at the light and shadows of his face illuminated by the inside lamps. And it seemed as though, for a moment, the mask of relentless cruelty fell from his features to reveal stark terror.

But it was only a moment, and I could not be certain I had really seen it. Abruptly, the eyes caught fire again, the thin mouth tightened, and Riker shoved through the doors with one long stride.

There was silence, utter ringing silence in that room. Even the scuffing of my bootheels sounded very loud as I edged cautiously to the doors.

Then, as I reached them, there was that sudden rustling, thumping, jingling combination of sounds that indicated general withdrawal from the two opposing men.

I looked in carefully.

Riker stood erect, his back to me, looking toward the bar. It now stood deserted save for one man.

Barth Selkirk was a tall man who looked even taller because of the black he wore. His hair was long and blond; it hung in thick ringlets beneath his wide-brimmed hat. He wore his pistol low on his right hip, the butt reversed, the holster thonged tightly to his thigh. His face was long and tanned, his eyes as sky-blue as Riker's, his mouth a motionless line beneath the well-trimmed length of his mustaches.

I had never seen Abilene's Hickock, but the word had always been that Selkirk might have been his twin.

As the two eyed each other, it was as though every watching man in that room had ceased to function, their breaths, frozen, their bodies petrified—only their eyes alive, shifting back and forth from man to man. It might have been a room of statues, so silently did each man stand.

Then I saw Selkirk's broad chest slowly expanding as it filled with air. And as it slowly sank, his deep voice broke the silence with the impact of a hammer blow on glass.

"*Well?*" he said and let his boot slide off the brass rail and thump down onto the floor.

An instant pause. Then suddenly, a gasping in that room as if one man had gasped instead of all.

For Selkirk's fingers, barely to the butt of his pistol, had turned to stone as he gaped dumbly at the brace of Colts in Riker's hands.

"Why you dirty—" he began—and then his voice was lost in the deafening roar of pistol fire. His body was flung back against the bar edge as if a club had struck him in the chest. He held there for a moment, his face blank with astonishment. Then the second pistol kicked thundering in Riker's hand and Selkirk went down in a twisted heap.

I looked dazedly at Selkirk's still body, staring at the great gush of blood from his torn chest. Then, my eyes were on Riker again as he stood veiled in acrid smoke before the staring men.

I heard him swallow convulsively. "My name is Riker," he said, his voice trembling in spite of efforts to control it. "Remember that. *Riker.*"

He backed off nervously, his left pistol holstered in a blur of movement, his right still pointed toward the crowd of men.

Then he was out of the saloon again, his face contorted with a mixture of fear and exultation as he turned and saw me standing there.

"Did you see it?" he asked me in a shaking voice. "Did you *see* it?"

I looked at him without a word as his head jerked to the side and he looked into the saloon again, his hands plummeting down like shot birds to his pistol butts.

Apparently he saw no menace, for instantly his eyes were back on me again—excited, swollen-pupiled eyes.

"They won't forget me now, will they?" he said and swallowed. "They'll remember my name. They'll be afraid of it."

He started to walk past me, then twitched to the side and leaned, with a sudden weakness, against the saloon wall, his chest heaving with breath, his blue eyes jumping around feverishly. He kept gasping at the air as if he were choking.

He swallowed with difficulty. "Did you *see* it?" he asked me again, as if he were desperate to share his murderous triumph. "He didn't even get to pull his pistols—didn't even get to *pull* them." His lean chest shuddered with turbulent breath. "*That's* how," he gasped, "*that's* how to do it." Another gasp. "I showed them. I showed them all how to do it. I came from the city and I showed them how. I got the best one they had, the *best one*." His throat moved so quickly it made a dry, clicking sound. "I showed them," he muttered.

He looked around blinking. "Now I'll—"

He looked around with frightened eyes, as if an army of silent killers were encircling him. His face went slack and he forced together his shaking lips.

"Get out of my way," he suddenly ordered and pushed me aside. I turned and watched him walking rapidly toward the hotel, looking at the sides and over his shoulder with quick jerks of his head, his hands half poised at his sides.

I tried to understand young Riker, but I couldn't. He was from the city; that I knew. Some city in the mass of cities had borne him. He had come to Grantville with the deliberate intention of singling out the fastest pistolman and killing him face to face. That made no sense to me. That seemed a purposeless desire.

Now what would he do? He had told me he was only going to be in Grantville for a while. Now that Selkirk was dead, that while was over.

Where would young Riker go next? And would the same scenes repeat themselves in the next town, and the next, and the next after that? The young city man arriving, changing outfits, asking for the most dangerous pistolman, meeting him—was that how it was going to be in every town? How long could such insanity last? How long before he met a man who would not lose the draw?

My mind was filled with these questions. But, over all, the single question—*Why*? Why was he doing this thing? What calculating madness had driven him from the city to seek out death in this strange land?

While I stood there wondering, Barth Selkirk's men carried out the bloodsoaked body of their slain god and laid him carefully across his horse. I was so close to them that I could see his blond hair ruffling slowly in the night wind and hear his life's blood spattering on the darkness of the street.

Then I saw the six men looking toward the Blue Buck Hotel, their eyes glinting vengefully in the light from the Nellie Gold, and I heard their voices talking low. No words came clear to me as they murmured among themselves, but from the way they kept looking toward the hotel I knew of what they spoke.

I drew back into the shadows again, thinking they might see me and carry their conversation elsewhere. I stood in the blackness watching. Somehow I knew exactly what they intended even before one of their shadowy group slapped a palm against his pistol butt and said distinctly, "*Come on.*"

I saw them move away slowly, the six of them, their voices suddenly stilled, their eyes directed at the hotel they were walking toward.

Foolishness again; it is an old man's trademark. For, suddenly, I found myself stepping from the shadows and turning the corner of the saloon, then running down the alley between the Nellie Gold and Pike's Saddlery; rushing through the squares of light made by the saloon windows, then into darkness again. I had no idea why I was running. I seemed driven by an unseen force which clutched all reason from my mind but one thought—*warn him.*

My breath was quickly lost. I felt my coattails flapping like furious bird wings against my legs. Each thudding bootfall drove a mail-gloved fist against my heart.

I don't know how I beat them there, except that they were walking cautiously while I ran headlong along St. Vera Street and hurried in the backway of the hotel. I rushed down the silent hallway, my bootheels thumping along the frayed rug.

Maxwell Tarrant was at the desk that night. He looked up with a start as I came running up to him.

"Why, Mr. Callaway," he said, "what are—?"

"Which room is Riker in?" I gasped.

"Riker?" young Tarrant asked me.

"*Quickly*, boy!" I cried and cast a frightened glance toward the entranceway as the jar of bootheels sounded on the porch steps.

"Room 27," young Tarrant said. I begged him to stall the men who were coming in for Riker, and rushed for the stairs.

I was barely to the second floor when I heard them in the lobby. I ran down the dimlit hall, and reaching Room 27, I rapped urgently on its thin door.

Inside, I heard a rustling sound, the sound of stockinged feet padding on the floor, then Riker's frail, trembling voice asking who it was.

"It's Callaway," I said, "the grocery man. Let me in, quickly. You're in danger."

"Get out of here," he ordered me, his voice sounding thinner yet.

"God help you, boy, prepare yourself," I told him breathlessly. "Selkirk's men are coming for you."

I heard his sharp, involuntary gasp. "*No*," he said. "That isn't—" He drew in a rasping breath. "How *many*?" he asked me hollowly.

"Six," I said, and on the other side of the door I thought I heard a sob.

"That isn't fair!" he burst out then in angry fright. "It's not fair, six against one. It isn't *fair!*"

I stood there for another moment, staring at the door, imagining that twisted young man on the other side, sick with terror, his heart jolting like club beats in his chest, able to think of nothing but a moral quality those six men never knew.

"What am I going to *do*?" he suddenly implored me.

I had no answer. For, suddenly, I heard the thumping of their boots as they started up the stairs, and helpless in my age, I backed quickly from the door and scuttled, like the frightened thing I was, down the hall into the shadows there.

Like a dream it was, seeing those six grim-faced men come moving down the hall with a heavy trudging of boots, a thin jingling of spur rowels, in each of their hands a long Colt pistol. No, like a nightmare, not a dream. Knowing that these living creatures were headed for the room in which young Riker waited, I felt something sinking in my stomach, something cold and wrenching at my insides. Helpless I was; I never knew such helplessness. For no seeming reason, I suddenly saw my Lew inside that room, waiting to be killed. It made me tremble without the strength to stop.

Their boots halted. The six men ringed the door, three on one side, three on the other. Six young men, their faces tight with unyielding intention, their hands bloodless, so tightly did they hold their pistols.

The silence broke. "Come out of that room, you Yankee bastard!" one of them said loudly. He was Thomas Ashwood, a boy I'd once seen playing children's games in the streets of Grantville, a boy who had grown into the twisted man who now stood, gun in hand, all thoughts driven from his mind but thoughts of killing and revenge.

Silence for a moment.

"I said, *come out!*" Ashwood cried again, then jerked his body to the side as the hotel seemed to tremble with a deafening blast and one of the door panels exploded into jagged splinters.

★   ★   ★

As the slug gouged into papered plaster across the hall, Ashwood fired his pistol twice into the door lock, the double flash of light splashing up his cheeks like lightning. My ears rang with the explosions as they echoed up and down the hall.

Another pistol shot roared inside the room. Ashwood kicked in the lock-splintered door and leaped out of my sight. The ear-shattering exchange of shots seemed to pin me to the wall.

Then, in a sudden silence, I heard young Riker cry out in a pitiful voice, "Don't shoot me any more!"

The next explosion hit me like a man's boot kicking at my stomach. I twisted back against the wall, my breath silenced, as I watched the other men run into the room and heard the crashing of their pistol fire.

It was over—all of it—in less than a minute. While I leaned weakly against the wall, hardly able to stand, my throat dry and tight, I saw two of Selkirk's men help the wounded Ashwood down the hall, the other three walking behind, murmuring excitedly among themselves. One of them said, "We got him good."

In a moment, the sound of their boots was gone and I stood alone in the empty hallway, staring blankly at the mist of powder smoke that drifted slowly from the open room.

I do not remember how long I stood there, my stomach a grinding twist of sickness, my hands trembling and cold at my sides.

Only when young Tarrant appeared, white-faced and frightened at the head of the steps, did I find the strength to shuffle down the hall to Riker's room.

We found him lying in his blood, his pain-shocked eyes staring sightlessly at the ceiling, the two pistols still smoking in his rigid hands.

He was dressed in checkered flannel again, in white shirt and dark stockings. It was grotesque to see him lying there that way, his city clothes covered with blood, those long pistols in his still, white hands.

"Oh, God," young Tarrant said in a shocked whisper. "Why did they kill him?"

I shook my head and said nothing. I told young Tarrant to get the undertaker and said I would pay the costs. He was glad to leave.

I sat down on the bed, feeling very tired. I looked into young Riker's open bag and saw, inside, the shirts and underclothes, the ties and stockings.

It was in the bag I found the clippings and the diary.

The clippings were from Northern magazines and newspapers. They were about Hickok and Longley and Hardin and other famous pistol fighters of our territory. There were pencil marks drawn beneath certain sentences—such as *Wild Bill usually carries two derringers beneath his coat* and *Many a man has lost his life because of Hardin's so-called "border roll" trick.*

The diary completed the picture. It told of a twisted mind holding up as idols those men whose only talent was to kill. It told of a young city boy who bought himself pistols and practiced drawing them from their holsters until he was incredibly quick, until his drawing speed became coupled with an ability to strike any target instantly.

It told of a projected odyssey in which a city boy would make himself the most famous pistol fighter in the Southwest. It listed towns that this young man had meant to conquer.

Grantville was the first town on the list.

Gary A. Braunbeck writes poetically dark suspense and horror fiction, rich in detail and scope. His occasional foray into the mystery genre is no less accomplished, having appeared in anthologies such as Danger in D.C. *and* Cat Crimes Takes a Vacation. *Here he weighs in with a tale of culinary crime in a small-town diner.*

Just Like Mom Used to Make

Gary A. Braunbeck

> Hard was their lodging, homely was their food;
> For all their luxury was doing good.
> —Sir Samuel Garth, *Claremont* (1715), 1.148

Of all the lamebrained and half-assed pearls of so-called wisdom that cluttered the intellectual landscape, none, Joel thought, was more inane than "The way to a man's heart is through his stomach."

Because if that were true, then—judging by his waistline—he was the most wooed man in the tri-state area. And he knew that wasn't the case by a long shot.

He tried once more to get his chef's smock buttoned all the way, and once more failed miserably.

"Joel," he whispered to himself. "Looks like it's time to renew that health-club membership."

Someone knocked on the door. "Mr. Hards, could you come out here, please?"

"Who is it?"

"Lisette."

Joel sighed. Lisette was the head waitress. Thirty-one and single. Red hair. Green eyes that made his overworked heart double its rate. Freckles on her face and neck he wanted to trace patterns on with his fingers. He'd never stand a chance with her. Fat guys never did with women like her.

"Be right there."

He was standing in the employees' restroom of Zeke's, the restaurant he co-owned with his mother, Virginia Hards. The place (named after his mother's pet name for him as a child) was a homey little family restaurant where you got a decent, tasty, home-cooked meal for a decent, tasty price. For as far back as Joel could remember his mother's fondest dream—well, the one that had taken the place of her *first* one—had been to someday own a restaurant.

Then Dad had smoked one too many pipes, drunk one too many beers, lost his temper one time too many, and kept one too many worries to himself, all of it heading for his heart. He'd complained of chest pains one night after dinner. Ten minutes later he'd keeled over. Five minutes later the ambulance arrived. By the time Joel and his mother pulled up to the emergency room, Dad was gone. Mom had insisted they use the majority of the insurance money to make a down payment on the restaurant because "He wouldn't've had it any other way." That had been three years ago.

Lisette knocked on the door again, harder this time. "Mr. Hards? We *really* need you to come out here. Sheriff Jackson and a couple of his deputies are here with a man from the Health Department."

"From the *what?*" He opened the door and stepped out. The smock was hanging open and he realized one second too late what a doofus he must've looked like.

"Where are they?"

"Outside by the delivery doors. Cletus said they've got some kind of court order."

Joel grabbed an apron and tied it over the smock, then, offering his best everything's-just-ducky smile to Lisette, walked out the door and up to Sheriff Cletus Jackson. "I just know you've got a good reason to be doing the Dirty Harry routine with me."

The Dirty Harry line was a private joke, the two of them being big Clint Eastwood fans who knew they didn't have a hope in hell of ever being that revered.

Jackson, a six-foot-two, two-hundred-and-eighty-pound Goliath who at first glance could scare a grizzly until you saw how perpetually sad his eyes were, gave a thin, humorless smile and held out a folded document that looked so Official and Serious, Joel felt guilty just because it seemed the thing to do.

Jackson quickly glanced at the man behind him, then said, "Joel, this's an order from the County Health Department. I'm afraid we have to close you down."

"*W-what*? For chrissakes, why?"

"Yesterday afternoon, did your mom send a batch of her hobo stew over to a private luncheon at Burt and Marlys McCarrick's?"

"Yes. She made it herself at Marlys's request."

Jackson wiped some sweat off his forehead. "Burt McCarrick woke up with severe stomach cramps and chest pains about one-thirty this morning. By the time Marlys called for an ambulance, he was in so much pain he couldn't stand—"

"God, it wasn't another heart attack, was it? Is he all right?"

Jackson bit his lower lip. "He died a little after five a.m. Marlys got the coroner out of bed to come down and perform an autopsy. According to her, Burt was the only person at the luncheon who ate the stew."

A low throbbing began somewhere behind Joel's eyes, and with every pulsing one word resounded in his skull: *botulism*.

Jackson put a hand on Joel's shoulder. "The meat was tainted. Coroner guessed the stuff had to've turned at least a week ago."

"No way. The stuff only came in yesterday morning. Mom wanted all the ingredients to be fresh."

Jackson pinched the bridge of his nose between his thumb and forefinger. He looked so tense you'd have thought he was about to snap right in two. "Did you help your mom prepare the stew?"

"No."

"Did anyone else?"

"Not that I know of."

The man from the Health Department cleared his throat and said, "I'm very sorry about this, Mr. Hards. My wife and I frequent your establishment and have always found the food and service to be exceptional. Please understand that this is SOP and I have no choice under the circumstances."

There was such genuine sympathy on the man's face, Joel couldn't get defensive.

"I, uh . . . I don't quite know how to tell the customers."

The HD man said, "I find a gas leak is a good way to clear a room. People won't ask too many questions and you don't have to worry about any immediate damage to your establishment's reputation."

Joel cast a worried glance at Cletus, who nodded his head and said, "I think that's the way to go, Joel. We'll wait back here until the place is empty."

"Thanks, Cletus. I . . . appreciate that."

Then, trying not to picture his mother's face when she heard the news, he strode back into the kitchen and through the doors that led to the dining room, his heart trying to squirt out through his ribcage.

After the customers—who'd been surprisingly understanding about the "small emergency in the kitchen"—had quickly and courteously left the restaurant, the HD man brought in his team—who looked more like extras from *The Andromeda Strain* or a Hazardous Waste Disposal unit.

A few of the employees (whom Joel had let in on what was happening) remained behind. The busboy rolled out his cart and began clearing one of the tables, but the HD man put a gentle hand on his shoulder and told him that he'd have to leave all the dirty plates right where they were.

As the team began taking out their testing equipment, Joel pulled Cletus aside and whispered, "All right, let's have the rest of it."

Cletus blinked. "How did you know there's a 'rest'?"

"Because in the fifteen years I've known you, you've never brought along deputies unless you think there'll be trouble."

Cletus sighed and shook his head. "I must be getting predictable in my old age. Joel, Marlys's son is screaming bloody murder about this. Man's the goddamn chief of staff at Licking Memorial and if he had his way, your mom would be in jail right now. But Marlys got him to agree to let me handle things. At least, for a little while." He exhaled, his shoulders slumping. "I'm afraid I have to bring your mom in for a few questions."

"Oh God, Cletus, you don't mean—there aren't any charges, are there?"

"Not yet. But the sooner we do this, the better." He shook his head again, his eyes looking even sadder than usual. "I hate this, Joel, I want you to know that. I'd like you to come with me to . . . talk to her."

Joel took a couple of deep breaths to slow the beating of his heart. The pulsing behind his eyes had now solidly taken root in the center of his skull. "Uh . . . sure. Sure." He looked around the dining room. "Just let me put a couple of things in order." He walked over to Lisette and— not thinking about what he was doing—took hold of her hand and pulled her aside.

"Listen, Lisette, I need you to stay here. On the clock, of course. You know where everything is: the order books, the inventory sheets— you've got the extra set of keys, right?"

"Yes." She made no move to pull her hand from his. Her green eyes were bright with concern. "Are you going to be okay, Mr. Hards?" Had her grip on his hand actually gotten tighter? "You look like you're about ready to cry."

A smile crossed Joel's face, felt uncomfortable about being in such an odd neighborhood, and disappeared. He let go of her hand and started to walk away, then turned around and said, "It might help if you'd start calling me 'Joel.' You've worked here for three years."

She gave a quick nod of her head, offering a tender grin that made Joel realize once again just how damn lonely he felt most of the time. Then she took out her keys and joined the HD men.

Joel pulled on his jacket and made a beeline for the exit. Wordlessly, Cletus Jackson followed.

Joel lived with his mother just off Mount Vernon Road in a mobile-home court. It wasn't the grandest place in the city, nor was it the worst; it was simply a place where decent, middle-class people came to feel that their dreams weren't the shabby things they often suspected them to be. Most claimed to be happy with their lives, but there was a certain grayness to the atmosphere, a certain heaviness to people's step, a certain dispiritedness to the smiles. Still, it beat the hell out of some of the places Joel and his mother had lived when he was growing up. So things must be Getting Better.

Yet as he pulled into the driveway next to Cletus's cruiser, Joel had a sick, broken-hearted feeling that everything they'd worked for was about to come crashing down on top of their heads.

He joined Cletus at the front door. "Do me a favor—let me tell her."

"I was hoping you'd offer. I like your mom a lot and I hate having to tell something like this to someone I like."

Joel unlocked the door. "Didn't look like you hated telling me."

"Yeah, but then you never could take a hint."

The two men looked at one another. Something passed between them, and their eyes brightened at the joke.

Joel swung open the door to see something that was both surprising and puzzling as hell.

His mother was sitting in the chair where she always did her needlework. She was reading something on a sheet of paper. Her hands were shaking. When she looked up and saw Joel standing there with

Cletus, she forced a smile onto her face, folded the sheet of paper and slipped it inside the knitting basket, then stood.

That in itself wasn't what surprised and puzzled her son—those honors went to the way she was dressed and the glassy sheen of her puffy, red-rimmed eyes. She looked as if she were about to attend a wedding: wearing her best dress, with her hair styled in a manner befitting a small woman of sixty-three who looked ten years younger, and her makeup, which she rarely wore, had been applied with a deft hand.

She looked quite lovely, except for how much she'd been crying.

She leaned up to give Joel a little peck on the check, then turned toward Cletus and said, "Hello, Sheriff."

"Virginia," said Cletus, shooting a quick glance to Joel that said, *What is this calling me "Sheriff" shit?* "You look really nice."

She wiped one of her eyes. "It's very gentlemanly of you to say so." She patted his arm with the brief, furtive affection of a distant aunt. "But I already know why you're here. Marlys called me."

Joel and Cletus exchanged glances that were equally perplexed.

"Mom," said Joel with as much tenderness as he could muster. "Cletus needs to—"

"I'll save you both some trouble," she said. Then she faced Cletus and said, "I knew that the meat in the stew was bad, Sheriff. I put it in there deliberately. I wanted to make Burt sick."

"Virginia," said Cletus. "You know you have the right to have an attorney present during questioning, don't you?"

"I do."

"Then you'd best think about anything else you want to say. We'll talk more after we get to the station and you've had a chance to call—"

"I do not need to call *anyone*, Cletus Randolph Jackson. I'm telling you that I purposefully poisoned Burt McCarrick."

"Jesus H. Christ, Mom!" blurted Joel. "Don't you realize you're basically confessing to—"

She faced her son. "I do."

"Mom, come on! We've been friends of the McCarricks' since I was twelve. I mean, I know we didn't always get along with their son, but there's never been any reason to—"

"I did it, Joel. I planned it, and I did it. And if you'll shut up— you're just like your father, *he* didn't know when to be quiet, either—if you'll keep quiet, I'd like to tell the sheriff here about it."

At any other time this Iron Maiden routine would have worked on Joel: the set of her jaw, the steely gaze, the strength with which she clutched her purse, but as he looked at her tight face he saw something that would have meant nothing to anyone else, but spoke volumes to him.

Her chin was quivering. Not a lot, not so that you'd notice it from two feet away, but just enough to let him know that she was lying. Of all the little tics that she'd developed over the years, this was the one she could never control. Joel had figured this one out when he'd been a child; it came in handy at Christmas when he was trying to guess what his presents might be.

"You're lying," he said.

She bit her lower lip. Hard. Enough to stop the quivering.

Joel looked at Cletus. "She's lying."

Cletus turned Virginia toward him. "Are you, Virginia? You pullin' a fast one on me?"

"No," she said. Hissed, actually. The rest of her words came out in a rapid, deadly, low cadence. "I knew that Burt would be the only one eating it. I took a package of spoiled meat out of the Dumpster in back of the restaurant, washed it off, re-wrapped it so it would look like part of a fresh order, and used that. I knew it would make him sick, and I knew that, with his heart, it might even possibly kill him. If the botulism didn't do it, his heart would. So do whatever you have to do. Just . . . let's get on with it, shall we?"

Cletus looked over her head at Joel. "I'm sorry, Joel."

His eyes sadder than Joel had ever seen them, Sheriff Cletus Jackson placed Virginia Hards under arrest.

When Joel was a child and wanted to hide while his parents were fighting (and it seemed to him that they fought a lot) he would sneak out and go back to the lonely haunts of his former neighborhood. As he grew older, the haunts and the neighborhood kept disappearing—most to the encroaching interstate—so he found himself leaving the trailer-park and returning to the house where his parents had fought so much. But even that was gone now, and all his memories of these places had diminished a little more each year until they became ghosts of an errant wish—that he might recapture some small, happy part of his past.

But such moments had never really existed, so he was just a thirty-four-year-old fat man, staring wistfully through slightly droopy eyes at something that had never been.

· After Cletus had taken his mother down to the station and Joel had called her lawyer ("I'll handle everything, Joel, you just wait for me to call. You'd only be in the way down there."), he realized there was only one place left for him to go.

He stared up at the sign that bore his pet name. He thought that maybe he smiled.

Zeke's.

At least that was still there. At least that wasn't a ghost.

Not yet, anyway.

"Are you okay?"

He blinked, then looked at Lisette, who was standing right next to him. When had she come outside?

"That's the second time today you've asked me that question."

"This hasn't exactly been a red-letter day for you."

"No, it sure hasn't."

Lisette cleared her throat, then stood a little closer. "I heard about what happened. One of the deputies heard from Cletus and was talking to his partner. I don't think they knew I could hear them." She touched his shoulder. "I'm sorry."

"Thanks." He continued staring at the sign, some distant part of himself trying to make sense of what had happened.

"What're you thinking about?" asked Lisette.

"Baryshnikov."

"Really?" Her voice was filled with surprise and delight. "I saw him dance once, with Twyla Tharpe. It was *so* incredible! What made you think of him?"

He turned to face her, his face expressionless. "Did you know I have two brothers and a sister? Yeah. They're all a little older than me and none of them live here, but they exist. You'd never know it from how much Mom and I hear from them, though. Usually around Christmas. A couple of gifts they order from an L. L. Bean catalogue and a card, maybe a phone call if they're feeling a little sentimental, but mostly they . . . don't bother."

"That's terrible."

Joel shrugged. "Maybe. Maybe not. They've got families of their own now, lives of their own. They know I'm here to take care of Mom. I can't say I wouldn't do the same thing if I had a . . . a wife and family.

"The point is, I was thinking of Baryshnikov because he was in a production of *The Nutcracker* on PBS a few years back. The Christmas right after Dad died, Mom and I were sitting there watching it and suddenly, right out of the blue, she just stood and turned off the set and said, 'Goddammit!' and walked into her room. I waited for her to come out but she never did.

"The next morning I found this scrapbook stuffed in the trash, along with a pair of ballet slippers. The slippers were quite old and looked like they'd belonged to a young girl. I looked at the scrapbook. Mom'd studied dance when she was a little girl. She'd wanted to be a ballerina. And I understood why she'd cry when she and Dad were fighting and he'd say something like, 'Why don't you go put on your red shoes?'"

Lisette stared at him for a moment, then, an apology in her smile, shrugged her shoulders.

"*The Red Shoes* was her favorite movie. I couldn't understand that, either, because she always cried when she watched it. But that morning, looking at her scrapbook, it hit me for the first time what she had given up to be a wife and mother. Other things kept popping into my head . . . all the dance specials she'd want to watch but couldn't because there was a football game or my sister wanted to see something else, all those times she'd talk about going to a BalletMet show over in Cedar City and we'd all make fun of it and she'd just smile and never mention it again. . . .

"Don't misunderstand. I'm not one of those guys who looks down on women who're homemakers—Lord knows that's a hell of a job—but Mom never told any of us that she wanted to be a dancer. I remember how sad it made her, for so many years. She put every-thing on hold to care for her family, and by the time they were able to care for themselves she was too old to realize the one great dream she'd had. So she learned how to cook. I mean, *really* cook. Exotic dishes, gourmet meals, stuff we'd never had when I was growing up. It was like she'd decided to funnel all those unused creative passions into her cooking. She traded in being a dancer for owning a restau-rant. Now she's deliberately pissing it all away and won't tell me why.

"I can't . . . I can't handle finding another scrapbook, Lisette. Especially one that I'm in. Do you know what I'm saying?"

"I think so, but . . . you're getting yourself really upset, Joel."

He faced her, taking her hands in his. "Look at me, Lisette. I mean, *look at me*. I'm an overweight, balding, thirty-four-year-old bachelor who lives with his mother. I have the social skills of a snail and if there're any grace notes in my character, I've not found them yet. I'm not whining about anything; most of what I've done has been by choice, including making this restaurant the focus of my life." He shook his head, much more violently than he'd intended.

"I love Mom, I do, but I can't let her do this to us. I can't believe that she'd purposefully use bad meat in the stew—"

"Wait a sec," said Lisette. "That's what caused all this, that batch of hobo stew we made the other night?"

Joel stared at her. "*We?* You helped her?"

"Only toward the end when it came time to mix everything in that big pot she uses."

"The ten-gallon pot? That one?"

"Yes. After the stew was ready we put some in a little pot for the McCarricks, put some in the refrigerator, and the rest she gave to Larry Blevins."

"Blevins? The shelter director?"

"Uh-huh. She asked me to call him and tell him to come by and pick up the rest of the stew. Said it ought to feed everyone down there for a couple of meals."

Joel's heart was slamming against his ribs. Taking a deep breath to keep himself calm, he put his hands on Lisette's shoulders and said, "Who put the meat into the stew?"

"Your mom."

"Who got it from the refrigerator?"

"She did."

Dammit! "Who cut it up and cooked it?"

"We both did."

"Did any of it smell bad to you?"

"No. It was all fresh. Looked and smelled real tasty."

"I'm going to kiss you now. Wait—no I'm not. I've got to call Blevins."

"Anything I can do?"

"Yes. Get on another line and call Cletus and tell him what you just told me."

"Okay."

Then Joel kissed her—once, on the lips, very quickly. He did not wait for her to say anything or to see the expression on her face. Which was too bad, because she was smiling.

Radiantly.

*   *   *

"Mr. Blevins? This is Joel Hards from Zeke's."

"Mr. Hards, hello! Listen, I didn't really have much time to thank your mother properly for—"

"That's what I'm calling about, sir. Have you served the stew to anyone at the shelter yet?"

"One of our volunteers should be returning the pot to you sometime this afternoon."

"So it's all been eaten?"

"It lasted about forty minutes. We've had . . . well, quite a few families staying with us. A lot of children."

"Mr. Blevins, please don't be alarmed by this question, but has anyone gotten sick from eating the stew?"

"Absolutely not. I had a bowl of it myself. No, everyone's fine. Do you mind if I ask why?"

Joel gave him an abbreviated version of the day's events, hitting all the high points except for his mother's confession.

"Good Lord," said Blevins. "Well, I can assure you, Mr. Hards, that no one here has suffered any adverse effects from the stew. In fact, today's the day our medical volunteers come in. Health exams, checking for head lice, things like that. I'd be more than happy to have them confirm that no one here's suffered food poisoning."

"That would be wonderful, sir. Now may I ask a favor?"

"Mr. Hards, you and your mother have always been exceptionally generous about sending food to us. It would be a pleasure to help you."

"Then please call Sheriff Cletus Jackson and tell him everything that you've just told me. Including the business about the medical exams."

"Consider it done. Tell your mother I hope this problem goes away quickly."

"So do I," said Joel. "I'll give her your best, sir. And as soon as we can re-open, we'll get back on schedule with our donations."

"God bless both of you, Mr. Hards."

"Thank you."

Joel hung up the phone, then leaned forward on his desk and pressed his hands against his eyes.

"Joel?"

He expected it to be Lisette—the voice had the same soft, singsong quality to it—but when he pulled his hands away it was Marlys McCarrick who stood in front of him. He blinked, thinking for a second he must be imagining this, but then Marlys sat down and pulled a small stack of papers from her purse.

It took Joel a moment to find his voice. "God, Marlys, I . . . I don't quite know what to say. I'm so sorry about Burt. He was a terrific guy. I"—he shrugged—"can't think of how else to put it."

"Do you mind if I have a cigarette?"

"Uh . . . no."

"Thanks. This has been about the worst day of my life." Her words were full of conviction, but everything else about her denied the statement. Her eyes looked as if she hadn't shed one tear over this, her makeup was perfectly applied, and her hands were so steady it was almost unnerving.

She lit the cigarette and tossed the match into the ashtray that Joel pulled from the bottom drawer—a leftover from his pack-and-a-half days.

Looking at her now, Joel couldn't help but marvel. Marlys McCarrick was the same age as his mother, but where Virginia Hards looked ten years younger than her age, Marlys could easily pass for forty-four. There had been rumors for a while that part of her youthful appearance was due to plastic surgery, but when Marlys's mother had come to town for a visit a few Thanksgivings ago, everyone saw that those rumors had been not only false, but pettier than anyone would ever admit: Marlys's mother, at age eighty-seven, looked about sixty.

"—is you."

Joel snapped out of his reverie, apologized, and asked Marlys to repeat herself.

"I said that, of all the people who have and are going to suffer as a result of this, the only genuine innocent is you. And odds are you'll be the one who gets the brunt of the grief." She leaned forward and put one of her exquisite hands on top of his. "I've always been fond of you, Joel. Burt used to say you were like the nephew we never had. I'm sorry about all of this."

"Thank you, Marlys, but . . . I'm sorry, it's just that you could've told me this over the phone. I guess I'm a little confused about why you're here."

She stubbed out her cigarette and unfolded the papers she'd taken from her purse. "Burt, Jr., was actually the one who called the coroner. When the man arrived, Burt, Jr., told him that the first thing we wanted to know was whether or not your mother's stew had contributed to Burt's death. When he found out that the meat in Burt's stomach was tainted, he went off, screaming about your mother.

"My son is not very fond of your mother, Joel. But I'll get to that. First, I think you should have a look at this." She tossed a sheet of paper onto his desk.

"What is this?" said Joel, picking it up.

"The rest of the autopsy findings." She reached over and pointed to a small block of words located halfway down the page. "That's the part that should interest you."

Joel read the results of the findings.

Felt his heart skip a beat.

Then read the words again.

"Oh Christ," he whispered. He looked at Marlys and saw the tears brimming in her eyes.

"It's really odd, don't you think," she said, "the different ways people can find to hurt one another. Most of us don't want any ugliness to come into our lives, at least directly. So if there's someone close to us, someone that we love who, for some reason, turns into the object of our wrath, we can't bring ourselves to vent that wrath on them because we love them. So we find someone to take their place. Someone outside the little protected circle of our life. And we make them suffer for the things someone else has done." She wiped her eyes, lit another cigarette, and took hold of Joel's hand.

"I have to ask you something now, Joel. Please don't ask me why right away, just answer the question first, and then I'll answer anything you want to know. Will you do that? Will you promise me you'll do exactly that?"

"You're scaring the hell out of me, Marlys."

"*Promise* me, please?"

He looked into her eyes and saw the layers of sorrow peeling back. Felt the slight trembling in her hand. Heard the barely restrained desperation in her voice.

She suddenly looked and sounded too much like his mother.

"I promise," he said.

"Thank you." She let go of his hand. "What do you remember about the night your father died?"

Forty-five minutes later Joel entered the trailer, went straight to his mother's knitting basket, and yanked out the sheet of paper she'd put in there earlier.

He tried to unfold it, everything he had within him at that moment was concentrated on that one task, but he couldn't do it.

He closed his eyes and took a deep breath, replaying his conversation with Marlys and, after that, random memories from his childhood.

When he opened his eyes again, the page, unfolded, was right in his line of sight.

He read the letter's salutation, then had to sit down and lay the page on top of the end table. His hands were shaking too badly.

As he read each line an eerie calmness settled over and within him.

He reached the end of the page.

He was very, very calm.

He read it again.

Quite calm, thank you.

Then he read it once more, just to make certain everything registered.

He nodded his head once.

Stood up.

Refolded the letter and put it in the pocket of his jacket, along with the page from the coroner's report that Marlys had given to him.

His eyes found a framed cross-stitch project of his mother's that was hanging on a far wall. An old wizard in a multicolored robe, standing in the middle of his alchemist's lab where his magic was given life.

Magic.

Tricks.

Deception.

Lies. Lies. Lies.

He didn't even realize he'd smashed it with his fist until he was halfway to the sheriff's office, when he saw the swelling knuckles and the blood running down the back of his hand. A small, jagged shard of glass was still embedded between the knuckles of his index and middle fingers. He plucked it out and tossed it through the open car window.

Then wrapped his hand in one of his mother's favorite scarves.

That he'd taken from her dresser drawer.

After heaving it across the bedroom.

When he found the other letters.

Before smashing her wooden knitting chair into kindling.

As he pulled into a parking space and killed the engine, he smiled.

He was doing just fine.

No, he wasn't.

But he would. Not. Cry.

He stuffed his bleeding hand into his coat pocket and walked up the cement steps, through the front doors, and up to the desk where one of Cletus's deputies sat, and told him that he needed to see the sheriff and he needed to see the sheriff now and his face must've looked pretty damned serious because the deputy turned three shades of white and said he'd be right back so Joel stood there with his bleeding hand and broken heart and calm demeanor and shifted his weight from foot to foot thinking he probably looked just like one of those Weebles that wobble but don't fall down and—

"What the hell happened to you, Joel?"

He looked into the face of a man. It took him a second to clear the red from his gaze, but once it had abated he smiled because it was Cletus's face he was seeing, and Cletus was a good guy, Cletus was a friend, Cletus wouldn't lie to him because they were both Clint Eastwood fans who knew they didn't have a hope in hell of ever being that revered.

"Where's my mother?" asked Joel. His voice didn't sound like his own.

Cletus put a hand on Joel's arm and said, "Lisette called, and so did Blevins. Everything's fine, my friend, your mom's lawyer is just doing some of the necessary paperwork. We'll be releasing her in a few minutes."

"That's nice, Cletus, but you didn't answer the damn question— *where is she?*"

Joel almost never swore and Cletus's sad eyes widened at the language. "She's in my office."

"We should go talk to her."

"You don't have to worry, Joel, everything's—"

Cletus fell silent when Joel pulled his wounded hand from his pocket. There was a sheet of paper in it.

"Read this," said Joel. "Specifically, read what's written in that block about halfway down the page."

Cletus did. "I already know about this. I've got a copy in my office."

"Burt had advanced stomach cancer. He'd have been dead in another four, five months."

"I know, Joel."

"But did you notice about the meat? It was pork. Mom never uses pork in her hobo stew. Only beef."

"That's what Lisette told me."

"Well, here's something she didn't tell you, because she didn't know. I knew it, but it had never really seemed like it was important.

You know what that is? There was no autopsy done on my father. Everyone *knew* about his condition, how bad his heart was. A quick examination and the doctors said 'coronary' and signed his death certificate and that was that."

"What in the hell are you talking about, Joel?"

He took Cletus's arm and led him into the hall toward the office. "I think I'll let my mom explain that to you."

And he smiled. There was no humor in it, but it was a smile, nonetheless.

Because everything was all right now.

And he was quite calm, thank you.

It took about ten seconds for Joel's rage to be replaced by sorrow when he laid eyes on his mother's face.

She looked so resigned.

So sad.

And, as always, so very, very alone.

She saw his hand, her bloody scarf wrapped around it, the letter he pulled from his pocket, and her face collapsed in on itself as she broke down. The sobs wracked her body and Joel almost went to her, almost held her and kissed her cheek and told her that it was all right, that he understood—

—but he didn't. He didn't understand any of it.

And so, for a few minutes, Virginia Hards wept without the comfort of her son's embrace.

Finally, when she was finished, after Cletus had given her some tissues and put a hot cup of coffee in her hands, only then did Joel toss the letter onto the desk and sit down in front of her.

"Would you mind, now, telling me what all this is about?" said Cletus.

"Burt McCarrick committed suicide," said Joel. "He told Mom in that letter. He told her how, and he told her why."

Cletus cast a worried glance at Virginia. "Is that true?"

"Read it for yourself," she whispered, her eyes never leaving her son's face.

Cletus read the letter. "I'll be goddamned."

"You can understand why," said Joel. "The woman he loves decides to cut off their affair because she can't live with the guilt anymore, the lies. Burt was always a little emotional, even when he still had his practice. He knew he was dying, anyway, so the last thing he did was make damn sure that he broke her heart the same way she'd broken his." He broke eye contact with his mother and turned to Cletus. "I don't know where he got the tainted meat, probably from the plastic container that's in their kitchen. Marlys says that's where that sort of stuff always goes. He must've put it in the stew before he ate at the luncheon. He wouldn't have been able to taste it, not with all the spices Mom puts in there."

"You expect me to believe that Burt poisoned himself so it'd look like your mom did it?"

"That's right."

Cletus shook his head. "I don't buy it."

"Then ask Burt, Jr. He knew about his father's cancer; he was the one who diagnosed it. But his dad wanted it kept a secret." Joel looked back at his mother. "Burt, Jr., knew about the two of you, but his dad talked him into keeping that secret, as well. And just so you know, Mom, Marlys's known about it for years."

"Oh God . . ." Virginia covered her mouth with her hand.

Cletus leaned against the wall and pushed his hat back on his head. "This still doesn't make sense. Why would Burt's son agree to go along with this?"

"Because he hates me," said Virginia. "I just never realized . . . how much." She reached over to take one of Joel's hands, but he pulled away.

"He wanted to see you ruined as much as his father did," said Joel. "For all I know, he might've even provided the meat for his dad. That's for him to say."

Cletus rose and started for the door. Joel grabbed his arm.

"Where're you going?"

"To have him brought in for questioning."

"Don't bother. Marlys will probably show up here with him in a little bit. Besides"—he looked back at his mother—"you only know half the story."

"Please, Joel," begged Virginia. "Don't make me tell it in front of you. I'll tell Cletus everything, *I swear*. Just don't make me say it in front of you."

"No. I want to hear you tell it. I want to sit here and watch your face while you tell Cletus how you and Burt McCarrick killed my father."

"How they *what*?" shouted Cletus.

"Tell him, Mom. Tell *us*. Go on."

Something in her face died. When she spoke, it was in the hollow voice of one whose heart has just been emptied of everything that matters.

"Your father was a cruel man, Joel. I knew after one year of marriage that we'd ruin each other if we stayed together. But things were different back then. You didn't run in for a divorce. You took the wedding vows seriously. By the time I knew things would never work, I was pregnant with your sister. It might be acceptable today for a divorced woman to be pregnant, but back then you *did not* do that sort of thing. You stayed with your husband. And that's what I did. He knew that the children would keep me in place, so he kept me pregnant. Even when I didn't want to have . . . relations with him, he went on ahead and did it, anyway. He was a mean, sadistic man.

"That's why I never really . . . showed any of you much love. I'd conceived all of you against my will. I was the worst with you, Joel, because you looked so much like him. You still do.

"Burt McCarrick and I met when I was in the hospital having your brothers. Twins were a big deal then, and everyone had to come by and have a look. Burt stuck around and talked with me a while, and before he left my room we both knew what was going to happen between us. We both wanted it.

"We'd been seeing each other secretly since before you'd even been born. Your father never suspected a thing. But the older you kids got, the more your father kept close tabs on me. It didn't matter that people's attitudes toward women got more modern, he had no use for that. No, he wanted his woman in his house to serve his needs whenever he wanted. I was a prisoner there when he was home. The only time I felt like I could breathe was when he'd leave for work and you kids'd be in school. That's when Burt would come over and we could be together in the way a man and woman in love were meant to be together. It was because of him that I started to learn how to really cook. We both came up with the recipe for the hobo stew. That's why he ate it all the time. It might sound funny to the two of you, but that recipe was like *our* child.

"This went on for years, our afternoons, even after your brothers and sisters had moved out.

"He saw what your father had been doing to me, and he hated it. I was miserable, Burt and Marlys hadn't been in love for quite some time . . . one afternoon we were lying together in the bed your father and I slept in, and I started crying and all . . . all the anger came out. I told him how much I despised your father, how I wished he'd leave. Because maybe if he was gone, I could treat my children with the decency and tenderness a mother should show her children.

"Burt never laughed about my wanting to be a dancer. He thought that was wonderful. But by then my chances of being a dancer were over and gone and buried.

"So that afternoon, when I cried in his arms, we made love again and then Burt told me how we could do it. It took me a long time to come around to his way of thinking—you'd moved back in with us by then, Joel, after the factory closed down and you lost your job there— but I finally agreed.

"I don't know what it was that he gave me, some kind of powder. He told me that if I sprinkled it over your father's food, it'd produce the same effects as a heart attack." She blinked, looked once at her son, then turned away.

"That's what I remembered about that night," said Joel. "I remember that, before you called the ambulance, you called Burt McCarrick."

"He was already at the hospital. He came over with the ambulance. I don't know what he did to your dad between the house and the hospital, but since it appeared he was having a heart attack I imagine it must've been something to . . . I don't know what, and I don't know how, but Burt finished your father off in that ambulance."

"I always wondered why Burt and Marlys never had to pay a check."

Virginia's eyes widened. "My God, Joel. Is that all you can say?"

"No. There's one more question."

"Ask me anything you want."

"Were you always stuffing food in my face because I liked your cooking so much, or were you doing it because I looked so much like Dad?"

"I don't—"

"You couldn't make him ugly, so you did it to me."

Tears burst from her eyes. "No, Joel, no. Please believe me, I never once wanted to hurt you because . . . oh, Jesus, no! I love you, hon. I always did. You were the only one who stood by me. I—"

Joel stood up and turned away from her. "Do what you have to, Cletus." Then he pulled a small stack of letters, still in their envelopes, from his other jacket pocket. The letters were held together by a satin ribbon. "I found these in Mom's dresser, wrapped in one of her scarves. They're all from Burt. They'll fill in some of the smaller details for you."

He tossed the letters on Cletus's desk, then walked over to the door, very slowly, looking down at his feet. He put his hand on the doorknob, then froze.

"Mom?" he said.

"What is it, honey?"

"I don't hate you. I could never do that."

He heard the sobs splutter from her, but could not bring himself to turn around and look at her.

"I'll be back in a little while. You won't have to go through this alone. I just need to be by myself for a bit."

"Where can I find you?" asked Cletus.

"Three guesses."

Then he opened the door and walked out.

Back at the restaurant the HD man and his team had already gone. The place was empty.

Except for Lisette.

Joel didn't say anything to her. He didn't need to. She saw the pain in his face and took him in her arms, and after a while they said things to each other that both had wanted to say for a long time but had never had the courage to voice.

Then they sat in silence, holding each other's hands.

Later, Joel took her back in the kitchen and turned on the stove and made them dinner.

A decent, tasty, home-cooked meal that, in its own way, helped to ease a man's confused heart. Helped him to sort things out, to look across the table at his companion and see promise where before there had only been despair.

And maybe even helped give him the strength he would need for what lay ahead.

A decent, tasty, home-cooked meal.

Just like Mom used to make.

Combine the beautiful, melancholy city of Seattle, Washington, with an irascible cop named J. P. Beaumont and you have the novels of J. A. Jance. A former high school teacher, librarian, and life insurance salesperson, she seems to have hit her true calling with the Beaumont novels, winning two American Mystery Awards for the books Without Due Process *and* Failure to Appear. *"Oil and Water" features a non-series character, who deserves to appear more often, investigating a domestic disturbance that is disturbing indeed.*

Oil and Water

J. A. Jance

I was headed into the precinct briefing room when Captain Waldron stopped me. "You're up, Detective Lanier. We've just had a 9-1-1 call reporting a homicide out in May Valley. Detective Barry's gassing up the car. He'll pick you up out front."

Of all the detectives who work for the King County Police Department, Detective James Joseph Barry was my least favorite possible partner. A recent transfer from Chicago P.D., Detective Barry shared his reactionary views with all concerned. Although barely thirty-five, his unbearably tedious monologues made Mike Royko's curmudgeonly rumblings sound like those of a lily-livered liberal.

But newly appointed to the Detective Division, I didn't dare question the captain when it came to handing out assignments. I shut my mouth, kept my opinions to myself, and headed for the door.

Moments after I stepped outside, the unmarked car skidded to a stop beside me. As I slipped into the rider's seat, Detective Barry made a big deal of checking out my legs. He was obvious as hell, but I ignored it.

"So," he said, ramming the car into gear and careening through the rain-slicked parking lot, "how come a great-looking babe like you isn't married?"

"Homicide dicks aren't much good in the marriage department," I told him evenly. "A fact of life your wife must have figured out all on her own."

Touché! The fleeting grimace on his face told me my remark had hit the intended target. "Shut up and drive, will you?" I said.

He did, for the time being. Meanwhile, I got on the horn to ask Records what they knew about where we were headed and what we'd be up against. From the radio I gathered that patrol officers were already on the scene. The victim was dead and the crime scene secure, so there was no need for either flashing lights or siren. Detective Barry made liberal use of both.

It was a chilly October night. After a delightful Indian-summer September, this was winter's first real rainstorm. The pavement was glassy and dangerously slick with mixed accumulations of oil and water. Instead of telling him to slow down, I made sure my seatbelt was securely fastened and thanked God for airbags.

Over the rhythmic slap of the windshield wipers, Barry launched off into one of his interminable stories about the good old days back in Chicago, this one featuring his late, unlamented, bowling partner—the beady-eyed Beady Dodgson.

"So I says to him, I says," 'Beady, you old billy goat. For chrissakes, when you gonna wash that damn shirt of yours?' And he says back, he says, 'Barry, you stupid mick, after the damn tournament. Whaddaya tink? You want I should wash away my luck?'"

Detective Barry liked nothing better than the sound of his own voice. However, boring tales of reminiscence were far preferable to questions about my current marital status which seemed to surface every time the two of us had any joint dealings. Detective Barry made no secret of the fact that he thought I should be home taking care of a husband and kids. He didn't approve of what he called *girl* detectives. Which is no doubt why Captain Waldron made sure he was stuck with me. Or vice versa.

"Turn here," I said. "Take the first right up the hill."

As we turned off the May Valley Highway and headed up a steep, winding incline, the headlights cut through sheets of slanting raindrops illuminating a yellow "Livestock" warning sign along the road. Detective Barry slowed the car to a bare crawl.

City born and bred, Detective Barry was in his element and totally at home when confronting a group of urbanized, street-toughened teenagers. It was strange to realize that he was petrified of encountering stray cattle or horses on one of King County's numerous rural roads.

At last the radio crackled back to life and the harried Records clerk's voice came over the air to deliver what scanty information was then available. The victim's name was de Gasteneau, Renée Denise de Gasteneau. A computer check of the de Gasteneau address in the 18500 block of Rainier Vista had turned up six priors in the previous six weeks—two domestics, one civil disturbance, and the rest noise complaints. Chances were Renée de Gasteneau was probably none too popular with her neighbors.

"One other thing," the operator from Records added. "Her husband's there on the scene right now. Emile de Gasteneau."

The name was one I had seen in local society columns from time to time but most recently in the police blotter. "Is that as in Dr. de Gasteneau, the plastic surgeon?" I asked.

"That's the one. When officers responded to the first domestic, they let him go. The second time they picked him up. He's out on bail for that one."

"Three's the charm," I muttered.

Domestic disturbances are tough calls for all cops. For me personally they were especially disturbing. "Why do women stay with men like that?" I demanded. "Why the hell don't they get out while there's still time?"

Detective Barry shrugged. "Maybe they stay because they don't have anywhere else to go."

"That's no excuse," I said. And I meant it with every ounce of my being.

I left the very first time Mark hit me—the only time Mark hit me—and I never went back. It was less than six weeks after our wedding—a three-ring circus, storybook, church, and country-club affair with all the necessary trimmings. I came back to the Park and Ride after work late one Friday afternoon and discovered that someone had broken into my little Fiat and stolen both the stereo and the steering wheel.

That Fiat was my baby. It was the first car I had chosen, bought, and paid for all on my own. When I told Mark about it, I expected some sympathy. Instead, he lit into me. He said I should have had better sense than to leave it at the Park and Ride in the first place. The argument got totally out of hand, and before I knew what was happening, he hit me—knocked me out cold.

Once I picked myself up off the kitchen floor, I called the cops. I remember trying to keep the blood from my loosened teeth from dripping into the telephone receiver. The two patrol officers who responded were wonderful. One of them kept Mark out of the room while the other one stuck with me. He followed me around the house while I threw my clothes and makeup into suitcases and plastic trash bags. He helped amass an odd assortment of hastily collected household goods— dishes, silverware, pots, and pans. I made off with Aunt Mindy's wedding present waffle iron, one of the two popcorn poppers, and every single set of matching towels and washcloths I could lay hands on.

The two cops were more than happy to help me drag my collection of stuff downstairs and out the door where they obligingly loaded it into a waiting Yellow cab. Now that I'm a police officer myself, I know why they were so eager to help me. I was the exception, not the rule. Most women don't leave. Ever.

By then our car was rounding a tight curve on the winding foothills road called Rainier Vista, although any view of Mount Rainier was totally shrouded in clouds. Ahead of us the narrow right-of-way and the lowering clouds were brightly lit by the orange glow of flashing lights from numerous emergency vehicles—several patrol cars and what was evidently a now totally unnecessary ambulance.

The figure of a rain-slickered patrol officer emerged out of the darkness. The cop motioned for us to park directly behind one of the medical examiner's somber gray vans.

"How the hell did the meat wagon beat us?" Detective Barry demanded irritably.

"Believe me," I said, "it wasn't because you didn't try."

The uniformed deputy hurried over to our car. Detective Barry lowered his window. "What's up?"

"The husband's waiting out back. I let him know detectives were on the way; told him you'd probably want to talk to him."

Barry nodded. "I'm sure we do."

"That's his Jaguar over there in the driveway," the deputy added.

A Jag, I thought. That figured. Mark loved his Corvette more than life itself. Certainly more than he loved me. He beat the crap out of me, but as far as I know, he never damaged so much as a fender on that precious car of his.

By the time Detective Barry rolled his window back up, I was already out of the car and headed up the sidewalk. He caught me before I made it to the front porch.

"Let me handle the guy, Detective Lanier," Barry said. "I know where he's coming from."

"I don't give a damn where he's coming from," I returned. "Just as long as he goes to jail."

"Jumping to conclusions, aren't we?" Barry taunted.

His patronizing attitude bugged the hell out of me. Yes, he had been a cop a whole lot longer than I had, transferring out to Washington State after years of being a detective in Chicago. But as a transferring officer, he had been cycled through King County's training program all the same, and he had spent his obligatory time in Patrol right along with the new hires. When it was time to make the move from Patrol to Detective Division, the two of us did it at almost the same time. Since scores on training exams are posted, I knew I had outscored him on every written exam we'd been given.

I shoved my clenched fists out of sight in the pockets of my already dripping raincoat. "Cram it, Barry," I told him. "I'll do my best to keep an open mind."

Looking at it from the outside, the house was one of those you expect to find featured on the pages of *House Beautiful* or *Architectural Digest*—vast expanses of clear glass and straight up-and-downs punctuated here and there by unexpectedly sharp angles. The place was lit up like the proverbial Christmas tree with warmly inviting lights glowing through every window. Appearances can be deceiving. Once inside, it was clear the entire house was a shambles.

Even in the well-appointed entryway, every available surface—including the burled maple entryway table—was covered with an accumulation of junk and debris. There were dirty dishes and glasses everywhere, along with a collection of empty beer and soda cans, overflowing ashtrays, and unopened mail. Under the table was a mound of at least a month's worth of yellowed, unread newspapers, still rolled up and encircled by rubber bands.

The human mind is an amazing device. One glance at that hopeless disarray threw me back ten years to the weeks and months just after I left Mark. Once beyond the initial blast of hurt and anger, I closeted myself away in a tiny, two-room apartment and drifted into a miasma of despair and self-loathing. It was a time when I didn't do the dishes, answer the phone, open the mail, pay the bills, or take messages off the machine. Even the simplest tasks became impossibilities, the smallest decisions unthinkable.

If it hadn't been for Aunt Mindy and Uncle Ed, I might be there still. The telephone company had already disconnected my phone for lack of payment when Aunt Mindy and Uncle Ed showed up on my doorstep early one Saturday morning. They knocked and knocked. When I wouldn't open the door, Uncle Ed literally broke it down. They packed me up, cleaned out the place, and took me home with them. One piece at a time, they helped me start gluing my life back together. Six months later I found myself down at the county courthouse, filling out an application to become a police officer.

Thrusting that sudden series of painful memories aside, I took a deep breath and focused my attention on the dead woman lying naked in the middle of the parquet entryway floor. Her pale skin was spotlit by the soft light of a huge crystal chandelier that hung down from the soaring ceiling some three stories above us.

Careful to disturb nothing, I stepped near enough to examine her more closely. Renée Denise de Gasteneau was white, blonde, and probably not much more than thirty. She lay sprawled in an awkward position. One knee was drawn up and thrust forward—as though she had been struck down in mid-stride.

While I bent over the body, Detective James Barry moved farther into the entryway and glanced into the living room.

"I'll tell you one thing," he announced. "This broad was almost as shitty a housekeeper as my ex-wife."

"Believe me," I returned coldly, "housekeeping is the least of this woman's problems."

Tom Hammond, an assistant from the Medical Examiner's office, was standing off to one side, watching us quizzically. "What do you think, Tom?" I asked.

"I've seen worse—housekeeping, that is."

"Forget the damn housekeeping, for godssake! What do you think killed her?"

"Too soon to tell," he replied. "I can see some bruising on the back of the neck, right there where her hair is parted. Could be from a blow to the back of the head. Could be she was strangled. We won't know for sure until we get her downtown."

"How long's she been dead?" Barry asked.

"Hard to say. Ten to twelve hours at least. Maybe longer."

About that time one of the county's crime-scene techs showed up with their photography equipment as well as the Alternate Light Source box that can be used to locate all kinds of trace evidence from latent fingerprints to stray strands of hair or thread or carpet fuzz. What crime techs need more than anything is for people to get the hell out of the way and leave them alone.

"Let's go talk to her husband," I said.

"Suits me," Detective Barry said.

We found Dr. Emile de Gasteneau sitting in an Adirondack chair on a covered deck at the rear of the house. He sat there, sobbing quietly, his face buried in his hands. When he glanced up at our approach, his cheeks were wet with tears. "Are you the detectives?" he croaked.

I nodded and flashed my badge in front of him, but he barely noticed. "I didn't mean for it to end this way," he groaned.

"What way is that, Dr. de Gasteneau?" I asked.

"With her dead like this," he answered hopelessly. "I just wanted to get on with my life. I never meant to hurt her."

My initial reaction was to Mirandize the guy on the spot. It sounded to me as though he was ready to blurt out a full-blown confession, and I didn't want it disqualified in a court of law on some stupid technicality.

Evidently Detective Barry didn't agree. He stepped forward and moved me aside. "How's that, Dr. de Gasteneau? How'd you hurt your wife?"

"I left her," the seemingly distraught man answered. "I just couldn't go on living a lie. I told her I wanted out, but I offered her a good settlement, a fair settlement. I told her she could have the entire equity from the house on the condition she sell it as soon as possible. I thought she'd take the money and run—find someplace less expensive to live and keep the change.

"Instead, she just let the place go to ruin. You can see it's a mess. There's a For Sale sign out front, but as far as I know, no one's even been out here to look at it. I think the real estate agent is ashamed to bring anyone by. I don't blame her. Who would want to buy a $750,000 pigsty—"

"Excuse me, Dr. de Gasteneau," I interrupted. "It sounds to me as though you're more upset by the fact that your wife was a poor housekeeper than you are by the fact she's dead."

The widower stiffened and glared at me. "That was rude."

"So is murder," I countered.

Giving up on any possibility of a voluntary confession, I took my notepad out of my pocket. "Are you the one who called 9-1-1?"

De Gasteneau nodded. "Yes."

"What time?"

He glanced at his watch—an expensive jewel-encrusted timepiece the size of a doorknob, with luminous hands that glowed in the dim light of the porch. "Right after I got here," he answered. "About an hour ago now."

Without a word, Detective Barry stepped off the porch and moved purposefully toward the Jaguar parked a few feet away in the driveway. He put his hand on the hood, checking for residual warmth, and then nodded in my direction.

"Since you and your wife were separated, why did you come here?"

"Mrs. Wilbur called me."

"Who's she?"

"A neighbor from just across the road. She was worried about Renée. She called my office and asked me to come check on her—on Renée."

"Why?"

"I don't know. She was worried about her, I guess. I told her I'd come over right after work."

"Why was she worried? Had she seen strange cars, heard noises, what?"

"I don't know. She didn't say, and I didn't ask. I came out as soon as I could. I had an engagement."

I was about to ask him what kind of engagement when Detective Barry sauntered back up onto the porch. "That's a pretty slick Jagwire you've got out there. Always wanted to get me one of those. What kind of gas mileage does that thing get?"

"It's not that good on gas," de Gasteneau admitted.

Jagwire! The man sounded like he'd just crawled out from under a rock. Renée de Gasteneau was dead, and here was this jerk of a Detective Barry sounding like a hick out kicking the tires at some exotic car dealership. How the hell did Captain Waldron expect me to work with a creep like that?

"How about if we step inside, Dr. de Gasteneau?" I said. "Maybe you can tell us whether or not anything is missing from your wife's house."

What I really wanted to do was to get inside where the light was better. I wanted to check out Emile de Gasteneau's arms and wrists and the backs of his hands to see if there were any scratches, any signs of a life-and-death struggle that might have left telltale marks on the living flesh of Renée de Gasteneau's killer.

Without a word the good doctor de Gasteneau stood up and went inside. "Just wait," Detective Barry whispered over my shoulder as we followed him into the house. "Next thing you know, he's going to try telling us a one-armed man did it. You know—like in *The Fugitive.*"

"Please," I sighed. "I got it. You don't have to explain."

As we trailed Dr. de Gasteneau from one impossibly messy room to another, I stole several discreet glances in the direction of his hands and arms. I was more disappointed than I should have been when there was nothing to see.

Checking throughout the house, it was difficult to tell whether or not anything was missing. Several television sets and VCR's were in their proper places as were two very expensive stereo systems. The jewelry was a tougher call, but as far as de Gasteneau could tell, none of that was missing, either.

"When's the last time you saw your wife?" I asked as we left the upstairs master bedroom and headed back toward the main level of the house.

He paused before he answered. "Two weeks ago," he answered guardedly. "But you probably already know about that."

"You mean the time when you were arrested for hitting her?"

"Yes."

"And you haven't seen her since then?"

"No."

"What time do you get off work?"

"Between four and four-thirty. I'm my own boss. I come and go when I damn well please."

"But you told the neighbor, Mrs. Wilbur, that you'd come here as soon as you could after work. The 9-1-1 call didn't come in until a little after eight. Where were you between four and eight?"

"I already told you. I had an engagement."

"With whom?"

"I don't have to tell you that."

"Phyllis—" Detective Barry interjected, but I silenced him with a single hard-edged stare. I was on track, and I wasn't about to let him pull me away.

"You're right," I said easily. "You don't have to tell us anything at all. But if you don't, I guarantee you we'll find out anyway—one way or the other."

It was nothing more than an empty threat, but de Gasteneau fell for it all the same. "I was seeing my friend," he conceded angrily. "We met for a drink."

Just the way he answered triggered a warning signal in my mind, made me wonder if we were dealing with a lover's triangle. "What kind of friend?" I asked. "Male or female?"

"A male friend," he answered.

So much for the lover theory, I thought. I said, "What's his name?"

De Gasteneau looked at Detective Barry in a blatant appeal for help, but I wasn't about to be derailed. "What's his name?" I insisted.

"Garth," de Gasteneau answered flatly. "His name's Garth Homewood. But please don't call him. Believe me, he's got nothing to do with all this."

"Why would we think he did?" I asked.

We were descending the broad, carpeted stairway when, suddenly, de Gasteneau sank down on the bottom step.

"Garth and I are lovers," he answered unexpectedly. "He's the whole reason I left Renée in the first place. I guess that's one of the reasons she was so upset about it. Maybe if I'd left her for another woman, it wouldn't have bothered her so much."

These are the nineties. Detective Barry and I are both adults and we are both cops. I guess de Gasteneau's admission shouldn't have shocked or surprised either one of us, but it did. My partner looked stunned. I felt like someone who pokes something he thinks is a dead twig only to have it turn out to be a quick brown snake. Once again I was struck by an incredible feeling of kinship toward the dead woman. Poor Renée de Gasteneau. It occurred to me that learning her husband was gay was probably as much a blow to her self-esteem as Mark Lanier's punishing balled fist had been to mine.

"Why?" I said. Not why did you leave her? That much was clear. But why did you marry her in the first place?

The last question as well as the unspoken ones that followed were more reflex than anything else. I didn't really expect Emile de Gasteneau to answer, but he did.

"I tricked her," he admitted, somberly. "I wanted an heir, a child. Someone to leave all this to." His despairing glance encompassed the whole house and everything in it. "Except it didn't work out. I picked the wrong woman. Renée loved me, I guess, but I didn't care about her. Not the same way she did for me. And when it turned out she couldn't get pregnant, it was too much. After a while, I couldn't bring myself to try anymore. It was too dishonest. Now she's dead. Although I didn't kill her, I know it's my fault."

The tears came again. While Emile de Gasteneau sat sobbing on the bottom stair, Detective Barry tapped me on the shoulder.

"Come on," he said, jerking his head toward the door. "Leave the guy alone. Let's go talk to the woman across the street."

I thought it was uncharacteristically nice of Barry to want to give the poor man some privacy, but outside and safely out of earshot, James Joseph Barry, ex-Chicago cop, let go with an amazing string of oaths.

"The guy's a frigging queer!" he raged. "For all we know, he's probably dying of AIDS. Jesus Christ! Did he breathe on us? You got a breath spray on you?"

Detective Barry's only obvious concession toward society's current mania for political correctness was refraining from use of the N-word in racially mixed company. The word "gay" had neither entered his vocabulary nor penetrated his consciousness. I, too, had been shocked by Emile de Gasteneau's revelation, but not for the same reason my partner was.

We walked across the road together and made our way down a steeply pitched driveway to the house we had been told belonged to a family named Wilbur. This one was somewhat older than Renée de Gasteneau's had been, and slightly less showy, but it was still a very expensive piece of suburban real estate.

Detective Barry continued to mutter under his breath as he rang the doorbell. An attractive woman in her late sixties or early seventies answered the door and switched on the porch light.

"Yes?" she said guardedly. "Can I help you?"

I moved forward and showed her my badge. "We're Detectives Barry and Lanier," I explained. "We're investigating the incident across the street. Are you Mrs. Wilbur?"

She nodded but without opening the door any wider. "Inez," she said, "what do you want?"

"I understand you were the person who called Dr. de Gasteneau. Is that true?"

"Yes."

"Why did you call him? Did you hear something unusual? See something out of the ordinary?"

"Well, yes. I mean no. It's just that Renée was always on the go, rushing off this way or that. When her car didn't move all day long, I was worried."

I looked back over my shoulder. From where I stood on the front step of Inez Wilbur's porch, only the topmost gable of the de Gasteneau roof was visible over the crest of the hill. Inez Wilbur seemed to follow both my movements as well as my train of thought.

"You're right," she put in quickly. "it's not easy to see from where you are, but I can see her house from upstairs, from my room . . ."

"Mama," a man's voice said from somewhere behind her. "Who is it?"

"It's nothing, Carl. Go back to your program. I'll be done here in a minute."

"But it's a boring program, Mama," he replied. "I don't like it."

The voice had the basso timbre of an adult, but the words were the whining complaints of a dissatisfied child.

"Please, Carl," Inez Wilbur said, with a tight frown. "Change channels then. I'll be done in a minute."

"Who's Carl?" I asked.

"He's my son," she answered. "He's not a child, but he's like a child, if you know what I mean. All this would upset him terribly."

"All what would upset him terribly?" I asked.

A look of anguished confusion washed over Inez Wilbur's delicately made-up face. "About Mrs. de Gasteneau."

"What about her?"

"She's dead, isn't she?"

"Mama," Carl said behind her, "who is it? Is it company? Are we going to have dessert now?"

Inez let go of the doorknob and covered her face with her hands. Slowly, as though being pushed by the wind, the heavy wooden door swung open.

A large, open-faced man with a wild headful of slightly graying hair stood illuminated in the vestibule behind her. He was wearing a short-sleeved shirt and expertly playing with a yo-yo. His muscular forearms were raked with long deep parallel scratches—a last desperate message from a dying woman.

"Hello, Carl," I said quietly. "My name's Detective Lanier and this is Detective Barry. We'd like to talk to you for a few minutes if you don't mind."

Inez stepped aside and let us into the house while Carl Wilbur's mouth broke into a broad, gap-toothed grin. "Detectives? Really? Do you hear that, Mama? They're cops, and they want to talk to me!"

Inez Wilbur's face collapsed like a shattered teacup, and she began to cry.

Detective Barry pulled his Miranda card out of his wallet. "I'll bet you've seen this on TV, Carl. It's called reading you your rights. You have the right to remain silent . . ."

★   ★   ★

It was six o'clock the next morning before we finally finished our paper. Inez Wilbur had tried to explain to Renée de Gasteneau that Carl was watching her, that she should always pull her curtains and be more careful about walking around the house without any clothes on. But Renée had ignored the warnings just as she had ignored Carl himself.

In the aftermath of Emile's defection, Renée de Gasteneau had searched for validation of her womanhood by taking on all comers. Carl Wilbur, her curious neighbor, had watched all the proceedings with rapt fascination, learning as he did so that there was more to life than he had previously suspected, that there were some interesting things that he wanted to try for himself. And when those things were denied him, he had responded with unthinking but lethal rage. He had thrown a lifeless Renée de Gasteneau to the floor, like a discarded and broken doll.

I was dragging myself out to the parking lot when Captain Waldron caught me by the front door. He hurried up to me, his kind face etched with concern.

"Are you all right?" he asked.

"Just tired. Worn out."

Detective Barry drove by out in the parking lot. He tapped on his horn and waved. I waved back.

"Tough case," Captain Waldron said, "but you handled it like a pair of champs. How do you like working with Detective Barry?"

"He's okay," I said.

Waldron nodded. "Good. I was worried about whether or not you two could get along."

I laughed. "Why? Because Barry's an asshole?"

"No, because of his divorce."

"What about his divorce?"

"You mean you don't know about that? It's common knowledge. I thought everyone knew. His wife left him because he beat her up and she turned him in. That's why he transferred out here from Chicago. Her father's a captain on the Berwyn P.D. somewhere outside of Chicago. I guess things got pretty sticky for a while, but with his track record for cracking serial-killer cases, the sheriff was willing to take him on."

"No questions asked?" I demanded.

Waldron shrugged. "I think he had to complete one of those anger-management courses."

"Did he?"

"As far as I know. I just wanted to let you know how glad I was that the two of you were able to get along."

"We got along, all right," I said. "Just like oil and water."

Some of the finest short fiction today is being written by Lawrence Block. His Matt Scudder novels show the everyday streets of New York City from the viewpoint of a private eye struggling to rebuild his life. As for shorter fiction, the tales of the laconic hit man Keller are a fine combination of philosophical musings on life with hard-edged suspense stories. A Keller collection has been promised in the near future. Hopefully it isn't far off. "Keller on Horseback" is one of his best.

Keller on Horseback

Lawrence Block

At the airport newsstand Keller picked up a paperback western. The cover was pretty much generic, showing a standard-issue Marlboro man, long and lean, walking down the dusty streets of a western town with a gun riding his hip. Neither the title nor the author's name meant anything to Keller. What drew him was a line that seemed to leap out from the cover.

"He rode a thousand miles," Keller read, "to kill a man he never met."

Keller paid for the book and tucked it into his carry-on bag. When the plane was in the air, he dug it out and looked at the cover, wondering why he'd bought it. He didn't read much, and when he did, he never chose westerns.

Maybe he wasn't supposed to read this book. Maybe he was supposed to keep it for a talisman.

All for that one sentence. Imagine riding a thousand miles on a horse for any purpose, let alone the killing of a stranger. How long would it take, a thousand-mile journey on horseback? A thoroughbred got around a racecourse in something like two minutes, but it couldn't go all day at that pace any more than a human being could string together twenty-six four-minute miles and call it a marathon.

What could you manage on a horse, fifty miles a day? A hundred miles in two days, a thousand miles in twenty? Three weeks, say, at the conclusion of which a man would probably be eager to kill anybody, stranger or blood kin.

Was Ol' Sweat 'n' Leather getting paid for his thousand miles? Was he in the trade? Keller turned the book over in his hands, read the paragraph on the back cover. It did not sound promising. Something about a drifter in the Arizona Territory, a saddle tramp, looking to avenge an old Civil War grievance.

Forgive and forget, Keller advised him.

Keller, riding substantially more than a thousand miles, albeit on a plane instead of a horse, was similarly charged with killing a man as yet unmet. And he was drifting into the Old West to do it, first to Denver, then to Casper, Wyoming, and finally to a town called Martingale. That had been reason enough to pick up the book, but was it reason enough to read it?

He gave it a try. He read a few pages before they came down the aisle with the drinks cart, read a couple more while he sipped his V-8 and ate the salted nuts. Then he evidently dozed off because the next thing he knew the stewardess was waking him to apologize for not having the fruit plate he'd ordered. He told her it didn't matter, he'd have the regular dinner.

"Or there's a Hindu meal that's going begging," she said.

His mind filled with a vision of an airline tray wrapped in one of those saffron-colored robes, extending itself beseechingly and demanding alms. He had the regular dinner instead and ate most of it, except for the mystery meat. He dozed off afterward and didn't wake up until they were making their descent into Stapleton Airport.

Earlier he'd tucked the book into the seat pocket in front of him, and he'd intended to let it ride off into the sunset wedged between the airsickness bag and the plastic card with the emergency exit diagrams. At the last minute he changed his mind and brought the book along.

He spent an hour on the ground in Denver, another hour in the air flying to Casper. The cheerful young man at the Avis counter had a car reserved for Dale Whitlock. Keller showed him a Connecticut driver's license and an American Express card, and the young man gave him a set of keys and told him to have a nice day.

The keys fit a white Chevy Caprice. Cruising north on the interstate, Keller decided he liked everything about the car but its name. There was nothing capricious about his mission. Riding a thousand miles to kill a man you hadn't met was not something one undertook on a whim.

Ideally, he thought, he'd be bouncing along on a rutted two-lane blacktop in a Mustang, say, or maybe a Bronco. Even a Pinto sounded like a better match for a rawboned, leathery desperado like Dale Whitlock than a Caprice.

It was comfortable, though, and he liked the way it handled. And the color was okay. But forget white. As far as he was concerned, the car was a palomino.

It took about an hour to drive to Martingale, a town of around ten thousand midway between Casper and Sheridan on I-25. Just looking around, you knew right away that you'd left the East Coast far behind. Mountains in the distance, a great expanse of sky overhead. And, right in front of you, frame buildings that could have been false fronts in a Randolph Scott film. A feedstore, a western wear emporium, a rundown hotel where you'd expect to find Wild Bill Hickok holding aces and eights at a table in the saloon, or Doc Holliday coughing his lungs out in a bedroom on the second floor.

Of course, there were also a couple of supermarkets and gas stations, a two-screen movie house and a Toyota dealership, a Pizza Hut and a Taco John's, so it wasn't too hard to keep track of what century you were in. He saw a man walk out of the Taco John's looking a lot like the young Randolph Scott, from his boots to his Stetson, but he spoiled the illusion by climbing into a pickup truck.

The hotel that inspired Hickok-Holliday fantasies was the Martingale, located right in the center of things on the wide main street. Keller imagined himself walking in, slapping a credit card on the counter. Then the desk clerk—Henry Jones always played him in the movie— would say that they didn't take plastic. "Or p-p-paper either," he'd say, eyes darting, looking for a place to duck when the shooting started.

And Keller would set a silver dollar spinning on the counter. "I'll be here a few days," he'd announce. "If I have any change coming, buy yourself a new pair of suspenders."

And Henry Jones would glance down at his suspenders, to see what was wrong with them.

He sighed, shook his head, and drove to the Holiday Inn near the interstate exit. It had plenty of rooms and gave him what he asked for, a nonsmoking room on the third floor in the rear. The desk clerk was a woman, very young, very blond, very perky, with nothing about her to remind you of Henry Jones. She said, "Enjoy your stay with us, Mr. Whitlock." Not stammering, eyes steady.

He unpacked, showered, and went to the window to look at the sunset. It was the sort of sunset a hero would ride off into, leaving a slender blonde to bite back tears while calling after him, "I hope you enjoyed your stay with us, Mr. Whitlock."

Stop it, he told himself. Stay with reality. You've flown a couple of thousand miles to kill a man you never met. Just get it done. The sunset can wait.

He hadn't met the man, but he knew his name. Even if he wasn't sure how to pronounce it.

The man in White Plains had handed Keller an index card with two lines of block capitals hand-printed.

"Lyman Crowder," he read, as if it rhymed with louder. "Or should that be Crowder?"—as if it rhymed with loader.

A shrug in response.

"Martingale, WY," Keller went on. "Why indeed? And where, besides Wyoming? Is Martingale near anything?"

Another shrug, accompanied by a photograph. Or a part of one; it had apparently been cropped from a larger photo and showed the upper half of a middle-aged man who looked to have spent a lot of time outdoors. A big man, too. Keller wasn't sure how he knew that. You couldn't see the man's legs, and there was nothing else in the photo to give you an idea of scale. But somehow he could tell.

"What did he do?"

Again a shrug, but one that conveyed information to Keller. If the other man didn't know what Crowder had done, he had evidently done it to somebody else. That meant the man in White Plains had no personal interest in the matter. It was strictly business.

"So who's the client?"

A shake of the head. Meaning that he didn't know who was picking up the tab or that he knew but wasn't saying? Hard to tell. The man in White Plains was a man of few words and master of none.

"What's the time frame?"

"The time frame," the man said, evidently enjoying the phrase. "No big hurry. One week, two weeks." He leaned forward, patted Keller on the knee. "Take your time," he said. "Enjoy yourself."

On the way out he'd shown the index card to Dot. He said, "How would you pronounce this? As in 'crow' or as in 'crowd'?"

Dot shrugged.

"Jesus," he said, "you're as bad as he is."

"Nobody's as bad as he is," Dot said. "Keller, what difference does it make how Lyman pronounces his last name?"

"I just wondered."

"Well, stick around for the funeral," she suggested. "See what the minister says."

"You're a big help," Keller said.

There was only one Crowder listed in the Martingale phone book. Lyman Crowder, with a telephone number but no address. About a third of the book's listings were like that. Keller wondered why. Did these people assume everybody knew where they lived in a town this size? Or were they saddle tramps with cellular phones and no fixed abode?

Probably rural, he decided. Lived out of town on some unnamed road, picked up their mail at the post office, so why list an address in the phone book?

Great. His quarry lived in the boondocks outside a town that wasn't big enough to have boondocks, and Keller didn't even have an address for him. He had a phone number, but what good was that? What was he supposed to do, call him up and ask directions? "Hi, this here's Dale Whitlock, we haven't met, but I just rode a thousand miles and—"

Scratch that.

He drove around and ate at a downtown café called the Singletree. It was housed in a weathered frame building just down the street from the Martingale Hotel. The café's name was spelled out in rope nailed to the vertical clapboards. For Keller the name brought a vision of a solitary pine or oak set out in the middle of vast grasslands, a landmark for herdsmen, a rare bit of shade from the relentless sun.

From the menu he learned that a singletree was some kind of apparatus used in hitching up a horse, or a team of horses. It was a little unclear to him just what it was or how it functioned, but it certainly didn't spread its branches in the middle of the prairie.

Keller had the special, a chicken-fried steak and some french fries that came smothered in gravy. He was hungry enough to eat everything in spite of the way it tasted.

You don't want to live here, he told himself.

It was a relief to know this. Driving around Martingale, Keller had found himself reminded of Roseburg, Oregon. Roseburg was larger, with none of the Old West feel of Martingale, but they both were small western towns of a sort Keller rarely got to. In Roseburg Keller had allowed his imagination to get away from him for a little while, and he wouldn't want to let that happen again.

Still, crossing the threshold of the Singletree, he had been unable to avoid remembering the little Mexican place in Roseburg. If the food and service here turned out to be on that level—

Forget it. He was safe.

After his meal Keller strode out through the bat-wing doors and walked up one side of the street and down the other. It seemed to him that there was something unusual about the way he was walking, that his gait was that of a man who had just climbed down from a horse.

Keller had been on a horse once in his life, and he couldn't remember how he'd walked after he got off it. So this walk he was doing now wasn't coming from his own past. It must have been something he'd learned unconsciously from movies and TV, a synthesis of all those riders of the purple sage and the silver screen.

No need to worry about yearning to settle here, he knew now. Because his fantasy now was not of someone settling in but passing through, the saddle tramp, the shootist, the flint-eyed loner who does his business and moves on.

This was a good fantasy, he decided. You wouldn't get into any trouble with a fantasy like that.

Back in his room Keller tried the book again but couldn't keep his mind on what he was reading. He turned on the TV and worked his way through the channels, using the remote control bolted to the nightstand. Westerns, he decided, were like cops and cabs, never around when you wanted them. It seemed to him that he never made a trip around the cable circuit without running into John Wayne or Randolph Scott or Joel McCrea or a rerun of *Gunsmoke* or *Rawhide* or one of those spaghetti westerns with Eastwood or Lee Van Cleef. Or the great villains—Jack Elam, Strother Martin, the young Lee Marvin in *The Man Who Shot Liberty Valance*.

It probably said something about you, Keller thought, when your favorite actor was Jack Elam.

He switched off the set and looked up Lyman Crowder's phone number. He could dial it, and when someone picked up and said, "Crowder residence," he'd know how the name was pronounced. "Just checking," he could say, cradling the phone and giving them something to think about.

Of course, he wouldn't say that; he'd mutter something harmless about a wrong number, but was even that much contact a good idea? Maybe it would put Crowder on his guard. Maybe Crowder was already on his guard, as far as that went. That was the trouble with going in blind like this, knowing nothing about either the target or the client.

If he called Crowder's house from the motel, there might be a record of the call, a link between Lyman Crowder and Dale Whitlock. That wouldn't matter much to Keller, who would shed the Whitlock identity on his way out of town, but there was no reason to create more grief for the real Dale Whitlock.

Because there *was* a real Dale Whitlock, and Keller was giving him grief enough without making him a murder suspect.

It was pretty slick the way the man in White Plains worked it. He knew a man who had a machine with which he could make flawless American Express cards. He knew someone else who could obtain the names and account numbers of bona fide American Express cardholders. Then he had cards made which were essentially duplicates of existing cards. You didn't have to worry that the card-holder had reported his card stolen because it hadn't been stolen; it was still sitting in his wallet. You were off somewhere charging the earth, and he didn't have a clue until the charges turned up on his monthly statement.

The driver's license was real, too. Well, technically, it was a counterfeit, of course, and the photograph on it showed Keller, not Whitlock. But someone had managed to access the Connecticut Bureau of Motor Vehicles' computer, and thus the counterfeit license showed the same number as Whitlock's, and gave the same address.

In the old days, Keller thought, it had been a lot more straight forward. You didn't need a license to ride a horse or a credit card to rent one. You bought or stole one, and when you rode into town on it, nobody asked to see your ID. They might not even come right out and ask your name, and if they did, they wouldn't expect a detailed reply. "Call me Tex," you'd say, and that's what they'd call you as you rode off into the sunset.

"Good-bye, Tex," the blonde would call out. "I hope you enjoyed your stay with us."

★   ★   ★

The lounge downstairs turned out to be the hot spot in Martingale. Restless, Keller had gone downstairs to have a quiet drink. He walked into a thickly carpeted room with soft lighting and a good sound system. There were fifteen or twenty people in the place, all of them either having a good time or looking for one.

Keller ordered a Coors at the bar. On the jukebox Barbara Mandrell sang a song about cheating. When she was done, a duo he didn't recognize sang a song about cheating. Then came Hank Williams's oldie, "Your Cheating Heart."

A subtle pattern was beginning to emerge.

"I love this song," the blonde said.

A different blonde, not the perky young thing from the front desk. This woman was taller, older, and fuller-figured. She wore a skirt and a sort of cowgirl blouse with piping and embroidery on it.

"Old Hank," Keller said, to say something.

"I'm June."

"Call me Tex."

"Tex!" Her laughter came in a sort of yelp. "When did anybody ever call you Tex, tell me that?"

"Well, nobody has," he admitted, "but that's not to say they never will."

"Where are you from, Tex? No, I'm sorry, I can't call you that; it sticks in my throat. If you want me to call you Tex, you're going to have to start wearing boots."

"You see by my outfit that I'm not a cowboy."

"Your outfit, your accent, your haircut. If you're not an easterner, then I'm a virgin."

"I'm from Connecticut."

"I knew it."

"My name's Dale."

"Well, you could keep that. If you were fixing to be a cowboy, I mean. You'd have to change the way you dress and talk and comb your hair, but you could hang on to Dale. There another name that goes with it?"

In for a penny, in for a pound. "Whitlock," he said.

"Dale Whitlock. Shoot, that's pretty close to perfect. You tell 'em a name like that, you got credit down at the Agway in a New York minute. Wouldn't even have to fill out a form. You married, Dale?"

What was the right answer? She was wearing a ring herself, and the jukebox was now playing yet another cheating song.

"Not in Martingale," he said.

"Oh, I like that," she said, eyes sparkling. "I like the whole idea of regional marriage. I *am* married in Martingale, but we're not *in* Martingale. The town line's Front Street."

"In that case," he said, "maybe I could buy you a drink."

"You easterners," she said. "You're just so damn fast."

There had to be a catch.

Keller didn't do too badly with women. He got lucky once in a while. But he didn't have the sort of looks that made heads turn, nor had he made seduction his life's work. Some years ago he'd read a book called *How to Pick Up Girls*, filled with opening lines that were guaranteed to work. Keller thought they were silly. He was willing to believe they would work, but he was not able to believe they would work for him.

This woman, though, had hit on him before he'd had time to become aware of her presence. This sort of thing happened, especially when you were dealing with a married woman in a bar where all they played was cheating songs. Everybody knew what everybody else was there for, and nobody had time to dawdle. So this sort of thing happened, but it never seemed to happen to him, and he didn't trust it.

Something would go wrong. She'd call home and find out her kid was running a fever. Her husband would walk in the door just as the jukebox gave out with "You Picked a Fine Time to Leave Me, Lucille." She'd be overcome by conscience or rendered unconscious by the drink Keller had just bought her.

"I'd say my place or yours," she said, "but we both know the answer to that one. What's your room number?" Keller told her. "You go on up," she said. "I won't be a minute. Don't start without me."

He brushed his teeth, splashed on a little aftershave. She wouldn't show, he told himself. Or she'd expect to be paid, which would take a little of the frost off the pumpkin. Or her husband would turn up and they'd try to work some variation of the badger game.

Or she'd be sloppy drunk, or he'd be impotent. Or something.

"Whew," she said. "I don't guess you need boots after all. I'll call you Tex or Slim or any damn thing you want me to, just so you come when you're called. How long are you in town for, Dale?"

"I'm not sure. A few days."

"Business, I suppose. What sort of business are you in?"

"I work for a big corporation," he said. "They fly me over to look into situations."

"Sounds like you can't talk about it."

"Well, we do a lot of government work," he said. "So I'm really not supposed to."

"Say no more," she said. "Oh, Lord, look at the time!"

While she showered, he picked up the paperback and rewrote the blurb. He killed a thousand miles, he thought, to ride a woman he never met. Well, sometimes you got lucky. The stars were in the right place; the forces that ruled the universe decided you deserved a present. There didn't always have to be a catch to it, did there?

She turned off the shower, and he heard the last line of the song she'd been singing. "'And Margie's at the Lincoln Park Inn,'" she sang, and moments later she emerged from the bathroom and began dressing.

"What's this?" she said. "'He rode a thousand miles to kill a man he never met.' You know, that's funny, because I just had the darnedest thought while I was runnin' the soap over my pink and tender flesh."

"Oh?"

"I just said that last to remind you what's under this here skirt and blouse. Oh, the thought I had? Well, something you said, government work. I thought maybe this man's CIA, maybe he's some old soldier of fortune, maybe he's the answer to this maiden's prayer."

"What do you mean?"

"Just that it was already a real fine evening, Dale, but it would be heaven on earth if what you came to Martingale for was to kill my damn husband."

Christ. Was *she* the client? Was the pickup downstairs a cute way for them to meet? Could she actually be that stupid, coming on in a public place to a man she was hiring to kill her husband?

For that matter, how had she recognized him? Only Dot and the man in White Plains had known the name he was using. They'd have kept it to themselves. And she'd made her move before she knew his name. Had she been able to recognize him? I see by your outfit that you are a hit man? Something along those lines?

"Yarnell," she was saying. "Hobart Lee Yarnell, and what he'd like is for people to call him Bart, and what everybody calls him is Hobie. Now what does that tell you about the man?"

That he's not the man I came here to kill, Keller thought. This was comforting to realize but left her waiting for an answer to her question. "That he's not used to getting his own way," Keller said.

She laughed. "He's not," she said, "but it's not for lack of trying. You know, I like you, Dale. You're a nice fellow. But if it wasn't you tonight, it would have been somebody else."

"And here I thought it was my aftershave."

"I'll just bet you did. No, the kind of marriage I got, I come around here a lot. I've put a lot of quarters in that jukebox the last year or so."

"And played a lot of cheating songs?"

"And done a fair amount of cheating. But it doesn't really work. I still wake up the next day married to that bastard."

"Why don't you divorce him?"

"I've thought about it."

"And?"

"I was brought up not to believe in it," she said. "But I don't guess that's it. I wasn't raised to believe in cheating either." She frowned. "Money's part of it," she admitted. "I won't bore you with the details, but I'd get gored pretty bad in a divorce."

"That's a problem."

"I guess, except what do I care about money anyway? Enough's as much as a person needs, and my daddy's got pots of money. He's not about to let me starve."

"Well, then——"

"But he thinks the world of Hobie," she said, glaring at Keller as if it were his fault. "Hunts elk with him, goes after trout and salmon with him, thinks he's just the best thing ever came over the pass. And he doesn't even want to hear the word 'divorce.' You know that Tammy Wynette song where she spells it out a letter at a time? I swear he'd leave the room before you got past *R*. I say it'd about break Lyman Crowder's heart if his little girl ever got herself divorced."

Well, it was true. If you kept your mouth shut and your ears open, you learned things. What he had learned was that "Crowder" rhymed with "powder."

Now what?

After her departure, after his own shower, he paced back and forth, trying to sort it all out. In the few hours since his arrival in Martingale, he'd slept with a woman who turned out to be the loving daughter of the target and, in all likelihood, the unloving wife of the client.

Well, maybe not. Lyman Crowder was a rich man, lived north of town on a good-size ranch that he ran pretty much as a hobby. He'd made his real money in oil, and nobody ever made a small amount of money that way. You either went broke or got rich. Rich men had enemies: people they'd crossed in business, people who stood to profit from their death.

But it figured that Yarnell was the client. There was a kind of poetic inevitability about it. She picks him up in the lounge, it's not enough that she's the target's daughter. She also ought to be the client's wife. Round things out, tie up all the loose ends.

The thing to do . . . well, he knew the thing to do. The thing to do was get a few hours' sleep and then, bright and early, reverse the usual order of affairs by riding off into the sunrise. Get on a plane, get off in New York, and write off Martingale as a happy little romantic adventure. Men, after all, had been known to travel farther than that in the hope of getting laid.

He'd tell the man in White Plains to find somebody else. Sometimes you had to do that. No blame attached, as long as you didn't make a habit of it. He'd say he was blown.

As, come to think of it, he was. Quite expertly, as a matter of fact.

In the morning he got up and packed his carry-on. He'd call White Plains from the airport or wait until he was back in New York. He didn't want to phone from the room. When the real Dale Whitlock had a fit and called American Express, they'd look over things like the Holiday Inn statement. No sense leaving anything that led anywhere.

He thought about June, and the memory made him playful. He checked the time. Eight o'clock, two hours later in the East, not an uncivil time to call.

He called Whitlock's home in Rowayton, Connecticut. A woman answered. He identified himself as a representative of a political polling organization, using a name she would recognize. By asking questions that encouraged lengthy responses, he had no trouble keeping her on the phone. "Well, thank you very much," he said at length. "And have a nice day."

Now let Whitlock explain that one to American Express.

He finished packing and was almost out the door when his eye caught the paperback western. Take it along? Leave it for the maid? What?

He picked it up, read the cover line, sighed. Was this what Randolph Scott would do? Or John Wayne, or Clint Eastwood? How about Jack Elam?

No, of course not.

Because then there'd be no movie. A man rides into town, starts to have a look at the situation, meets a woman, gets it on with her, then just backs out and rides off? You put something like that on the screen, it wouldn't even play in the art houses.

Still, this wasn't a movie.

Still . . .

He looked at the book and wanted to heave it across the room. But all he heaved was a sigh. Then he unpacked.

He was having a cup of coffee in town when a pickup pulled up across the street and two men got out of it. One of them was Lyman Crowder. The other, not quite as tall, was twenty pounds lighter and twenty years younger. Crowder's son, by the looks of him.

His son-in-law, as it turned out. Keller followed the two men into a store where the fellow behind the counter greeted them as Lyman and Hobie. Crowder had a lengthy shopping list composed largely of items Keller would have been hard put to find a use for.

While the owner filled the order, Keller had a look at the display of hand-tooled boots. The pointed toes would be handy in New York, he thought, for killing cockroaches in corners. The heels would add better than an inch to his height. He wondered if he'd feel awkward in the boots, like a teenager in her first pair of high heels. Lyman and Hobie looked comfortable enough in their boots, as pointy in the toes and as elevated in the heels as any on display, but they also looked comfortable in their string ties and ten-gallon hats, and Keller was sure he'd feel ridiculous dressed like that.

They were a pair, he thought. They looked alike, they talked alike, they dressed alike, and they seemed uncommonly fond of each other.

Back in his room Keller stood at the window and looked down at the parking lot, then across the way at a pair of mountains. A few years ago his work had taken him to Miami, where he'd met a Cuban who'd cautioned him against ever taking a hotel room above the second floor.

"Suppose you got to leave in a hurry?" the man said. "Ground floor, no problem. Second floor, no problem. Third floor, break your fockeen leg."

The logic of this had impressed Keller, and for a while he had made a point of taking the man's advice. Then he happened to learn that the Cuban not only shunned the higher floors of hotels but also refused to enter an elevator or fly on an airplane. What had looked like tradecraft now appeared to be nothing more than phobia.

It struck Keller that he had never in his life had to leave a hotel room, or any other sort of room, by the window. This was not to say that it would never happen, but he'd decided it was a risk he was prepared to run. He liked high floors. Maybe he even liked running risks.

He picked up the phone, made a call. When she answered, he said, "This is Tex. Would you believe my business appointment canceled? Left me with the whole afternoon to myself."

"Are you where I left you?"

"I've barely moved since then."

"Well, don't move now," she said. "I'll be right on over."

Around nine that night Keller wanted a drink, but he didn't want to have it in the company of adulterers and their favorite music. He drove around in his palomino Caprice until he found a place on the edge of town that looked promising. It called itself Joe's Bar. Outside, it was nondescript. Inside, it smelled of stale beer and casual plumbing. The lights were low. There was sawdust on the floor and the heads of dead animals on the walls. The clientele was exclusively male, and for a moment this gave Keller pause. There were gay bars in New York that tried hard to look like this place, though it was hard for Keller to imagine why. But Joe's, he realized, was not a gay bar, not in any sense of the word.

He sat on a wobbly stool and ordered a beer. The other drinkers left him alone, even as they left one another alone. The jukebox played intermittently, with men dropping in quarters when they could no longer bear the silence.

The songs, Keller noted, ran to type. There were the tryin'-to-drink-that-woman-off-of-my-mind songs and the if-it-wasn't-for-bad-luck-I-wouldn't-have-no-luck-at-all songs. Nothing about Margie in the Lincoln Park Inn, nothing about heaven being just a sin away. These songs were for drinking and feeling really rotten about it.

"'Nother damn day," said a voice at Keller's elbow.

He knew who it was without turning. He supposed he might have recognized the voice, but he didn't think that was it. No, it was more a recognition of the inevitability of it all. Of course it would be Yarnell, making conversation with him in this bar where no one made conversation with anyone. Who else could it be?

"'Nother damn day," Keller agreed.

"Don't believe I've seen you around."

"I'm just passing through."

"Well, you got the right idea," Yarnell said. "Name's Bart."

In for a pound, in for a ton. "Dale," Keller said.

"Good to know you, Dale."

"Same here, Bart."

The bartender loomed before them. "Hey, Hobie," he said. "The usual?"

Yarnell nodded. "And another of those for Dale here." The bartender poured Yarnell's usual, which turned out to be bourbon with water back, and uncapped another beer for Keller. Somebody broke down and fed the jukebox a quarter and played "There Stands the Glass."

Yarnell said, "You hear what he called me?"

"I wasn't paying attention."

"Called me Hobie," Yarnell said. "Everybody does. You'll be doing the same, won't be able to help yourself."

"The world is a terrible place," Keller said.

"By God, you got that right," Yarnell said. "No one ever said it better. You a married man, Dale?"

"Not at the moment."

"'Not at the moment.' I swear I'd give a lot if I could say the same."

"Troubles?"

"Married to one woman and in love with another one. I guess you could call that trouble."

"I guess you could."

"Sweetest, gentlest, darlingest, lovingest creature God ever made," Yarnell said. "When she whispers 'Bart,' it don't matter if the whole rest of the world shouts 'Hobie.'"

"This isn't your wife you're talking about," Keller guessed.

"God, no! My wife's a round-heeled meanspirited hardhearted tramp. I hate my damn wife. I love my girlfriend."

They were silent for a moment, and so was the whole room. Then someone played, "The Last Word in Lonesome Is Me."

"They don't write songs like that anymore," Yarnell said.

The hell they didn't. "I'm sure I'm not the first person to suggest this," Keller said, "but have you thought about—"

"Leaving June," Yarnell said. "Running off with Edith. Getting a divorce."

"Something like that."

"Never an hour that I don't think about it, Dale. Night and god-damn day I think about it. I think about it, and I drink about it, but the one thing I can't do is do it."

"Why's that?"

"There is a man," Yarnell said, "who is a father and a best friend to me all rolled into one. Finest man I ever met in my life, and the only wrong thing he ever did in his life was have a daughter, and the biggest mistake I ever made was marrying her. And if there's one thing that man believes in, it's the sanctity of marriage. Why, he thinks 'divorce' is the dirtiest word in the language."

So Yarnell couldn't even let on to his father-in-law that his mar-riage was hell on earth, let alone take steps to end it. He had to keep his affair with Edith very much backstreet. The only person he could talk to was Edith, and she was out of town for the next week or so, leaving him dying of loneliness and ready to pour out his heart to the first stranger he could find. For which he apologized, but—

"Hey, that's all right, Bart," Keller said. "A man can't keep it all locked up inside."

"Calling me Bart, I appreciate that, I truly do. Even Lyman calls me Hobie, and he's the best friend any man ever had. Hell, he can't help it. Everybody calls me Hobie sooner or later."

"Well," Keller said, "I'll hold out as long as I can."

Alone, Keller reviewed his options.

He could kill Lyman Crowder. He'd be keeping it simple, carrying out the mission as it had been given to him. And it would solve every-body's problems. June and Hobie could get the divorce they both so desperately wanted.

On the downside, they'd both be losing the man each regarded as the greatest thing since microwave popcorn.

He could toss a coin and take out either June or her husband, thus serving as a sort of divorce court of last resort. If it came up heads, June could spend the rest of her life cheating on a ghost. If it was tails, Yarnell could have his cake and Edith, too. Only a question of time until she stopped calling him Bart and took to calling him Hobie, of course, and next thing you knew she would turn up at the Holiday Inn, dropping her quarter in the slot to play "Third-Rate Romance, Low-Rent Rendezvous."

It struck Keller that there ought to be some sort of solution that didn't involve lowering the population. But he knew he was the person least likely to come up with it.

If you had a medical problem, the treatment you got depended on the sort of person you went to. You didn't expect a surgeon to manipulate your spine, or prescribe herbs and enemas, or kneel down and pray with you. Whatever the problem was, the first thing the surgeon would do was look around for something to cut. That's how he'd been trained; that's how he saw the world; that's what he did.

Keller, too, was predisposed to a surgical approach. While others might push counseling or twelve-step programs, Keller reached for a scalpel. But sometimes it was difficult to tell where to make the incision.

Kill 'em all, he thought savagely, and let God sort 'em out. Or ride off into the sunset with your tail between your legs.

First thing in the morning Keller drove to Sheridan and caught a plane to Salt Lake City. He paid cash for his ticket and used the name John Richards. At the TWA counter in Salt Lake City he bought a one-way ticket to Las Vegas and again paid cash, this time using the name Alan Johnson.

At the Las Vegas airport he walked around the long-term parking lot as if looking for his car. He'd been doing this for five minutes or so when a balding man wearing a glen plaid sport coat parked a two-year-old Plymouth and removed several large suitcases from its trunk, affixing them to one of those aluminum luggage carriers. Wherever he was headed, he'd packed enough to stay there for a while.

As soon as he was out of sight, Keller dropped to a knee and groped the undercarriage until he found the magnetized hide-a-key. He always looked before breaking into a car, and he got lucky about one time in five. As usual, he was elated. Finding a key was a good omen. It boded well.

Keller had been to Vegas frequently over the years. He didn't like the place, but he knew his way around. He drove to Caesars Palace and left his borrowed Plymouth for the attendant to park. He knocked on the door of an eighth-floor room until its occupant protested that she was trying to sleep.

He said, "It's news from Martingale, Miss Bodine. For Christ's sake, open the door."

She opened the door a crack but kept the chain fastened. She was about the same age as June but looked older, her black hair a mess, her eyes bleary, her face still bearing traces of yesterday's makeup.

"Crowder's dead," he said.

Keller could think of any number of things she might have said, ranging from "What happened?" to "Who cares?" This woman cut to the chase. "You idiot," she said. "What are you doing here?"

Mistake.

"Let me in," he said, and she did.

Another mistake.

The attendant brought Keller's Plymouth and seemed happy with the tip Keller gave him. At the airport someone else had left a Toyota Camry in the spot where the balding man had originally parked the Plymouth, and the best Keller could do was wedge it into a spot one aisle over and a dozen spaces off to the side. He figured the owner would find it and hoped he wouldn't worry that he was in the early stages of Alzheimer's.

Keller flew to Denver as Richard Hill, to Sheridan as David Edwards. En route he thought about Edith Bodine, who'd evidently slipped on a wet tile in the bathroom of her room at Caesars, cracking her skull on the side of the big tub. With the Do Not Disturb sign hanging from the doorknob and the air conditioner at its highest setting, there was no telling how long she might remain undisturbed.

He'd figured she had to be the client. It wasn't June or Hobie, both of whom thought the world revolved around Lyman Crowder, so whom did that leave? Crowder himself, turned sneakily suicidal? Some old enemy, some business rival?

No, Edith was the best prospect. A client would either want to meet Keller—not obliquely, as both Yarnells had done, but by arrangement—or would contrive to be demonstrably off the scene when it all happened. Thus the trip to Las Vegas.

Why? The Crowder fortune, of course. She had Hobie Yarnell crazy about her, but he wouldn't leave June for fear of breaking Crowder's heart, and even if he did, he'd go empty-handed. Having June killed wouldn't work, either, because she didn't have any real money of her own. But June would inherit if the old man died, and later on something could always happen to June.

Anyway, that was how he figured it. If he'd wanted to know Edith's exact reasoning, he'd have had to ask her, and that had struck him as a waste of time. More to the point, the last thing he'd wanted was a chance to get to know her. That just screwed everything up when you got to know these people.

If you were going to ride a thousand miles to kill a man you'd never met, you were really well advised to be the tight-lipped stranger every step of the way. No point in talking to anybody, not the target, not the client, and not anybody else either. If you had anything to say, you could whisper it to your horse.

He got off the fourth plane of the day at Sheridan, picked up his Caprice—the name was seeming more appropriate with every passing hour—and drove back to Martingale. He kept it right around the speed limit, then slowed down along with everyone else five miles outside Martingale. They were clearing a wreck out of the northbound lane. That shouldn't have slowed things down in the southbound lane, but of course it did; everybody had to slow down to see what everyone else was slowing down to look at.

Back in his room he had his bag packed before he realized that he couldn't go anywhere. The client was dead, but that didn't change anything; since he had no way of knowing that she was the client or that she was dead, his mission remained unchanged. He could go home and admit an inability to get the job done, waiting for the news to seep through that there was no longer any job to be done. That would get him off the hook after the fact, but he wouldn't have covered himself with glory, nor would he get paid. The client had almost certainly paid in advance, and if there'd been a middleman between the client and the man in White Plains, he had almost certainly passed the money on, and there was very little likelihood that the man in White Plains would even consider the notion of refunding a fee to a dead client, not that anyone would raise the subject. But neither would the man in White Plains pay Keller for work he'd failed to perform. The man in White Plains would just keep everything.

Keller thought about it. It looked to him as though his best course lay in playing a waiting game. How long could it take before a sneak thief or a chambermaid walked in on Edith Bodine? How long before news of her death found its way to White Plains?

The more he thought about it, the longer it seemed likely to take. If there were, as sometimes happened, a whole string of intermediaries involved, the message might very well never get to Garcia.

Maybe the simplest thing was to kill Crowder and be done with it.

No, he thought. He'd just made a side trip of, yes, more than a thousand miles—and at his own expense yet—solely to keep from having to kill this legendary Man He Never Met. Damned if he was going to kill him now, after all that.

He'd wait a while anyway. He didn't want to drive anywhere now, and he couldn't bear to look at another airplane, let alone get on board.

He stretched out on the bed, closed his eyes.

He had a frightful dream. In it he was walking at night out in the middle of the desert, lost, chilled, desperately alone. Then a horse came galloping out of nowhere, and on his back was a magnificent woman with a great mane of hair and eyes that flashed in the moonlight. She extended a hand, and Keller leaped up on the horse and rode behind her. She was naked. So was Keller, although he had somehow failed to notice this before.

They fell in love. Wordless, they told each other everything, knew each other like twin souls. And then, gazing into her eyes, Keller realized who she was. She was Edith Bodine, and she was dead; he'd killed her earlier without knowing she'd turn out to be the girl of his dreams. It was done, it could never be undone, and his heart was broken for eternity.

Keller woke up shaking. For five minutes he paced the room, struggling to sort out what was a dream and what was real. He hadn't been sleeping long. The sun was setting; it was still the same endless day.

God, what a hellish dream.

He couldn't get caught up in TV, and he had no luck at all with the book. He put it down, picked up the phone, and dialed June's number.

"It's Dale," he said. "I was sitting here and—"

"Oh, Dale," she cut in, "you're so thoughtful to call. Isn't it terrible? Isn't it the most awful thing?"

"Uh," he said.

"I can't talk now," she said. "I can't even think straight. I've never been so upset in my life. Thank you, Dale, for being so thoughtful."

She hung up and left him staring at the phone. Unless she was a better actress than he would have guessed, she sounded absolutely over-come. He was surprised that news of Edith Bodine's death could have reached her so soon, but far more surprised that she could be taking it so hard. Was there more to all this than met the eye? Were Hobie's wife and mistress actually close friends? Or were they—Jesus—*more* than just good friends?

Things were certainly a lot simpler for Randolph Scott.

The same bartender was on duty at Joe's. "I don't guess your friend Hobie'll be coming around tonight," he said. "I suppose you heard the news."

"Uh," Keller said. Some backstreet affair, he thought, if the whole town was ready to comfort Hobie before the body was cold.

"Hell of a thing," the man went on. "Terrible loss for this town. Martingale won't be the same without him."

"This news," Keller said carefully. "I think maybe I missed it. What happened anyway?"

He called the airlines from his motel room. The next flight out of Casper wasn't until morning. Of course, if he wanted to drive to Denver—

He didn't want to drive to Denver. He booked the first flight out in the morning, using the Whitlock name and the Whitlock credit card.

No need to stick around, not with Lyman Crowder stretched out somewhere getting pumped full of embalming fluid. Dead in a car crash on I-25 North, the very accident that had slowed Keller down on his way back from Sheridan.

He wouldn't be around for the funeral, but should he send flow-ers? It was quite clear that he shouldn't. Still, the impulse was there.

He dialed 1-800-FLOWERS and sent a dozen roses to Mrs. Dale Whitlock in Rowayton, charging them to Whitlock's American Express account. He asked them to enclose a card reading, "Just because I love you—Dale."

He felt it was the least he could do.

Two days later he was on Taunton Place in White Plains, making his report. Accidents were always good, the man told him. Accidents and natural causes, always the best. Oh, sometimes you needed a noisy hit to send a message, but the rest of the time you couldn't beat an accident.

"Good you could arrange it," the man said.

Would have taken a hell of an arranger, Keller thought. First you'd have had to arrange for Lyman Crowder to be speeding north in his pickup. Then you'd have had to get an unemployed sheepherder named Danny Vasco good and drunk and sent him hurtling toward Martingale, racing his own pickup—Jesus, didn't they drive anything but pickups?—racing it at ninety-plus miles an hour, and proceeding southbound in the northbound lane. Arrange for a few near misses. Arrange for Vasco to brush a school bus and sideswipe a minivan, and then let him ram Crowder head-on.

Some arrangement.

If the man in White Plains had any idea that the client was dead as well or even who the client was, he gave no sign to Keller. On the way out Dot asked him how Crowder pronounced his name.

"Rhymes with 'chowder,'" he said.

"I knew you'd find out," she said. "Keller, are you all right? You seem different."

"Just awed by the workings of fate," he said.

"Well," she said, "that'll do it."

On the train back to the city he thought about the workings of fate. Earlier he'd tried to tell himself that his side trip to Las Vegas had been a waste of time and money and human life. All he'd had to do was wait a day for Danny Vasco to take the game off the boards.

Never would have happened.

Without his trip to Vegas, there would have been no wreck on the highway. One event had opened some channel that allowed the other to happen. He couldn't explain this, couldn't make sense out of it, but somehow he knew it was true.

Everything had happened exactly the way it had had to happen. Encountering June in the Meet 'n' Cheat, running into Hobie at the Burnout Bar. He could no more have avoided those meetings than he could have kept himself from buying the paperback western novel that had set the tone for everything that followed.

He hoped Mrs. Whitlock liked the flowers.